PRAISE FOR

Charming the Shrew

"Move over Shakespeare, no one writes a more lovable shrew than Laurin Wittig."
—Sherrilyn Kenyon, *New York Times* bestselling author

"A wild romp across Scotland . . . definitely a writer to watch!" —Mary Jo Putney, *New York Times* bestselling author

"*Charming the Shrew* has everything needed for the perfect story: treachery, greed, insecurity, humor, hot love scenes, a really good fight scene and judgment before a reputable king . . . Make sure *Charming the Shrew* is at the top of your reading list, and let the call of the Highlands whisk you away to a time and place where love is a rarity, but when found, it is found forever."
—*Romance Reviews Today*

"In this exhilarating Highlands adventure, Wittig knows how to merge passion, wild adventure, history and danger into a perfect tale that takes your breath away and tugs at the heart." —*Romantic Times Bookclub*

"Charming, fun and captivating . . . a powerful historical romance, not to be missed!" —*The Road to Romance*

"A wonderfully touching story . . . I highly recommend *Charming the Shrew* to all lovers of historical romance."
—*RomanceandFriends.com*

continued . . .

Daring

the

Highlander

Laurin Wittig

BERKLEY SENSATION, NEW YORK

THE BERKLEY PUBLISHING GROUP
Published by the Penguin Group
Penguin Group (USA) Inc.
375 Hudson Street, New York, New York 10014, USA
Penguin Group (Canada), 10 Alcorn Avenue, Toronto, Ontario M4V 3B2, Canada
(a division of Pearson Penguin Canada Inc.)
Penguin Books Ltd., 80 Strand, London WC2R 0RL, England
Penguin Group Ireland, 25 St. Stephen's Green, Dublin 2, Ireland (a division of Penguin Books Ltd.)
Penguin Group (Australia), 250 Camberwell Road, Camberwell, Victoria 3124, Australia
(a division of Pearson Australia Group Pty. Ltd.)
Penguin Books India Pvt. Ltd., 11 Community Centre, Panchsheel Park, New Delhi—110 017, India
Penguin Group (NZ), Cnr. Airborne and Rosedale Roads, Albany, Auckland 1310, New Zealand
(a division of Pearson New Zealand Ltd.)
Penguin Books (South Africa) (Pty.) Ltd., 24 Sturdee Avenue, Rosebank, Johannesburg 2196,
South Africa

Penguin Books Ltd., Registered Offices: 80 Strand, London WC2R 0RL, England

This is a work of fiction. Names, characters, places, and incidents either are the product of the author's imagination or are used fictitiously, and any resemblance to actual persons, living or dead, business establishments, events, or locales is entirely coincidental.

DARING THE HIGHLANDER

A Berkley Sensation Book / published by arrangement with the author

PRINTING HISTORY
Berkley Sensation edition / May 2005

ISBN: 0-425-20292-5

BERKLEY® SENSATION
Berkley Sensation Books are published by The Berkley Publishing Group,
a division of Penguin Group (USA) Inc.,
375 Hudson Street, New York, New York 10014.
BERKLEY SENSATION and the "B" design are trademarks belonging to Penguin Group (USA) Inc.

PRINTED IN THE UNITED STATES OF AMERICA

10 9 8 7 6 5 4 3 2 1

For David and Dale Wittig,
the best brothers-in-law a girl could wish for.

And for the many neighbors, friends and family
who also came to our aide
with good humor, strong backs and hot meals
after Hurricane Isabel graced us with her fury.
You all have my love and undying thanks.

Acknowledgments

Many thanks to my dear friends and fellow writers Elizabeth Holcombe and Pamela Palmer Poulsen for their massive and timely support, encouragement and wisdom during the writing of this book. Thanks, as always, to my family, Dean, Samantha and Alex who make everything possible.

Prologue

Scotland, Mid-January, 1309

An icy blast of Highland wind whipped over the top of
Dunbeg, shoving against Ailig MacLeod as if to keep
him from cresting the last hill on his long journey home, as
if the wind itself knew his clan would hate him for the
news he brought.

Shoving his thrashing hair out of his face, he pulled his
horse to a stop and studied the glen below. Assynt Castle
crouched amongst piles of soot-encrusted snow. Its gray
imposing bulk uncomfortably straddled the narrow strip of
land between the glorious open freedom of the white-clad
mountains and the dark, frigid depths of the frozen loch.
The horse danced sideways and Ailig loosened the grip he
had on it with his knees.

Assynt Castle. Home.

Heavy gray clouds raced across the sky, spitting icy pellets down his neck, pulling his attention away from the
castle and what awaited him there. He watched the clouds

flee the glen, driven by the rising wind, and, for just a moment, he considered following them.

But he couldn't.

Less than a month ago he'd left this glen with his four older brothers in pursuit of their runaway sister. Now he was the only one returning. Catriona, his sister, had run off and married a good man of her own choosing, a man Ailig respected and admired. But she had been promised to another, the dog-faced chief of a neighboring clan. The ramifications of her escape were but the least of what awaited him at Assynt.

His foolish eldest brother, in league with Catriona's dog-faced intended, had conspired to kill the king. And now it had come to this. He shook the icy snow out of his eyes and returned his attention to the castle.

Ailig, who had never gotten along with his brothers, nor his own father, was all that stood between the clan and the king's vengeance. 'Twas up to him to fulfill the king's command, a task that would mark him as little better than a traitor in his father's eyes.

But the clan must be protected. He'd not let the king destroy his family, his home. He'd not let his father throw away this chance at a future just because he had no use for his youngest son. For anything less than doing as the king commanded would doom them all.

Ailig sat up straighter, picked up his reins and took a long, deep breath. No matter how confident he wished to be, 'twas a daunting future that awaited him, a future he could delay no longer. He twitched the reins and the horse started forward, heading downhill towards the castle and the dubious welcome awaiting them. 'Twould be no welcome at all when his father learned that the king demanded that which Ailig had never wanted, which his father would bitterly decry.

He'd demanded Ailig rip the reins of power from his own father. He'd demanded Ailig become chief.

chapter 1

Morainn MacRailt hugged the sunset-colored plaid, her latest creation, to her stomach as she stood looking out over the frozen expanse of Loch Assynt. The castle loomed behind her, but she was not ready to enter it. She'd been putting it off all day, chiding herself for being a coward. It wasn't like her to avoid confrontation, but she was tired of fending off her would-be suitor. She missed the days when she could hide behind her mourning. No one had approached her about marrying again until her official mourning period had ended just a fortnight earlier.

She let her gaze wander over the double-peaked expanse of snow-draped mountain on the opposite shore, then up to the scudding clouds retreating down the length of the glen.

She hadn't always been a coward, but marriage hadn't turned out the way she had expected. They had both quickly seen their mistake but 'twas too late when they discovered it. They were married and there was nothing to undo that, until Hamish's early death one night while reaving the MacTavishs' cows with the chief's sons.

She should have felt a stab of pain at the mention of him, or at least guilt, but lately even that had faded to a small hollow ache that was becoming all too easy to live with. Not that anyone else need know that.

She had been mortified that her first reaction to the news had been relief. She *had* been sad. He had not deserved to die so young, but deep inside where she would never let anyone see it, she had felt a door open. She had felt her true self pour forth again from where she had locked it away trying to be a good wife.

But she would never do that again. And she'd never marry again. She had thought herself in love with Hamish, but the flush of infatuation had quickly burned out and she'd been left living with a man she did not particularly like, and one who no longer liked her overmuch, either. For three years they had avoided each other as much as possible, speaking little. He had been miserable and she blamed herself for that, but she had also been miserable and that, too, she blamed on herself. He was older than she was. He knew what he wanted in a wife. She was much younger and had been so lonely after the death of her mother and the emotional retreat of her father that the gratitude at the attention Hamish heaped on her had felt like love. What did she know of love? Nothing, it turned out.

She let the calm and quiet of the winter landscape seep into her, fortify her. She drew the sharp-edged air into her lungs. Sick of her own cowardice, she faced the castle only to find herself being watched.

Baltair, the clan's champion, stood between her and the

castle. A slow smile spread across his ruddy face, pulling his narrow lips tight, and his crooked nose even further out of line than it usually was. The man really shouldn't smile. His eyes went to slits and he looked almost as if he were grimacing.

She'd like to grimace, too, but she managed to stop at a frown.

"Is there something you need?" she asked, clutching her bundle of plaid tightly to her like armor. The man was relentless and she was tired of it. He didn't seem to understand her when she told him she was not looking for a husband. Why couldn't anybody understand that? One thing *she* was beginning to understand was that when Baltair got it into his wee little mind that he wanted something . . . say, her . . . he was just as unyielding and just as hard of hearing as the stone wall his chest resembled.

"Why are you always in such a hurry to get away from me, Morainn?" he asked, his voice low as if he spoke to a lover.

She clamped down on the urge to kick him in the shin . . . or maybe higher. She satisfied herself with the thought, not the action, and cocked her head at him. "I have much to do. Do you not as well?"

"Not so much that I cannot take time to woo my future bride." His nose shifted direction subtly with each word he spoke. His hair, so dark a brown 'twas almost black, writhed around his face in the breeze that was growing stronger, and colder, by the moment. "You used to have sweet words for Hamish. Do you not have a sweet word for me?"

Sweet words meant little and she certainly didn't have any for this big muttonhead. He was cut from the same rough cloth as the chief's offspring, wild, willful, and too sure the world should bow down at his feet—something she would never do.

"Hamish was my husband. You are not."

"Aye, but I will be." Baltair grinned at her.

"Only if I am dead and lying in my grave," she muttered, stepping around him. Unfortunately, he followed her, his long legs catching him up quickly.

"Was that an acceptance?" he asked.

She stopped in her tracks and glared at him. Irritation was an emotion she did not like and this man gave it to her in heaps.

"Baltair MacLeod, have you no ears? Can you not understand my words? I. Will. Never. Marry. Again. Not you, not anyone. Shall I repeat it again more slowly so you will understand it this time?"

The grin left his face and his eyes went black and stony. "You will marry again, Morainn, and 'twill be to me. I am champion now," he said. "'Tis time for me to take a wife, have bairns."

A jolt ran through Morainn, but she did not let him see how his words pierced through her. Once she had wanted bairns but she had given up that dream.

"You are a good weaver, a good cook, or so Hamish used to say. I am sure Hamish trained you well in the other wifely duties," he continued, leering at her. "'Twould be a good match for you to wed me."

She was actually grateful he had continued, thus stoking her ire and steeling her will.

"'Twould be a good match for *you* to wed *me*," she said, "but 'twill not happen." Morainn's patience was at an end. "I have much to do before the light fails." She stepped around him again and set off for the castle.

She had not gone three steps before Baltair spun her around. She lost her grip on the plaid as he pulled her so close his nose doubled in her vision. She arched her back to get enough distance to judge his intent. 'Twas a mistake, for he took the opportunity to kiss her.

Revulsion combined with anger and all her control fled. She struggled to get loose, shoving against his rocklike chest, trying with all her might to wrench away from him, but he was too big, too strong, too determined.

Too gone.

One moment she was caught in the vise of his embrace, his hard lips pressed against hers, the next he was whirling around, trying to keep his balance. She stumbled backward, catching her own balance with difficulty.

"It doesn't look like the lass wants to be kissed, Baltair," came a smooth voice from behind the champion.

Baltair shifted to his left just enough so she could see who her new hero was. Flaxen hair danced about an oh-so-handsome face. A smile skirted the corners of his mouth, somehow balancing between a smirk and a grin. His eyes stayed on Baltair but she could feel his attention on her. Quickly, he glanced at her.

"Are you well, Morainn?"

His smoky-gray eyes held her gaze for a moment. His full-blown smile slammed into her with enough force to make her step backward. She stumbled on an icy patch and Ailig reached out to steady her, rescuing her once more. She wasn't sure she was comfortable seeing one of the chief's sons as her rescuer, especially not given the may-hem his smile was causing in her gut and the odd way her arm tingled where he held it. She stepped away from him, removing herself from his grip.

Ailig gave her a quizzical look, his honey-brown brows drawn down over eyes gone the color of clouds.

A ilig was puzzled by Morainn's lack of greeting. He knew she did not think much of him, but he had expected some word of thanks at the least. Her wildly curling brown hair showed glints of copper in the fading sunshine, though most of her curls were severely tamed in a thick braid that hung over one shoulder. Her smile was cautious.

"Did he harm you?" he asked.

She glared at Baltair, and Ailig was startled at the look of hatred Baltair flung in his direction.

"He did not. 'Tis only that he is hard of hearing, or gone completely daft."

"'Tis none of your affair, wean," Baltair said to Ailig as he grabbed Morainn's elbow and pulled her against his side. Morainn tried to pull her arm free but the man obviously had a tight grip upon her.

An unfamiliar protectiveness insinuated itself into Ailig's thoughts. He stepped closer, facing down the much larger man.

"I'd say 'tis none of yours, either, from the look on the lass's face. Release her."

"I do not take orders from you, bairnie. I am champion. I answer to the chief alone. I do not think you are that person."

"Not yet," Ailig said.

Rage painted Baltair's face a brilliant red and Ailig

prayed the man would give in to it. He'd like nothing better than a good fight to rid himself of the nervous energy that plagued him, but now wasn't the time for it.

"Not ever!" Baltair roared, shoving Morainn behind him, then surging toward Ailig.

A rage of his own swept through Ailig as he ducked the meaty fist that whistled just over his head.

"I've no time to fight you now." He whirled to his left as the big man charged at him, grabbing Baltair's arm as he passed. Before the larger man could react, Ailig had spun him so that his arm was twisted up against his back, his shoulder in danger of wrenching out of its socket.

Baltair's fists were clenched and his chest heaved as he tried to get loose. "You always were too much of a coward to fight fair."

"Calling me names will not change the fact that Morainn did not want your kiss, Baltair. 'Twould seem you are the coward for forcing yourself on someone unable to defend herself."

He heard Morainn gasp behind him.

"I *can* defend myself!"

He grinned at the spirit in her voice. He glanced over his shoulder at the beautiful woman glaring at the both of them, hands on her hips and challenge in her sparkling eyes. In truth, he could not fault Baltair for wanting to kiss her, only for acting upon it when the lass clearly did not want his attentions.

"If I release you"—Ailig pulled harder on Baltair's arm, making his point—"will you leave us and cease bothering Mistress Morainn?"

"You cannot hold me here forever, wee Ailig."

Ailig figured that was as close as he was likely to get to

an affirmative answer from the man, so he released him with a shove toward the gate.

"You can take your anger out on me later, Baltair, and I will relish the excuse to break your nose again, but for now I must see the chief."

"'Twas a lucky punch, pup, and many years ago. 'Twill never happen again." He scowled at Morainn. "We are not done, lass." He shifted the scowl back to Ailig. "'Twill be my pleasure to beat you to a bloody pulp, just as soon as the chief is done with you."

The man rubbed his shoulder, then turned his back on both of them and stomped through the gate into the castle.

"Do not look at me like that, Morainn. Had I known you could defend yourself I would have happily watched you scratch his eyes out."

He watched as her glare shifted into an embarrassed smile. "I do appreciate your rescue," she said, looking down at the snow-crusted ground. "He took me by surprise."

As she took him. He vaguely remembered her as a little girl, all gangly arms and legs, but now . . . now she was grown up, and the sharp elbows and knees had given way to womanly curves. His body surged, surprising him, and he quickly turned back to gather the reins he'd dropped when he'd vaulted off his horse.

"Are you well?" he asked over his shoulder.

"Aye," she said, her voice tentative. "Did you find your sister?"

He nodded. "Catriona is well." But he could say no more. Not yet. He turned back to face her, his horse following behind. "I must speak to the chief."

She nodded and stepped back, breaking a thread that he

hadn't even realized had connected them, even if only for a moment.

"You were in mourning when I left, were you not?" he asked, though he wasn't sure why.

"I was," she said, then looked to the castle. "Thank you for your help, but I would not keep you from doing what you must."

Reluctantly he agreed. "Perhaps I shall see you at the evening meal?" Ailig said as he mounted his horse.

"I do not take my meals in the castle."

"Pity," he said, mostly to himself. He leaned on his saddle and looked down at her. The icy snow pellets had shifted to light fluffy flakes that caught on her coppery-brown hair and melted where they landed on her softly freckled nose and cheeks.

"You've grown up, Morainn," he said.

"Most people do," she said, looking up at him.

"Aye, but not many turn out as bonny as you have." He smiled at the pink that stained her cheeks and urged the horse on his way. At least there was one bright spot to returning to Assynt. He looked up at the castle looming over him and realized 'twas likely the only bright spot he would find for a very long time.

A few people bustled through the shadowed inner bailey, casting curious glances at him as he approached the stable. Grimy, snow-blanketed, well-trod paths leading amongst the outbuildings, the Great Hall, and the two towers showed that the denizens of Assynt Castle still kept to their work.

A lad darted out of the stable and took the reins as Ailig divested the horse of his belongings.

"Be sure he gets oats and a good brush," he said, his voice more brusque than he had intended. For all that seeing the beautiful Morainn had buoyed his spirits, the thought of finally confronting his father with his news, and the king's command, had him on edge. The lad grunted his assent as he led the tired horse away.

Ailig hooked his traveling sack over his shoulder and made for the chief's tower. He'd had a full fortnight to mull over what he must do next, but he still didn't know how to break the tidings to his father—nor to anyone else for that matter—but that, at least, would be his father's trouble.

He stepped out of the windy cold of the bailey and into the damp, bone-chilling cold of the stone tower. He took the winding stairway, two steps at a time, his sack bouncing against his back as if urging him on. Passing the first landing, he moved upward to the second, the one that led to his own chamber. He thought fleetingly of a long night's sleep in his own bed; of the feather-filled mattress covered in soft linen sheets, and, for warmth, a heavy woolen blanket and another of furs his sister had made for him several winters ago. If the beautiful Morainn were to join him there . . .

But no. Before comfort, before rest, sustenance or anything involving a very bonny woman, before anything else, duty called and 'twould accomplish nothing to put it off. He laid his bag next to a plain door, much like the one at the bottom of the stairs and raised his fist. Each rap of his knuckles against the hard wood tightened the knots across his shoulders.

At the muffled reply "enter," Ailig lifted the latch and pushed open the heavy door, ducking slightly as he stepped under the low lintel and into the chief's outer chamber.

His father, Neill, chief of Clan Leod, sat at the battered table he used as a desk, scratching away at a parchment, mumbling to himself, ignoring Ailig as he always had. Ailig cleared his throat.

"Da."

"What? What is it?" Neill asked without raising his head from his work. His stringy gray hair fell about his face and he was crouched so close to the table Ailig could swear his nose almost touched the parchment. 'Twas the same way he dealt with the clan's business, and his own family, so close he could see the immediate situation, but never far enough away to see all that happened around him. He'd even missed the treachery brewing right under his nose.

"Da!"

Neill finally looked up from his work and seemed to take a moment to shift his concentration away from the parchment and toward the door where Ailig stood. After a moment his eyes focused. He sighed and leaned back in his plainly carved chair.

"Where are your brothers? And Catriona?" He looked past him, as always, as if expecting his four other sons and a runaway daughter to file in behind him.

The time had finally come to deliver the news that would destroy any hope of ever winning this man's elusive, ungraspable respect. He took a seat across from his father, took a deep breath and dove in.

"Catriona has wed another," he said, starting with the

easiest thing he had to tell. "My brothers will not be re-turning."

His father looked at him, his eyes narrowed. But he did not reply to this news.

"Calum, Gowan and Jamie serve in the king's army until such time as the Bruce deems their service done."

Still his father said nothing, but he leaned forward, bracing his elbows on the table and lacing his fingers to-gether.

When Ailig said nothing, the auld man raised an eye-brow.

"You do not wish to tell me the rest? Where is Broc, my heir? And what of Duff? We shall have to tell the Mac-Donells who yet reside here what has happened to their chief."

So the MacDonells were still here. That was a compli-cation he'd rather not have. Ailig took a deep breath and met his father's cold eyes. "Duff has been taken to the gaol at Dingwall Castle. He awaits the king's justice for trea-son."

Now there was a spark of worry in Neill's eyes. "And Broc . . . ?"

Ailig swallowed, unsure how the chief would take what he must say next, and still 'twas not the worst news he must deliver, at least not as far as Neill was concerned.

"Broc . . . is dead."

"Nay!" Neill surged to his feet. He banged the table once with his fists. "It cannot be! What have you done with him? Where is he?" Neill was leaning over the table, his eyes so wide the whites around them shone. "Where is he?!"

"He was buried in Culrain. 'Twas where we met up with

the king." Worried at the wild look in his father's eye, Ailig rose and poured a cup of ale from a pitcher set on one corner of the table. "There is more, sir, but I would have you calm yourself. Drink this." He held the cup out for his father to take.

The chief stared at the cup for a moment, as if he could not understand what it was his son offered him. He looked up at Ailig with grief-filled eyes, red rimmed. His skin was ashen and he looked as if he had aged a decade in but a moment. At last, he reached out and took the ale, downing it in one long gulp, then he lowered himself back into his chair, staring past Ailig.

"What more can there be?" he finally whispered.

Indeed, what could be worse than learning of the death of your eldest child, the one who would follow you as chief of the clan? What could be worse than knowing your next three children were fighting bloody battles in the king's army that they weren't likely to survive? What could be worse than your only daughter, betrothed to one man, running off and marrying another?

What could be worse?

Ailig forced himself to sit absolutely still, schooling his features into cool indifference. The king had laid the fate of Clan Leod in Ailig's hands, and he would not shirk that responsibility.

"The king commands that you relinquish your place as chief of Clan Leod of Assynt," Ailig said at last, firmly, matter-of-factly, without emotion.

Neill stared at his youngest son as if he were a stranger. "I will not."

"You must. Da, the king will set his men upon us, turn us out of Assynt, out of our homes, scatter us into the bens and lay a price upon the head of every man, woman and child amongst us if you do not. We will all be hunted down and slaughtered."

Neill sat back in his chair heavily, resting one elbow on the chair's arm and his head in his hand. "But Broc is dead."

"He is."

"And the others are serving in the king's army."

"They are."

Ailig could see the exact moment his father began to understand what the king had commanded. He glared up at his youngest son.

"Who is the traitor who seeks to steal my place upon the command of a king who knows nothing of Highland custom?" 'Twas not so much a question as an accusation.

Ailig forced himself to hold his father's glare with his own.

"'Tis I."

chapter 2

Morainn had watched Ailig disappear into the castle with her emotions churning. On one hand she was grateful that he had turned up when he had, but on the other she was irritated that she had needed anyone's help. Especially someone who made her skin heat up just by looking at her, or made her heart race by touching her.

As he rode away from her toward the castle, she'd seen him square his shoulders and sit a little taller in the saddle, but she had the distinct impression it was not for her benefit. Nay, 'twas more like the way she'd seen warriors ride out to battle, and she wondered what sort of battle he expected to find within his own home. 'Twas only then that she realized that he had left Assynt with all his brothers and the chief of the MacDonells—and he'd returned alone.

A sharp wind slapped at her, bringing the smell of ice off the loch. She shook herself out of the reverie she'd fallen into. 'Twas none of her affair what went on in Ailig's life, nor what troubled him.

She looked about for her plaid, picked it up out of the purple-shadowed snow and shook it out. She needed to get this to Una. She folded the plaid and set out for the castle, determined to get in and back out without meeting Baltair or Ailig again.

Morainn passed through the gate and into the castle's bailey. The big laundry caldron stood alone in the far corner of the open courtyard, so Morainn made for the bothy behind it. She came to a halt before the rickety door and knocked quietly. The door opened slowly and a tiny little girl peered up at her with thin, white-blond hair and big, sky-blue eyes.

"Are you come to see Mama?" she chirped, reaching up hesitantly to touch the fabric.

Morainn squatted down until she was almost eye level with the lass. "Aye, Lili. Do you like this?" She pushed the fabric closer so the child could pet it as if 'twere a wee pup.

Lili smiled shyly at Morainn. "'Tis very pretty. Mama says when I get bigger she'll have you teach me how to weave."

"I'd be honored to teach you as my own mother taught me." The door swung wide and Morainn stood up again.

"Mind your manners, child," Una said with a smile in her voice as she wiped her hands on the barmcloth tied at her waist. She pushed straight blond hair back from her heat-flushed face. "Invite Morainn to come in."

Lili stepped back into the comfort of her mother's skirts and mumbled the invitation. Morainn entered the humid room and spied an empty basket sitting in the middle of the floor as if Una had only just finished emptying it. Freshly washed clothes and linens draped the lines of rope that stretched from one wall to the other and back again. Three small fires burned in battered braziers around the space, warming the air.

Morainn handed her plaid to Una. "This is the wool I need wauked. Will you add it to the rest?"

Una took the plaid and opened it, holding it to the uncertain light from the braziers.

"'Tis beautiful," she said, her voice hushed as if she beheld something sacred.

"'Tis only a trial."

"Well, I shouldn't go saying that to Morna. Her best work cannot compare to your worst, never mind something as beautiful as this."

Una folded it up again. "We shall be waulking in another sennight. Will you not join us this time? I should think you'd like to be the one to say when 'tis sufficiently done, especially with this piece." She sent a sly look at Morainn but Morainn ignored it.

"I trust your eye, if not your intent." Una was forever trying to pull her back into the life of the castle.

"Your mourning is done, sweetling. It has been two full years since Hamish went, God rest his soul. He was a good man, and he would not like to see you so alone all the time."

Morainn rubbed her hands together over the nearest brazier, her back to Una so the woman could not see how much her words troubled her. She could not explain to her friend why she chose to keep herself distant from the clan so much of the time. 'Twould be humiliating to admit that she did not trust her own feelings. Una would never un-

derstand that she did not want to put herself in a position
where she was not completely sure of herself.

"I swear my hands shall never be warm again,"
Morainn said.

There was a little snort from behind her. "The draft
through this pitiful roof won't help, but perhaps once the
weather grows warm they shall thaw. Or you could find
some braw man to warm them for you. I saw Baltair passing through the bailey just before you came . . ."

"I have no interest in Baltair," she said, pleased that at
least in this she could tell her friend the truth. "I shall await
the turning of the seasons . . ." She faced Una again. "But
'twas another nice try."

Una shrugged. "Your mourning time is passed, lass.
'Tis high time you started to live your life again. I mourned
my Rabby's passing as hard as any, but there comes a time
where you have to go on. Hiding will not heal anything."

Morainn gave Una a quick hug. "I know. I know." She
reached for the door, her back to Una once more. "I shall
think about joining in the waulking this time. Good-bye,
Lili," she called to the little girl playing in the corner as she
escaped the bothy and Una's well-intended pushing.

*A*ilig opened his eyes the next morn to find the sky, visible through two small windows, just lightening to a
steely, predawn gray. Of course this time of year, when the
sun only rose above the bens for a few hours, predawn was
sleeping late. He scanned the cold chamber, taking in the
details of a room he knew well: the large bed, made more
comfortable by weeks of sleeping on the ground or cold,
hard bits of floor; the stand in the corner, near one of the

windows, that held a basin and a pitcher of water that was likely to have a skin of ice over its surface; a trunk at the foot of the bed held his clothes. A tapestry, which his sister had insisted he have, hung on one wall. 'Twas of Saint George slaying the dragon as the princess and her parents looked on. Catriona had always thought it funny, but the story had somehow comforted Ailig so he kept it. The rest of the chamber was unremarkable, a hearth, a candle stand in one corner and little else.

He sat up and threw off the covers, determined to face the day as soon as possible. He pushed himself out of the warm bed and into the cold room, moving first to stir up the fire. Crossing to the basin, he poured icy water into it, then splashed his face with the cold liquid in the hope that it would clear his muzzy head.

As he dressed, he decided that the first thing he required, even before his father told the clan the tale, was information. It could not wait for the formal announcement. There was no time to waste as he'd been privy to precious little of the chief's plans for the clan. He must learn what most needed tending to within the castle and without. He must learn if the MacDonells, who yet remained within these walls, were biding peacefully—he doubted that greatly—or if they were stirring up trouble and what it would take to get them to leave for their own castle. And he must learn who would support him as chief . . . and who would not.

But that information would have to come as he could find it, since he dared not ask anyone openly yet. The rest he could approach more directly. Perhaps.

His thoughts turned to Morainn. She had looked so . . . He searched for the right word. Beautiful, aye, enough to take a man's breath away, but that wasn't what had struck him the most. She held herself away, separate, as if she challenged anyone to get close to her. 'Twas a silly thought when Baltair had been about as close to her as a man could get with his clothes on, but the impression had stuck with him.

His stomach grumbled, pulling him from his wandering thoughts, and he realized it had been nearly a full day since last he ate. He'd been too tired to bother last night. For now, he would go to the Great Hall, break his fast, and look over those assembled there, learn what he could before seeking out the chief again.

He donned his clothes, tunic, trews, a pair of fur-lined brogues, and a length of plaid that he swathed about him like a cloak, then quickly left his chamber.

As he neared the Great Hall he heard the sound of loud voices. One shouted above the rest, but Ailig could not make out the words over the din. He turned the corner into the hall and stopped in the doorway.

The MacDonells were all gathered there, some half-score of unkempt warriors, hunkered around a trestle table laden with the morning meal. One striking warrior stood upon the table, his black hair tied back from his ruddy face, his thick eyebrows drawn down over serious eyes and his large booted feet planted firmly between the platters of meat. He stood with his fists upon his hips as if he commanded a mighty Viking ship, come to conquer and pillage all that he surveyed.

Ailig guessed that this was the one whose voice had risen above the others.

"We will have the truth, lads," the man said. A roar of agreement rose around him. "We will know what these conniving MacLeods have done with our chief!" Another roar of approval. "We will have the lass *and* the tocher that comes with her!" Another roar.

The MacDonells surged to their feet, beating the table with their fists. A self-satisfied smile exploded on the man's face as he regarded his loud kinsmen.

'Twas not the quiet breaking of a fast Ailig had hoped for, but 'twas revealing. He crossed his arms and leaned against the door frame, awaiting a lull in the rabble-rousing.

He might not like what he saw and heard, but he'd not give the MacDonells the satisfaction of thinking they had rattled him. Ailig had much practice in feigning a bored disinterest. He'd oft struck such a pose when faced with the troubles his brothers inevitably spawned.

He scanned the crowded hall for Baltair—after all, the clan's champion should be here keeping an eye on their "guests." If he looked for Morainn at the same time who would blame him? The lass intrigued him and he did have it in mind to wed once all was settled with the king.

Another shout from the MacDonells forced Ailig to shove his errant thoughts away. He could not let himself get distracted by thoughts of Morainn or any woman. For now, he must stay focused and do what was necessary to see to the clan's future, including the formidable task of ridding the castle of this rabble as quickly as possible.

The MacDonell troublemaker jumped down from the table, slapping several of his fellows on the back, and taking his place at the far end of the table he had been standing on.

Ailig pushed away from the doorway and carefully sauntered past the MacDonells without looking at any of them. He schooled his expression to show his complete lack of concern with the mummery they had just executed. When he reached the deserted chief's table upon the dais at the far end of the hall, he slouched into a large chair at one end.

Tonight he would sit in the chief's chair, carved with the symbol of Clan Leod, a bull's head with the clan's motto, "Hold Fast," in Latin above. The sides and arms were richly carved with twining branches of juniper burnished to a rich golden glow where generations of MacLeod chiefs had rested their hands. Ailig knew 'twas an imposing chair and 'twould be an imposing image of the future chief, comfortable in his surroundings when he sat in it at the evening meal.

He was not above a bit of theatrics himself and only wished he dared sit there now. But he could not, would not, until he had been made chief.

A kitchen lad brought him a wooden bowl and a horn spoon. Another brought a platter of salted beef, sliced thin, and another brought a pot of porridge. The first returned with a pewter mug. He nodded at the boy, quietly thanking him as he poured ale into it.

Ailig served himself a generous portion of porridge and snagged a piece of beef. 'Twas dry, tough and salty, just like the beef he'd been eating on his travels the past fortnight. Their "guests" must have eaten all the fresh meat for the kitchen to be serving salt beef so early in the winter. Perhaps he could escape the castle confines to hunt. Perhaps he could lure the MacDonells into a hunt, then have the gate barred against them after they left. Nay, he could not, for 'twould be an inexcusable breach of hospitality.

Ailig sighed. He could not force the MacDonells to

leave, so he would bide his time until he found a way to convince them that leaving was their own idea.

But he'd not wait too long.

Absently, Ailig lifted his spoon and tasted his porridge. Unpleasantly surprised, he looked down at his bowl. There were singed bits of oats floating amidst undercooked porridge. There were gray lumps amidst a watery base. He shoved it away and reached for the beef. At least that would satisfy his hunger, even if it was tough and salty.

As he chewed and watched the Great Hall fill with the castle dwellers, he considered those gathered there. The elders who served as the chief's council were conspicuously absent. They were probably meeting with the chief. A spurt of anger charged through Ailig. He should have been included in any such meeting. He took a deep breath and tried to let the anger slide away from him. Soon enough he would be the chief and he'd choose his own counselors.

He concentrated on the hall before him again, casting about for something to distract him from what his father might or might not be telling the elders council. Many warriors of the clan were here, along with many of the clan's women and weans, breaking their fast. All appeared to be doing their best to avoid the MacDonells, keeping their backs to them when possible, averting their eyes, the women keeping their weans close by their sides instead of letting them run about as was more usual.

Several young men entered the hall at the far end, laughter introducing them to the gathering. Ailig scowled when he recognized Baltair standing a full head taller than those around him. The champion should have been here earlier. The group took a table near the door and called for food and ale. Ailig recognized others, and slowly came to see that here was the future of the MacLeods. These were the men who would first lead the clan, then someday serve as the elders of the chief's council. These were the men he would most need to support him in his efforts as chief. These were the men he would have to convince to support the king, perhaps even to serve in the king's army.

Unfortunately, almost all of them were nit-brained friends and supporters of his brothers.

He really hated these men.

Ailig rose, leaving behind the remains of his disappointing meal. Slowly, to give himself time to assess the warriors, he moved along the shadows toward the other end of the hall. They were laughing, eating, drinking and telling ribald jokes. He stopped halfway and leaned against the wall, watching the byplay between them. One man knocked a cup of ale from another's hand while gesturing madly about what he and a woman had done in the night. Two others exchanged knowing glances but Ailig couldn't decide if it was because they knew the woman or they doubted the man. Several of the younger men sat on the edges of the group, laughing at the banter but not really participating.

"Do you ken the lot of them?" a voice asked at his shoulder.

Ailig quickly looked behind him and found a stranger at his elbow. The man was slight of build, thin and wiry, with the straight white-blond hair of the Norsemen. The hard planes of his face spoke of strength and determination though his eyes were hooded, as if he could not be bothered to look fully at anything around him.

"Aye, I know them, though I do not know who you are."

"Skaeth," was all the man said, never taking his eyes off the men at the far table.

"Just Skaeth?"

"Aye. Just Skaeth, but you be the young MacLeod, Ailig, are you not?"

Ailig nodded and directed his attention back to join Skaeth's at the warrior's table. "What brings you to Assynt Castle, Just Skaeth?"

"Nothing brings me here. 'Tis simply where I was when the snows hit. I'm a mercenary. Thought perhaps you could use my services until the snows thaw and I can be on my way again."

Ailig didn't say anything right away. "Where are you on your way to, Just Skaeth?" He could almost feel the man glowering at him, but it did not stop Ailig from prodding him.

"'Tis none of your affair. I am here now and would prefer to earn my way rather than to impose upon you and yours as a guest for the entire winter. I tried to speak to the chief but was told to speak to the brothers, that one of you would do the hiring."

Ailig kept his gaze on the warriors at the table and tried to hide his surprise at the mercenary's words. "And pray, who told you that?"

"'Twas the auld man with the bright blue eyes and the large ears."

"Angus Mhór?"

"Aye, 'twas his name."

Ailig considered this information for a moment. Angus Mhór was the youngest of the elders, only recently added to his father's council and Angus Mhór was no admirer of Broc's. Interesting. "How long have you been here?"

"A sennight, give or take a day."

"And what have you learned of my clan in that sennight?"

The man snorted. "Do you want the truth, or are you looking to be flattered?"

Ailig faced the man. He considered his features again, strong bones, hooded eyes, a mouth that promised brutal truths, and there was a wariness about him that fit with what he said he was. Here was a man used to intrigue, used to being on the outside, looking in. A man who had nothing to lose by telling the truth. And truth was something Ailig could use.

"I would be the last person to look for flattery. The truth is what I need. I would ask that of you."

Skaeth took his turn to consider Ailig and, though he could not tell what decision the man came to, Ailig could tell when the decision was made. Skaeth's shoulders relaxed, almost imperceptibly. Ailig returned his attention to the warriors.

"The big one—" Skaeth began.

"Baltair," Ailig supplied.

"He thinks to be in charge, but he's not an agile thinker, that one."

Ailig agreed. Baltair had been chosen as champion for his loyalty and strength, not for his mental abilities.

"The two on either side are strong warriors. I've seen 'em training, but they are none too smart outside of warfare. The three on the edge, now they are the interesting ones. The one in the green cloak—"

Ailig leaned his head to see around the bulk of Baltair. "Ah, Tamas MacRailt." He'd not noticed the brother to Morainn's dead husband, Hamish, earlier. What was he doing keeping company with the likes of Baltair? Tamas was one of the few people in this castle he thought he could call friend. Perhaps he had been wrong about him.

"Tamas then." Skaeth's voice jerked his attention back to the man beside him. "He's the one I'd turn to with a problem. He's quite useful with sword, knife or bow, though not as good as some of the others, but he's smart, creative. He makes up for his weaker strike by studying his foe for openings, weaknesses, mistakes—then he takes advantage of them."

The man described Tamas well, at least the Tamas he thought he knew.

"And you learned all this by watching them train?"

"Aye. You can learn a lot about a man by watching him train. Shall I go on?" Skaeth asked.

"You speak of the warriors but you tell me nothing of the clan."

"What is a clan without its warriors?"

Ailig had no answer for that. He'd have to gather information about the clan from another source. "So you think Tamas is the smartest of the lot?"

"By far."

"And you wish employment for the winter?"

"Aye."

"Very well. You shall have it. There is no coin to pay you but you may find a pallet in the guards' tower. Report to the captain of the guard and have him assign you."

"I do not make for a good guard."

Ailig glanced back at the man, surprised. "But you said you are a mercenary."

"I am, but not a guard. If I wished for such a dull job I

would not be wandering the Highlands in winter now would I?"

This tweaked Ailig's curiosity. "What, then, do you wish to do?"

"I would like to work in the training yard."

"Work?"

"I can spar with your warriors, help them to hone their skills."

"What makes you think you can teach them anything they do not already know?"

"I told you. I have been watching them. There is much I can teach them. 'Twill benefit your clan to have better-trained warriors and guards."

Ailig narrowed his eyes at the man. There was no shortage of pride in him, no shortage of confidence, and yet he was slight compared to the warriors. He was no taller than Ailig, if not slightly shorter, and Ailig was the shortest of the MacLeod brothers.

"I can prove my worth to you, if you like," Skaeth said. "Meet me in the training yard in an hour's time and you can decide for yourself if I have anything to teach your warriors."

"Good. If I find you do not, you will join the guard or leave the castle."

"Agreed."

"An hour then, for now I have other things I must attend to," Ailig said, dismissing the man.

Skaeth slipped away as quietly as he had come.

Ailig stood watching the warriors for a few more minutes. He'd like to speak to Tamas but now was not the time. Baltair was regaling the table with a story of one of his romantic conquests and Ailig was only glad that the lass whose name was being loudly used was not present to experience the embarrassment. 'Twas not the time to talk to any of them.

Staying to the shadows near the wall, Ailig tried to make his way to the door without drawing attention to himself.

"Wee Ailig!" Baltair bellowed at him. "Do you think to slink away and not tell us what you know of Broc and Duff?"

For a split second Ailig thought of bolting for the door as he had often done as a wean. Running had usually been the best option, but he could not do that now. He'd been expecting a confrontation; he'd only hoped to postpone it until his father had spoken to the clan.

He changed direction and walked deliberately to the table, never taking his eyes off Baltair's.

"I do not slink," he said when he arrived beside him.

"Nay, you slither," Baltair said. "Where are Broc and Duff?"

"I cannot say. The MacLeod will soon tell the tale to all here gathered. But you shall have to await his pleasure."

"When will he tell it?"

Ailig shrugged as he tried to gauge the mood of the other warriors. "I do not know."

"But you ken Broc and Duff's fate," Baltair growled. "Tell us now!" he said rising to his feet to face Ailig.

Ailig forced himself to stand his ground, though clearly Baltair was seeking to intimidate with his greater height.

"I will not," he said, carefully keeping his voice level and detached. "I am bound by my word to my father. Would you have me betray my chief's trust? Would you betray it?" He managed to slide the smallest hint of sarcasm into his question, and it won him a scowl from the man.

The sudden loud clattering of a spilled food tray startled them all and was quickly followed by oaths.

"I'm sick of this shite hole," one of the MacDonells shouted.

Ailig couldn't clearly hear the rest of the conversation, but there was a lot of grumbling about their hosts and their accommodations and the food.

Baltair stared at Ailig. "Since you are so beholden to the chief, perhaps you can get him to rid us of those vermin," he said. "I have tried, but was told to await Broc's and Duff's return." He took a step closer. "Why do I have the idea that they will not be returning soon?"

"The chief has his reasons for allowing our guests to remain," Ailig said, "though I am not privy to them."

Without so much as a good-bye, he strode for the door. Baltair was going to be trouble and 'twas up to the chief, the current chief, to rein him in before his misplaced loyalty overruled his thick head.

As he passed the last trestle table he glanced back at the hall. The mercenary, Skaeth, was seated not far from the MacDonells, flirting with a lass and seemingly oblivious to the roiling emotions around him. But there was something about the way he was angled, so that he could see both the MacDonell table and the one Baltair commanded, that told Ailig the man was quite aware of what was going on around him.

Ailig envied the mercenary. He could choose his fights while Ailig had forever had his fights forced upon him.

chapter 3

The sun had risen enough to turn the sky a smoky blue when Ailig reached the bailey stair. He resolved to speak to Skaeth about the MacDonells when they met to spar. He doubted not that the mercenary would have some interesting insights into their guests.

"Ailig!" He stopped halfway down the steps to see who had called him. "A word, please," Tamas said, as he jogged down the stairs to meet him.

Initial pleasure that his friend had followed him out was tempered by the knowledge that Tamas had been happily seated at Baltair's table.

"If Baltair sent you to fetch the news you'll have to go back without it. I cannot tell you what happened, either."

Tamas stopped, then descended more slowly, a scowl on his normally smiling face. "I am no errand boy for Baltair." He stood on the same step as Ailig and faced him. "You think because I choose to show the MacDonells where my loyalties lie it means I have lost my sense about the likes of Baltair?"

Ailig looked down for a moment, then focused back on Tamas. "You are right. I should not be so suspicious. 'Tis only that I'm not sure who to trust after these past few sennights. What did you wish to speak to me about?"

"Will you walk with me?" Tamas raised his hand in the direction of the gate.

Ailig shrugged and they set off down the rest of the stairs. Tamas seemed to be gathering his thoughts, so Ailig matched his stride and they walked in silence as he tried to decide how to ask about Morainn without seeming too obvious. They did not stop until they were outside the castle gate and facing Quinag, the mountain that commanded the opposite side of the frozen loch; its slopes were covered in snow this morning and its peak was crowned in wispy clouds.

"There is much to set to rights in this castle," Tamas said after a moment.

"I doubt it not," Ailig said, throwing a rock toward the ice-crusted shore of the loch. "Is there trouble with the guard?"

Tamas picked up a rock and tossed it in a high arc toward the loch. It landed with a hollow thunk on the ice and skittered away across the surface where it would await the spring thaw to finish its journey to the depths of the dark waters.

An image skittered through his mind of him standing on that ice, waiting for it to crack and sink beneath him. Almost unconsciously he checked his stance, making sure his feet were well planted.

"I cannot speak to the guard," Tamas said, "though I believe they are alert, at least when Baltair is visible. The lads tend to relax when his back is turned. Come to think of it, perhaps there is a problem there . . ."

"I shall see to it immediately," Ailig said, pivoting on his heel toward the castle, glad for something substantial he could work on.

"Wait," Tamas said, grabbing him by the arm. "'Twas not what I wished to speak to you about."

"Oh?"

"'Tis the castle . . . the food, the maids who tend the fires, hell, even the privy chutes are a disgrace."

"The . . . food?" Ailig shook his head, not understanding. The food was awful, but that was not his concern.

"Aye. The food has been ghastly since the Shrew ran away. There are other troubles, but the food is definitely the most pressing." Tamas threw another rock onto the ice. "'Tis what always sets off the MacDonells. But our own folk grumble over the same salt beef and horrid porridge every morn, too, with little better at the other meals."

He faced Ailig. "I," he said, poking himself in the chest with his thumb, "have been forced to sup with my mum each evening." The look of horror on Tamas's face almost made Ailig laugh, but he sensed the man was serious so he covered his mouth with a fist and cleared his throat to keep from offending him.

"The lads," Tamas continued, "take turns coming home with me. They appreciate the meal, but the company . . . well, no one ever said my mum was easy to live with."

Ailig knew the auld woman; everyone knew the difficult Agnes. He remembered wondering how Morainn, with her sunny disposition, could bear to live with such a sour person when she married Hamish.

"Morainn, does she still bide in her father's cottage?" The question was out before he realized he had voiced it.

Tamas gave him a considering look. "Aye. 'Tis hers now that he is gone."

"And she lives there . . . alone?"

Tamas smiled and Ailig realized he had asked too many questions. "I only ask because I met her yesterday when I returned. Baltair was . . . bothering her."

Tamas shook his head. "She'll never have that lad but he is determined."

"Determined, or daft. 'Twas very clear she did not want his attentions."

Tamas tensed. "What happened?"

"He kissed her. I stopped him. He was none too pleased."

"She should have told me."

"I handled it."

"She is my responsibility."

"I was there."

The two glared at each other for a moment. Tamas broke away first. "I suppose it is a good thing you were, but I shall have a word with Baltair."

"I do not think she wishes either of us to help her."

Tamas snorted. "You ken her well. The lass is too independent for her own good."

Ailig stared out at the mountain, remembering how he and Tamas had spent hours scrambling over the lower slopes of the bens when they were weans. 'Twould be fun to set out for the wilder parts of the Highlands again. But they were no longer children. Besides, he had too many things to tend to here at the castle, and if Tamas was right, the kitchen seemed to be the first thing that required his attention.

"You are telling me," he said, pulling himself back to the original topic of this conversation, "that since Catriona left, the castle has gone to wrack and ruin and my father has done naught to correct it?"

"Just so. Baltair has told him, several times, of the troubles. He just tells Baltair to see to it, but that lad is good for naught save fighting. There hasn't been a decent meal in weeks. The maids tend the fires when it suits them, which isn't often. The privies need cleaning out and those lads have an uncanny way of disappearing whenever someone goes looking for them with a shovel. The storage rooms are a shambles. 'Twould seem that any time something is needed everything else gets tossed out of the way until you cannot find anything without shifting everything. Shall I go on?"

Ailig encouraged him and Tamas continued his list— the farrier, the smith, the guard.

When at last the man fell silent all Ailig could do was shake his head.

"I don't think anyone ever appreciated how Catriona kept everything running smoothly around here," Tamas said. "Not that she did it in the most pleasant way . . . She could take lessons from my good sister on that score."

"Morainn."

Tamas cast a sly look at him. "The very one."

Ailig considered Tamas's description of the shambles the castle had fallen into in such a short span of time. "Cat would be confounded to hear such a tale, with herself as the heroine." He chuckled and felt the knots across his shoulders loosen, ever so slightly. It had been too long since he had laughed.

"So what are you going to do about it, Ailig?" Tamas stepped in front of him, blocking his view of the ben and forcing him to focus on Tamas's determined face.

Ailig snapped his attention to his companion. "Why do you assume 'tis up to me?"

"You are the only son of the chief here, now. 'Tis your duty."

"Aye, 'tis." Ailig could see questions simmering in Tamas's eyes, but the man did not ask them. "I suppose I need to find someone else to see to the kitchen and stores. I don't know the first thing about running a kitchen, though I can assure the fires are tended, and I could sort out how to clean the privy chutes. It seems to me, though, that the lads have earned the right to keep that job a bit longer than they first anticipated—once we find them."

Ailig's mind was running over all the tasks that Cat had done for the castle, all the people she had overseen.

"I said I have a suggestion," Tamas was saying, as if 'twas not the first time he'd said it.

Ailig looked at him expectantly.

"Morainn is the best cook west of Inverness. She's very capable and she's a widow with no weans to mind nor any other family." He seemed to watch Ailig particularly closely as he said this. "I think she'd suit you perfectly."

"Suit me?"

"To oversee the kitchen, plan the meals, see to the stores. She would need to move into the castle, though. The job would require early hours and late. I would not like her having to go out in the cold to go to her cottage at the end of each day, nor trekking through the cold of a dark morn."

Ailig tossed a rock in the air and caught it again. He doubted not that Tamas had ulterior motives for the suggestion, not the least of which was avoiding his own mum each evening. But 'twould serve to improve the fare served in the Great Hall, to the benefit of the clan. And if Ailig had a certain interest in perhaps getting to know the lass a bit better, where was the harm in that?

"I agree," he said, almost to himself, throwing another stone out toward the loch. This time it hit with a dull thud, then disappeared through the ice. "I think she will be perfect."

"Just so," Tamas said with a grin. "Let us find her now and convince her." He gestured for Ailig to follow him and they quickly left the frozen loch behind.

M orainn *stepped out of her cottage and pulled the* door closed behind her, making sure the latch held against the ever present bone-chilling wind. She was waiting for that day when she stepped outside to find the air almost imperceptibly softer, smoother, a harbinger of spring. But today was not that day.

She clutched her cloak tightly about her lest the fierce gusts succeed in their efforts to pull it from her. Forcing her shoulders to relax, she reminded herself that she was going to see Una for the second day in a row so she might discover what trouble Ailig MacLeod had brought back with him. Curiosity had kept her awake much of the night, curiosity and worry.

Ailig's braw form and brilliant smile had nothing to do

with her restless night, despite the fact that each time she'd dozed off her dreams had been filled with a sandy-haired warrior whose eyes were the palest of grays.

She pressed the heel of her hand to her chest. Nay, 'twas not that he was bonny to look upon, nor that he had rid her of Baltair's unwanted attentions that kept him in her mind. 'Twas that the brothers MacLeod excelled at bringing trouble home with them and she expected no less this time.

The last time they had gone out and fewer returned, it had been Hamish they had left behind, lying dead upon the moor. She might not have had a happy life with Hamish, but no one deserved to be left for dead that way. Ailig returning alone could not bode well for the clan.

So she would see Una. Una knew everything that happened in the castle, for sooner or later everyone passed by the laundress's bothy in the course of a day.

She knew Una would take her curiosity and questions as a sign that she was interested in Ailig, but there was naught she could do about that. Were she to be interested in any man, 'twould never be one of the chief's sons. But she was determined to get the latest news. Forewarned was forearmed her father always said, so she set off at her usual brisk pace. As she came round a bend in the path that skirted a large boulder she hesitated.

Two men stood face-to-face near the loch, deep in conversation. She could not make out their faces at this distance, but as she looked more closely her heart thudded. Something about the way the one stood, his feet planted solidly beneath him, his arm folded across his chest, reminded her of Ailig as he rode into the castle yesterday—determined and ready to do battle. The other looked familiar, too, but it wasn't until they seemed to come to some sort of agreement and turned toward the path that she realized 'twas Tamas.

Curiosity seized her, speeding her steps.

Ailig noticed her first, raising his hand in greeting. Awareness skipped over her skin, irritating her. Just the sight of the braw man had her thoughts rushing to things best not considered. She focused on her curiosity, pushing away the unwanted attraction. 'Twas possible she would not have to visit with Una after all. Perhaps she could find out what was going on right now. And if Ailig was close-mouthed, she was not above grilling Tamas later.

"You are out early," Tamas said when they met, a cat-in-the-cream smile spread over his narrow face. "Is your work done so soon today?"

"Nay. I had an errand that would not wait," she said. "And what brings the two of you this way?"

Tamas said nothing. Ailig stood there, his face arranged pleasantly, as if he waited patiently.

But for what?

She regarded his stance, hands clasped behind him, chin slightly raised, as if daring anyone to challenge him. His face showed cares in the crinkles around his silvery eyes, but there was an air of confidence about him. Confidence looked good on him. Too good. She forced her attention to her brother-in-law.

"You two are plotting something," she said, cocking an eyebrow and daring him to deny it.

The men looked at each other quickly, then Ailig smiled at her and 'twas like the sun breaking over the bens, casting shafts of light through her.

"You are very perceptive, Morainn," he said. "We have been plotting a decent meal for the clan."

"What?" 'Twas not at all what she had expected him to say.

The plan came at her rapid-fire from both men and she let them get it all out. She tried to listen intently as they practically stumbled over each other to explain why she was the only one who could sort out the castle's kitchen, but the seriousness on Ailig's face kept distracting her, drawing her attention to his eyes, his mouth . . .

"Well?" Tamas asked. Ailig said nothing but did not take his eyes off hers, and she found herself pulled by his regard. 'Twas almost a physical sensation, as if he guided her to him with a gentle but insistent hand. She realized she was breathless, her heart hammering and a most curious fluttering sensation filled her stomach. 'Twas not unlike the way Hamish had made her feel when he was wooing her. 'Twas a feeling that had disappeared within days of her wedding. And here she was, allowing herself to be swept up in those feelings again. 'Twas physical desire, nothing more. And she did not have to act upon it. Would not.

"Will you move into the castle, Morainn, and see that the kitchen runs smoothly again? Tamas assures me that you are the best cook west of Inverness and that a good meal would boost the spirits of the castle folk more than anything else."

He was smiling at her again, but she would not give into a charming smile. Once was enough to teach her not to trust those lovely fluttery feelings. She'd promised herself not to make the same mistake again. She stepped back and saw doubt edge into Ailig's eyes.

"I cannot. I know nothing about running a castle's kitchen." She stepped back again. "Besides, 'tis Catriona's

task. Where is she?" she asked, steering the conversation
to the questions she wanted answered and away from the
man who was so . . . distracting.

"I cannot tell you aught, except Catriona would be
pleased to know someone capable was seeing to her responsibilities."

She considered Ailig for a moment, trying to look past
his braw good looks to the man beneath. He had not given
her an answer. She narrowed her eyes at him, ignoring the
fidgeting Tamas at his side.

"Why are you concerned about the food? Is it not the
chief's job to see to the running of the castle?"

"My father has long delegated such tasks to his children. You ken that, Morainn. Please." In one stride he
closed the distance between them and took her hand in his.
He looked deeply into her eyes until she was aware of
nothing but the compelling man standing in front of her.
"Will you not do this for the clan?"

All the reasons she should say no raced through her
mind, and yet she hesitated.

"Why do you really want the kitchen sorted out?" she
asked, pulling her hand from his but standing her ground.
She'd not retreat again. If he thought his charm could sway
her, he was in for a rude surprise.

He looked at her for a long moment, then he stepped
back and looked at Tamas, as if deciding what or how
much he could say. She knew there was trouble.

"If you wish me to help you, you must tell me the
truth," she said. "I deserve no less if you truly wish my
aid." She held her breath, waiting to see if he would con-
fide in her or if he would try to charm her instead.

Tamas said nothing, but he watched Ailig intently, as if

this were a question he wanted answered as badly as she did.

"This must go no further," Ailig said at last.

Morainn and Tamas nodded.

"There are things afoot that bode ill for Assynt if changes are not made. If I can get the castle running smoothly—if *we* can," he said looking at both of them, "'twill go far towards setting things to rights. I cannot tell you more yet, but if you care aught for this clan, I beg you do this. For the clan's future. For your own future."

'Twas an impassioned plea and verified her sense that Ailig had brought trouble back with him. She looked at Tamas but said nothing. He simply nodded his head at her and that shook her more than she could have imagined. He trusted Ailig, trusted what the man had told them. Should she? Could she?

She took a deep breath. She had little to lose by trying her hand in the kitchen, and possibly much to lose if she did not. Besides, Ailig would not be in the kitchen, nor would Baltair, so she would be safe from the charm of one and the stubbornness of the other as much as if she kept to her own cottage. She had little to lose . . .

Suddenly, she realized she had made up her mind.

She would help, but she would not give in to the men completely. She had her own life to consider, her own needs, including the need to distance herself from Ailig MacLeod.

"I will not move into the castle." She held up her hand to stop them before either could frame a response. "But I will see to the kitchen . . . on one condition."

"We both agree you should move into the castle," Ailig said. Tamas nodded at his side.

"That I will not do."

"Why?" Tamas asked. She just stared at him. "You will have to be in the castle all day anyway. Why not take advantage of Ailig's offer and avail yourself of some of the comforts, and company, of the castle?"

Disappointment stabbed into her. Had her trust been so quickly misplaced? "So this *is* an attempt to marry me off." She turned back toward her cottage.

"Nay!"

"Morainn." Ailig caught her arm gently and she halted, unable to ignore neither the soft entreaty in his voice nor the subtle thrill that ran over her arm where he touched her. "Please."

She looked up at him, studying his face. Something dark dwelt behind his eyes, but she could not tell if 'twas concern, or pride, or something else.

"I will help the clan, Ailig." She loosed her arm from him and gripped her cloak tightly about her in an effort to keep him from touching her again. "But I like my life just as it is. I like my wee little cottage. I like my own bed. Besides, 'tis only a short walk from the castle to my home. Surely that will not be a burden on my time."

"You will not be dissuaded, will you?" he asked, his voice hushed.

"I will not."

"Stubborn to the last," Tamas said.

"That's me." She smiled at him, despite the knot in her belly.

"I do still have that one condition," she said.

"She always has conditions," Tamas said.

She stuck out her tongue at him and Ailig chuckled. The knot in her stomach loosened ever so slightly.

"Name your condition, lass," Ailig said. "We are in no position to say you nay."

"Good. Una's bothy needs rethatching."

"Una?"

"The laundress. She is a widow. She lives there with her little girl. 'Tis one thing to have the snow and wind come in on the laundry, but 'tis another to have it come in on Una and her child. I want her to have a new roof."

"That is your condition?" Ailig asked.

"Aye."

Tamas started to decline but Ailig stopped him with a quelling look.

"You will sort out the kitchen and see that the meals improve and in exchange we will see . . ."

"Una's bothy is rethatched. That is my condition."

Ailig grinned and Morainn felt a kick in her stomach. 'Twas a brilliant grin, one she could watch for a long, long time. It heralded adventure and she had not had any adventures in far too long. Though how sorting out a kitchen run amok could be an adventure she didn't know.

"Done," Ailig said.

"But 'tis winter—" Tamas said.

"You would have her wait until the weather is mild before you stop the wind that blows through there?" Morainn asked, taking care to lace a bit of rebuke through her words.

"Oh, very well," Tamas said.

Ailig pressed his hand to Morainn's back and steered her toward the castle before she could step out of his way.

"Will you come now?" He managed to usher her towards the castle even as he asked the question, Tamas falling in step on the other side of her as if he thought to block any escape. "We have much to do if you're to get a decent meal arranged for this evening," he continued. "Would you like to tell Una she'll be getting a new roof or shall we send Tamas?"

She took a deep breath and let it out slowly. "Tamas can tell her, then he can see to gathering the bracken needed." She flashed an evil grin at her brother-in-law.

"And that will be so much fun in the snow." Tamas rolled his eyes at her.

"Aye, 'twill," Ailig said.

She'd loosened her grip on her cloak and Ailig quickly took advantage, tucking her arm though his and pulling her close. She could feel the warmth of him along her side, feel the corded tendons of his forearms beneath her fingers as he led her into the castle. He smiled down at her and matched his stride to hers. The man was too bold and Morainn could only wonder what she had gotten herself into.

Ailig strode through the gate and into the bailey with Morainn and Tamas, pleased that he had found two allies so quickly. That one was bonny and challenging, was more than he could have hoped for.

The bailey should have been nearly empty in the face of the cold wind, so he was surprised by the small crowd . . . crowds . . . that were streaming out the postern gate, towards the practice yard.

He glanced at Morainn, who was looking at him, her eyes full of curiosity. Tamas had moved off to speak with someone near the stable.

"I am to meet someone out there," Ailig said. " 'Twould

appear 'twill not be a private meeting. Would you mind postponing your introduction to the kitchen staff? I fear this must be dealt with immediately."

"'Tis too late for the midday meal to be changed, anyway. A delay matters little," she said, slipping her arm free of his.

Ailig sighed, already missing the way his skin awakened at the touch of her fingers through his tunic. "Let us see what the crowd gathers for," he said, gesturing towards the postern gate across the bailey.

As they emerged from the small gate into the outer bailey, Ailig saw that the crowds were gathering about the snow-rimmed dirt square used by the men of the clan to practice their fighting skills. To one side of the dirt square stood a handful of MacLeod warriors, Baltair, and several others he had seen at the breaking of the fast that morning. On the opposite side stood the MacDonells.

It reminded him of the quiet before battle, the calm before a blizzard. Skaeth, the mercenary, leaned against the curtain wall, separate from both groups of warriors, as if he were the only person present.

"Wait here," Ailig said. "I shall return as soon as this is finished."

"Don't get hurt," she said, with the glimmer of a smile playing over her full lips. Ailig acknowledged the words with a slight bow before he sauntered toward the sparring ground.

He passed between the gathered warriors without acknowledging any of them and stopped in front of Skaeth, who made no move from his position.

"Why have you gathered an audience?" Ailig asked, his voice lowered so it would not carry to either group.

"I have gathered nothing. We must have been overheard this morn. You ken gossip runs through a castle faster than whiskey flows down a Highlander's gullet. 'Twould seem you are the draw. The question is, do they want to see you win . . . or lose?"

Skaeth pushed away from the wall and moved to the center of the square. He pulled a battle-ax from the loop at his belt, widened his stance and bent his knees slightly. He cocked an eyebrow at Ailig.

Ailig took a steadying breath, dropped his plaid makeshift mantle to the ground and drew his broadsword. 'Twas as good a time as any to show the clan that he was capable. If he could impress them here, then later, when his father declared him chief, perhaps they would be more inclined to accept him.

He quickly assessed his companion. Facing Skaeth was like facing a cat-a-mountain. Though slight, the man was a coil of strength, and Ailig found himself shaking off the image of himself as a helpless hare.

He waited for some comment from the crowd, but there was only silence. An eerie, unnatural silence. The wind that had buffeted him by the loch had died until there was nary a breeze to ruffle the cloaks and plaids of the spectators. Nary a person so much as whispered. They stood, silent, still, as if the world paused for just a moment as he teetered on the edge of an abyss. They only waited to see if he would fall in.

A movement caught his eye, yanking him from his strange musings. He parried just in time to stop Skaeth's first blow. The man was quick, light on his feet, spinning and shifting direction without effort. 'Twas all Ailig could do to defend himself. Never was there an opportunity to take control of the contest. Never did Ailig even come close to taxing Skaeth's abilities. The man fought like no one he had ever met. Where Ailig was used to the brute strength favored by his brothers, and indeed most Highlanders, this man traded upon his speed, his agility and his brains, for Ailig could see Skaeth considering, weighing options, watching, not unlike Ailig himself tended to do, but faster and more efficiently, seeming to act on decisions almost before he had made them.

Ailig was tiring more quickly than he would have liked, thanks to long days in the saddle followed by a restless night's sleep. He'd seen enough of the man's skills and needed to finish this little demonstration before he made a beginner's mistake and looked the fool in front of those he had intended to impress.

He shifted quickly to his right, then swung hard at Skaeth's head with a loud grunt. The other man seemed to know what he was going to do before Ailig did. He blocked the blow and somehow managed to wrest the sword from Ailig, sending it flying through the air to land point down in the dirt at Baltair's feet.

The MacDonells hooted and shook their fists in the air. The MacLeods fell to grumbling. Skaeth crossed to the sword, drawing it from the dirt and tossing it hilt first back to Ailig.

Irritation burned through Ailig as he tried to figure out how Skaeth had disarmed him. He could not decide if he should banish the man from the castle or reward him for his skill. 'Twould be a fine skill to have in his own personal arsenal.

The two men watched each other for a moment, then Ailig made up his mind, smiled and held out his hand.

Slowly, Skaeth took it in his own. A smile danced through his eyes, though his mouth never so much as twitched.

"I think you'll do," Skaeth said.

Ailig didn't have time to wonder at the mercenary's odd words. "And you will do, provided you can promise me your loyalty for as long as you remain in Assynt.

"For as long as I remain, I will work for you and against your enemies."

'Twas not precisely the vow he was seeking, but he was satisfied that Skaeth's loyalty did not lie with Baltair or the MacDonells.

"Very well."

Ailig turned to address the crowd, particularly Baltair.

"Skaeth will be training our guards and warriors," he said, raising his voice to carry throughout the practice yard. "Any who have a problem with that . . . too bad," he added, looking Baltair in the eye.

"We'll see what the chief has to say about that," Baltair said through gritted teeth.

"'Tis sure I am we will," Ailig said to himself. "Come to my chamber this afternoon," he said to Skaeth. "I would have you show me what you did to take my sword."

Skaeth nodded his head once, then slid his axe back into its loop as Ailig resheathed his broadsword.

Baltair moved slowly to face Ailig and Ailig knew 'twas a moment he must win.

"'Tis true what Broc always said about you," Baltair growled. "You are a wee daft eedjit. He always said all that learning your uncle gave you was useless. How could you let that mercenary best you in front of everybody? And you'd have him train the rest of us so we can learn to lose our swords in a fight?" He leaned in to Ailig. "You'll not last long in this place that way."

The last words were ground out and he had no doubt that his life was being threatened. 'Twas time to put Baltair in his place. Soon he would have a new chief.

"'Tis not your place to second-guess my purposes. Stand down, Baltair, or be prepared to leave the castle."

"Is that a threat, wee daftie?"

"'Tis. But the clan needs all its warriors at the moment, so I would ask you to step back and think before you threaten me again."

"Where is Broc?" he asked, his eyes narrowed, his stance that of a warrior prepared to battle if he did not like the answer.

Ailig noticed the other MacLeods ranged behind Baltair even as he noticed Skaeth had moved to his side, though he stood a step behind as a champion did. He could not spare a glance at the MacDonells, but he was sure they watched, waiting to see what would come of this confrontation, waiting to hear the answer to Baltair's question.

Ailig shook his head, then stepped around Baltair to reclaim his mantle. Baltair snagged his arm and swung him around.

"I asked you a question, eedjit!"

"Perhaps you should look down before you go calling me more names," Ailig said.

Confusion crossed Baltair's face until Ailig pushed his dagger closer to those private parts Baltair held most dear. Skaeth stifled a snort, but not before Ailig heard it. He pressed his lips together and would not let the sudden bubble of laughter out. He had always wanted Baltair in just this position. 'Twas a heady feeling to finally gain one of his dreams.

He watched Baltair swallow before he raised up on his toes slightly and stepped back from Ailig.

"Someone will answer my question," he said, glaring at Ailig.

"Aye, someone will. The tale will be told in good time. But 'tis the chief who decides when that time is."

He turned to all those gathered, awaiting the outcome of their confrontation, and found Morainn still standing at the edge of the crowd. Tamas stood by her side. Her eyes were wide, but there was a smile on her face and he felt an odd surge of success to see it there.

He gave a small bow to her, then said loudly, "With a bit of luck, and Mistress Morainn's guidance, I trust we'll have a meal worth eating this evening."

All eyes turned to the lass. She rolled her eyes and shook her head. Ailig prayed Tamas was right about Morainn's skill. He could use a good meal to placate the clan this night.

Baltair gathered up his lads and they made for the gate. The MacDonells dispersed, but managed to linger near the gate and Ailig had the distinct impression they were attending to his every move. Skaeth walked over to him.

"When shall we start?" he asked.

"Start?" Ailig's mind was still on Baltair and the MacDonells and the way Morainn's eyes glowed when she smiled.

"Ailig?"

"Aye?"

"Your training. When shall we start?"

Ailig blinked at him. "Training?"

"If you think to survive amongst this lot, you bloody well need it," Skaeth said. "You are clever and quick, but you are no match for a Highlander bent on your death, at least not yet."

"I have done well against many a Highlander—"

"Aye, but I'm thinking they had no reason to wish you dead . . . until now." At Ailig's surprised expression Skaeth shrugged. "Am I wrong?"

Ailig looked about him, but everyone was far enough away not to overhear their conversation. "Nay, you are not wrong. 'Tis only a matter of a short time and all will know what has happened, what will happen and how it all came to pass. I will be no one's hero once the tale is told, even though I had little to do with the outcome."

"So, when shall we start?"

"Why do you care what happens to me? You are not a MacLeod. You are here but for the winter. Why do you care?"

Skaeth's face shuttered. His eyes narrowed until Ailig could not tell their color any longer. "'Tis the right of the mercenary to choose which side he will fight on. I have ever chosen the underdog." He started to walk away, then stopped and faced Ailig. "'Tis a more challenging fight."

They simply stared at each other for a moment, assessing.

"How is it you know so much of what is happening here?"

"'Tis another job of the mercenary. Before you can choose sides, you must know who the players are and what they play for. Only then can you know what price to set."

"And your price is?"

"Dinna fash yerself. 'Twon't be more than you are willing to pay."

Ailig watched Skaeth as he disappeared through the postern gate back into the bailey. As he crossed the dirt square to speak to Morainn and Tamas, a lad raced out of the gate and pelted toward him, drawing to an abrupt halt just before he barreled into Ailig.

"The chief and the council summon you," he said, his breath coming in short gasps.

Ailig felt a surge of anticipation and trepidation burn over his skin. He sent the lad off and strode to where Morainn and Tamas awaited him.

"Tamas," he said as soon as he was close enough to speak without bellowing. "Will you help Morainn get settled with the kitchen staff? I must see the council."

"Aye."

Morainn reached out and tentatively touched his arm. "Good luck," she said.

"I shall need it," he said, unaccountably moved by her simple show of support.

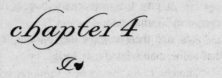

chapter 4

"To the kitchen then," Moirann said to Tamas. Relief tinged with disappointment spread through her as she watched Ailig disappear through the postern gate.

"Aye, there is much to be done if you're to insure a proper meal this evening," Tamas said, but neither of them moved.

"What do you think the counsel wants with him?" she asked.

Tamas shrugged and linked his arm with hers as Ailig had done, leading her back towards the castle. "Something about his travels, no doubt."

"No doubt . . . but what? He looked almost relieved to be summoned, as if he had been awaiting it."

"He did seem in a hurry, as we should be." He tugged her along at a faster clip.

"Don't you find his actions odd?" she asked.

"Should I?"

"He closets himself with the chief, is eager to speak to the council and this . . ." She gestured back towards the sparring yard.

"'Tis a pity that mercenary bested him in front of everyone," Tamas said.

"Aye, and then he gave the training of the guard into that same man's hands. It seems out of character for a MacLeod."

"He is not like his brothers. I thought you knew that."

"He has always tagged along behind his brothers. How could he be different from the rest of them?"

Tamas shook his head. "You have reason to dislike Broc. There is no doubt he was responsible for getting Hamish killed, but I did not think you would judge others by the company they were forced to keep."

His voice was soft, and yet the words felt like a slap.

She looked at her feet for a moment, considering what Tamas had said and what she had seen. "I still think 'tis odd. Is this the way a lesser son would act, be he MacLeod or anyone else?"

Tamas's brow lowered and he cocked his head, as if listening for something. "'Tis not. 'Tis the act of a man in charge . . . or one who expects to be in charge." He looked at Morainn. "Do you think . . . ?"

She shrugged, but in her bones she knew they were circling in on the trouble Ailig had only alluded to. There was more than the threat of the king. There was the reason for the threat and it had something to do with the missing MacLeods and the MacDonell chief.

"Keep your ears open," Tamas said as they arrived at the stair that led up to the kitchen. "And I will do the same. If 'tis as you suspect, 'twill not sit well with the clan. I'd not like to see the king's threat come to pass. Ailig is going to need all the help we can give him."

"You trust him, do you not?"

"Of course. I would not have let you get entangled in this if I did not."

She took a deep breath and let it go slowly. "To the kitchen then. I promised I'd try to sort out the place and I'd best be started. Full and satisfied bellies may be the only way I can help the clan, so that is what I shall do."

Tamas led Morainn into the kitchen tower and before they even entered the kitchen proper they were greeted with yelling and cursing the likes of which Morainn had never heard before. Men's bellows mixed with women's screeches and the occasional child's howl. She could not decide if they approached wild animals gone mad or a re-creation of the Tower of Babel. They stopped in the door-way and witnessed pandemonium.

She looked at Tamas and his eyes were as wide as she was sure hers were. What had she gotten herself into?

"Who is in charge?" she asked him.

"It does not look as if anyone is," he said, wading into the fray.

Morainn followed along behind as he made a path through the mayhem. The floor was littered with bits of vegetables, feathers, bones and other things she'd rather not think about. In the scullery corner the washtubs were piled full of pots, pans, dishes, trays, ewers and apparently every serving utensil and goblet in the castle, but no one was bothering to wash any of it.

Tamas stopped in the middle of the overheated, over-crowded, over-loud space and let out an ear-piercing whistle. Instantly every voice ceased and all eyes were on the two of them.

"The chief wishes a decent meal this evening and has deemed you lot unable to provide that."

Morainn raised her eyebrows at his invocation of the chief, but said nothing.

"Mistress Morainn has been given the task of seeing that a meal worthy of the chief is served. If you wish to keep your place here, you will do as she says. If you do not wish to keep your place, leave now."

Looks were exchanged and one woman stepped forward. "Why should we take orders from the likes of her?"

Morainn set her hands on her hips and leveled her steeliest stare at the woman. "Because if you do not, you will be cast out of the castle to fend for yourself in the midst of winter."

"We'll not be threatened. We're too used to that," a man said from near the hearth. A laugh went up and Morainn thought she might be able to manage this lot.

"I am not Catriona," she said. "I do not scream, but I will expect each and every one of you to work hard and follow my instructions." She stepped in front of Tamas then. "Where is the scullery maid?" she asked the woman who had spoken.

"Abed, most like. She's a lazy chit."

Morainn spied a lad of no more than ten summers sitting near the scullery tubs. "What's your name?" she said, pointing at him.

"Alasdair," he said, jumping to his feet.

"Do you know where the scullery maid sleeps?"

He nodded vigorously.

"Go and get her and bring her to me. Do not come back without her. Do you understand, Alasdair?"

He bobbed his head so hard she feared 'twould come loose from his neck.

"Go. Get her and return quickly."

She continued to pick people from the crowd and assign them tasks until each person was engaged in either preparing the midday meal or cleaning up the abysmally dirty kitchen. Before she knew it, platters were heading for the hall and the meal was served.

Hours later Morainn wiped her moist forehead on her sleeve and realized she could not say when Tamas slipped away. Once everyone had been assigned a job, she'd tackled planning the menu. What should have been an easy thing to do had turned exceedingly difficult when she ventured into the storerooms to find everything in disarray. She had rapidly rearranged the menu to include things she could actually find.

Everyone had worked hard for the first hour, but then several of them had drifted away. Alasdair, the lad who had found the scullery maid, had quickly shown a knack for locating those gone missing. Considering she'd only been there half a day, 'twas not a bad start. Tomorrow she'd have to arrive very early if they were to serve a decent morning meal. No one cared enough to see it done without prodding. But they would. If she had anything to say about it, they would.

Exhaustion dragged at her, but her curiosity would give her no rest. Rumors had run rampant through the kitchen all afternoon that the chief would reveal Ailig's news this night. She had not had a chance to search out Una or to even step into the Great Hall for more than a moment all during the evening meal, but no one had left yet, so perhaps she had not missed the announcement. Now all was done, save the last of the cleaning up. If 'twas not done well tonight, the kitchen workers would find themselves roused from their beds even earlier than usual to finish it on the morrow. She'd not yell as the Shrew had done, but she would not excuse laziness.

She made one last quick circuit of the kitchen, encouraging where she could, correcting where she couldn't, but always in a calm and even tone.

She removed her barmcloth, folding the apron and laying it atop a pile of dirty linens. She glanced around once more, raising an eyebrow when she caught the glance of a lad who was supposed to be hauling water for the washing but had yet to set to lifting a single bucket. He grabbed two of them and headed for the door that led out to the bailey and the well. She said a quick silent prayer for patience as she slipped out of the kitchen and into the Great Hall.

She hesitated behind the wooden screen that separated the serving area from the main part of the hall to smooth her gown. She pulled down her sleeves where she had pushed them up to her elbows and tried to tame the tendrils of hair that curled wildly about her face.

Taking a deep breath, she stepped into the crowded room. A fire crackled on the hearth along the outer wall. Two rows of crowded trestle tables ranged up and down the hall, a narrow aisle between them, with wider ones along each side. 'Twould seem the entire clan, not just the castle folk, had supped here this night.

She looked to the far end at the long table, raised on a dais just slightly above the level of the rest of the hall. There sat the chief, several of the elders of the clan and

Ailig. Her stomach flipped when his eyes met hers, but she told herself 'twas hunger, nothing more. There sat a serious young man, with an air of expectation about him. Whether the expectation was for good or bad, she could not tell, but the set of his shoulders and the straight line of his mouth told her he was ready for it.

Before she could find a place to sit that still had food upon the table, the chief rose and prepared to address the gathering. Quickly she filled a trencher from the nearest platter, oblivious to what the food was, then found a seat nearer to the dais.

"There is much to tell, none of it good," the chief began. He spoke without looking directly at anyone. Ailig shifted in his seat, ever so slightly, but he, too, did not meet anyone's eye. She checked the expressions on the faces around her and found curiosity equal to her own on most.

"My daughter will not return to Assynt."

A cheer went up from many in the hall while others merely smiled. Morainn couldn't say she was surprised, given Ailig's adamant need for her to take over the woman's duties in the kitchen. While the MacLeods congratulated themselves at their good fortune, the Mac-Donells stayed in their places, but the grumbling was loud from that quarter. For all the lass was a shrew, she was supposed to marry their chief.

Neill continued once the noise settled down. "The king believes Broc and Duff MacDonell plotted against him."

Morainn gasped. A round of shouts echoed in the hall as several MacDonells rose to their feet. This was so much worse than anything she could have imagined—a plot against the king! Scanning the crowd she found disbelief in some, outrage in others, and in a few, a knowing smile, as if they had shared in the conspiracy. She knew little of King Robert, but she doubted any king would suffer such a plot against his life without dire consequences.

Dire consequences. 'Twas what Ailig had confided that morn—now she knew why the king threatened such a thing.

"I do not believe it any more than you," Neill shouted, regaining the attention of the hall, "but that signifies little." He glanced down the table at Ailig who met him with a steady look. "The king believes it." He stood a little straighter and turned his attention directly to the table full of MacDonell warriors. "Duff, your chief, has been taken prisoner by the king. He will be tried for treason."

For one short moment there was stunned silence, then the MacDonell warriors surged to their feet with shouts of disbelief. Morainn jumped when the MacLeod warrior next to her rose abruptly and vaulted the table, joined by others from all over the hall. The two factions converged in front of the chief. Shouts of "liar" combined with "Give us the truth!" Morainn couldn't breathe for fear the disbelief and confusion would turn to fury. She stood and backed up against the wall, ready to bolt if it should come to a fight, but unable to leave without hearing the rest.

She could see Tamas and others trying to calm the angry warriors enough to have them take their seats but 'twas futile. She could only hope this was the worst of the tale, for the fate of Broc and the other brothers was still unknown.

When the warriors had settled enough to listen, though they would not leave their place in front of the dais, Neill continued.

"Three of my sons, Calum, Gowan, and Jamie, are serving at the king's pleasure in his army. I do not know when—or if—they shall return."

He took a drink from his pewter cup and Morainn could swear she saw his hand shake. The entire gathering seemed to hold its breath. After a moment he looked up, but again met no one's eyes.

"Broc is dead," he said, letting his words land amidst the crowd like boulders cast from a trebuchet.

Some gasped, some shook their heads, others leveled hateful glares at Ailig. He did not duck his head. He did not react in any way to his father's blunt statement.

He seemed to brace himself without ever shifting position. She could not say what it was that made her know this, but she was sure of it. Whatever came next had to do with Ailig's part in all this and he did not expect the clan to like whatever his father must say.

"There is more," the chief said, his voice tired and his face strangely ashen. "'Tis clear Broc can no longer . . ." He stopped speaking for a moment, swallowed hard, then continued. "He can no longer follow me as chief, and my other sons, all save Ailig, are in the king's service."

He paused and seemed to sway. He took another long draught from his cup.

"The king . . ." He sighed. "The king seeks to punish me. He has commanded Ailig to become chief . . . immediately."

Morainn sucked in her breath, surprised in spite of her earlier speculation, as shouts and boos met this news. She tried to catch Ailig's eye, to see what he was feeling, thinking, but he would not look at her, nor at anyone. He appeared tense, but calm. He must know the outcome of all of this already, she decided. That would explain much about his behavior today with her, with the mercenary in the training yard and even with Baltair.

"The king has commanded Ailig," the chief said again, trying to raise his voice above the outcry, "but . . ." Ailig's attention turned swiftly to his father. Morainn tensed, pressing the flats of her fingers to her mouth. Neill waited until they quieted. "But Highland custom holds that we choose our own chiefs and in our own time—not the king. He may command his earls and barons. He may command his Lowlanders and even his army, but we are Highlanders. MacLeods. He may not tell us who to choose, or when. That is for me, and the council, and for you to decide."

Agreement rose as one voice from all save the Mac-Donells. Men banged their tankards on the tables, splashing ale.

"The king, however," Neill continued, "sees otherwise and has threatened to turn us out of our homes and hunt us down like animals should we not do as he wishes."

Now there was stunned silence, though the MacDonells had satisfied smiles on their faces.

"But we will not let the king decide our fate," Neill said into the stillness. "Wee Ailig—"

Morainn glanced at Ailig, but the man's face was stone. He did not react, even to the derogatory name his own father used.

"—must prove himself worthy to be chief. If he were to be chief I would have him earn that privilege, not have it handed to him by the king of the Lowlanders."

This, too, met with loud agreement. Morainn could not take her eyes off Ailig. She waited for him to explode as his brothers would do, to shout, to bluster at anyone who would challenge him, to show some emotion, or even simply to defend himself. Something. Anything. But all she could see was the slight upward tilt of his chin and the strain that settled around his eyes.

She could not tell if he was surprised by his father's lack of support. Did he know this was coming and thus steeled himself to the reaction of those gathered there?

"What about the betrothal?" a voice rang out over the crowd. "Will there be no justice there? Will you not honor that pact?"

Morainn strained to see over the others standing near her and gained a glimpse of a tall man with black hair standing directly in front of the chief. She recognized him as Gofraig, Clan Donell's champion.

"Your daughter was to wed our chief and bind the clans together as allies. Why has she not returned to honor that pact?"

"My sister has married another," Ailig said, his voice steady and hard. "She'll not be returning to marry your chief, nor anyone else."

"But she was promised. We were promised. We were to be allies, and now, with the king's wrath focused upon us all, we will need any such allies as we can get. I demand you honor the betrothal."

"And how would we do that with Dogface in the king's gaol and Catriona married to another?" Ailig asked, his voice so hard and cruel it shocked Morainn. "Why would we wish to make another betrothal with the MacDonell clan?"

"We *could* make another betrothal." A deep voice that Morainn knew all too well joined the heated discussion. Baltair stood from his table and wandered towards the front as if he were mulling over a deep problem. Morainn did not trust the hint of a smirk that danced at the edges of his mouth. "We could offer a comparable alliance."

"I have but the one daughter," Neill said, sliding into his chair. "Thank goodness."

"Aye," Baltair said. "But you have a son who is here and unwed."

"We were promised a tocher for the Shrew," Gofraig said.

Neill glared at the man. "'Tis that which you most want, is it not?"

"It matters not what I most want. 'Tis owed to us. We will have it."

Morainn's heart was in her throat. An arranged marriage to one of the MacDonells? Would he agree?

"Will you leave if we satisfy the betrothal agreement?" Neill asked.

Ailig rose before Gofraig could answer. "The king trusts neither clan. Do you think I would endanger my people more than my brother and your chief have already done? I take my responsibilities to these people far too seriously to allow that. No betrothal. No alliance. No marriage between us. You have no further business here."

He looked at his father, who was staring at Ailig as if he had grown a second head. "You have pressed the bounds of hospitality and it is time for all of you"—Ailig shifted his glare back to Gofraig—"to return to your own lands. We will provision you for your journey, but do not ask for more from us. We are all pressed to please the king now thanks to both Broc and Duff, and despite what our chief thinks. You would be best served to take stock, as we must do here, and plan that appeasement."

"He is not the king of the Highlands," Gofraig said. "We do not bow before him."

"He has the support of the noblemen," Ailig replied. "He is the future of Scotland. You would be wise to heed his wishes—and mine—now."

Ailig held his temper in check, just, as the crowd erupted again, distracted from the real issue by Baltair's ill-conceived suggestion and Ailig's refusal. He was supposed to have been named chief; that was what was most important here, but no, his father and the council had betrayed him, had betrayed their own clan. But he would still become chief. He had to.

Ailig looked out over the crowd. Some were sitting quietly, as if stunned by the tale their chief told. Some gesticulated wildly, arguing with their neighbors. He dragged air into his lungs and found himself seeking out Morainn. She had been to one side, sitting in the shadows. He had felt her watching him, but he could not find her now. She was probably as shocked and as angry as the rest of the clan appeared to be and would have nothing more to do with him, despite the obvious attraction that sizzled between them. Anger fueled by regret for something that might have been churned deep within him.

Disaster had just crashed over them all. Their future, once sparkling before them, had been snatched away by their own chief. A scorching wrath singed his insides, incinerating any remorse he might have harbored at forcing Neill from his position. The man was no fit leader, denying the strength of the king to punish them, then trying to make a pact with the MacDonells when 'twas clear 'twould only serve to further anger the king.

Ailig aimed his fury back at the auld men sitting at the high table, their heads bent in discussion. His father ignored everything, seated in his chief's chair, his eyes closed and his face sagging as if under a great weight.

Ailig shook his head. The clan was in danger, yet the chief and the council would play games with their future. Perhaps he had not made the severity of the king's displeasure clear, or else they trusted him so little that it did not matter. Nay, they had no reason to distrust him. He had ever done what was needed for this clan. Still, if the council and his father thought to punish and humiliate him by denying the king's command, they had underestimated him.

Without taking his leave of any of the other men, he shoved his chair back and stepped away from the table. He had nothing to say to any of them.

"Ailig." Angus Mhór stopped him with a steely hand on his arm as he passed his chair. The youngest of the elders' council rose and moved a little away from the table, pulling Ailig with him. "Do not despair. You have allies in this. Use them to your advantage, to the clan's advantage, and the best man will become chief. This I guarantee."

"Can you? Will your assurances be good enough for the king? If we are turned out of our home and hunted like the hares of the moors 'twill be the fault of the council and of my father. But I *will* do all in my power to see that it does not come to pass."

"Aye, lad. And that is all I ask of you." With that he released Ailig's arm and returned to the table.

Ailig stood there for a moment, wondering at the words

of the elder, wondering why he had not made the council see what he apparently saw, do what he knew they must do.

He wanted to leave the hall but was unwilling to run the gauntlet of angry and confused MacLeods and angrier and more confused MacDonells. He had no stomach for any of them this night. He withdrew to the back of the dais and opened the door leading to the wine cellar below. From there he could make his way to the bailey and be free of the crowd.

"Wee Ailig!"

He winced at the name, cursing his father for shaming him earlier with it in front of the entire clan. He turned and was surprised by a swift punch to his face. Caught off guard he staggered backward, nearly falling through the doorway until he braced himself and blinked rapidly to clear his vision.

The MacDonells stood there, ranged about him, obliterating any sight of the rest of the hall. They could kill him where he stood and no one outside this group would be able to tell who had done the deed. That would be an unforgivable breach of the customs of hospitality. But then he had flirted with that breach tonight himself in telling them to be gone.

"You think to throw us out without any restitution for our troubles? We were to return with our chief, his wife and the tocher that was to come with her. We will not return to our home empty-handed and shamed by your clan. A deal was made. We have not broken it."

Ailig searched his painful head for the man's name . . . Gofraig, aye, Gofraig, champion of Duff MacDonell. Damn. 'Twas the same man who stood upon the table rallying his men this morn. The man was a pain in Ailig's arse and had a fist like iron.

But Ailig refused to acknowledge the blow.

"And what do you propose we pay you, a pound of flesh?"

"'Twould be a good start."

"You've already got it. Broc is dead. My other brothers are bound in service to the king. Duff was just as much a part of this plot as Broc. We owe you nothing."

"And what of the king?" Gofraig stepped forward, but Ailig had nowhere to go as the door frame was already against his back. "Will he seek to punish Dun Donell as he promises to punish Assynt?"

"Ask the chief," he said.

"I am asking you. 'Twould seem you are the lone survivor of the quest to regain the runaway bride. And now the king commands you to be chief? 'Tis muckle suspicious if you ask me."

"Then 'tis a good thing I did not ask you," Ailig said. "The chief will answer your questions . . . or not . . . as he sees fit."

"I'm asking you," Gofraig said again, this time jabbing Ailig's chest with a thick finger.

"And I am not chief, in case you did not understand my father. 'Tis not my responsibility to explain anything to you."

A short, squat, very dark man roared and made to pull his dagger, but someone jerked him backward by his plaid and quickly stilled the hand upon his dagger hilt.

"I do not think that is a wise idea," a slightly bored voice said and Ailig was pleased to see Skaeth was the one who had halted the dark man's actions. 'Twould seem he had at least one ally within these walls.

Gofraig glared at Skaeth, then turned his attention back to Ailig. Skaeth winked at Ailig, as if to say, I've got your back, just as Tamas appeared behind Gofraig and gave him the slightest of nods. Ailig felt his breath ease.

"If my clan is in peril," Gofraig said, "'tis your clan's fault. Your sister lured Duff into danger. If she had done as she was told, they would be wed and all would be well. Your own brother would probably still be alive, unless you lied about that, too. Perhaps he is in the king's care, like Duff, but you would wrest the power from him and be named chief in his absence. Aye, it makes more sense than your daft tale. And where is the shrew? 'Tis she who is responsible for this horror. We will have our vengeance upon her!"

Gofraig was shouting now and the look in his eyes worried Ailig. He was not rational and that made him dangerous. The crowd shifted nervously about them, readying for battle. Ailig glanced at Skaeth, who yet kept a grip on the dark man, then at Tamas. They would not be enough against a half score of MacDonells.

"Where is she?!" Gofraig demanded again.

"Safe from you and my own brothers. She is not responsible for the troubles my brother and your chief brought upon themselves. She will not return. The king blessed her marriage."

Gofraig watched him for a moment, his eyes narrowed, his fists clenching and unclenching. Ailig held his tongue, for enough had been said. The truth was between them and he but awaited Gofraig's acceptance of it.

"You are a liar," Gofraig finally said from between

clenched teeth. "Your brothers no doubt hold Duff hostage somewhere, though what you think to gain from such I do not ken yet. But I will. I will find out what you are scheming, why you are scheming."

"Were it not for the bounds of hospitality I would call you out for that," Ailig said, anger boiling in his veins again. He had been reasonable, rational, and yet this one would call him a liar, blame him for things the swine knew nothing of. "If you were to leave this castle, as I . . . suggested . . . then hospitality would be satisfied and I could meet you upon yon hill and beat the truth into you."

The MacDonells surged but Ailig had his dagger out and at Gofraig's throat before they realized the threat.

"I do not wish to sully the MacLeod's good name with the blood of our guest spilled in our own hall, but I will. I have told you what you asked. 'Tis not my fault if you are too daft to ken the truth when you hear it. Now leave this hall, and if you ken what is best for all here gathered, you will leave Assynt Castle by first light."

"You are a liar, wee Ailig." Gofraig raised his chin slightly and stepped back. "*You* cannot turn us out. Your father granted us leave to bide here as long as necessary, and 'twould appear that he is still chief. We go nowhere until we learn Duff's true fate and are satisfied that you will not set the king upon us. This I promise you, for as long as we bide here, I will be a thorn in your side."

"I doubt it not," Ailig said.

"You will not forget how the MacDonells were wronged in this scheme," Gofraig continued without stopping. "No one will forget."

Ailig said nothing. He had said enough and 'twas clear the man had made up his mind about Ailig and everything else. He would not be swayed by something as simple as the truth. Ailig slowly sheathed his dagger, all the while silently begging Gofraig to make a move at him so he could use the blade with a clear conscience. He was tired of the posturings and machinations, and he'd like nothing better than to take out his frustration and anger on the face of his latest antagonist.

At last Gofraig blew out a breath. "Come, lads," he said, whirling on his heel and stomping off the dais.

"That went well," Skaeth said.

Ailig looked at the man.

"You did not get skewered, so I'm thinking 'twas well done."

"I suppose it was," he said.

"Now you'll just have to watch your back a bit more, and your front, too," Tamas said. "I'm guessing that lot goes for a frontal assault more than the backstabbing sort of revenge."

"I would not put it past them to try both," Ailig said, watching as the last of them threw a scowl at him before he passed out of the hall.

"We have your back, Ailig," Tamas said. "We have your back."

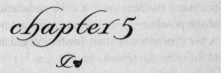

chapter 5

Morainn cursed Tamas's name as her viselike grip on the handles of the wooden tray sent tremors through it. The flask of whiskey and the cup she carried rattled as she climbed the narrow stair of the chief's tower. She didn't want to go to Ailig's chamber and it wasn't fair of Tamas to convince her she should. She didn't trust herself around Ailig at the moment.

He'd been so strong, so . . . The word heroic came to mind but she shoved it away. The MacLeod sons weren't heroic. They were troublemakers, bullies, no one to admire. And yet Ailig had stood up to the chief and the Mac-Donell man with a quiet dignity that went against everything she expected from him. She didn't want to admire the strength he had shown, didn't want to consider that Tamas might be right about him.

Because even if he wasn't like his brothers, she needed to believe he was. She needed to believe he wasn't someone she could have feelings for. She needed to believe she hadn't reacted so intensely when he'd been attacked. The tray rattled as her hands shook with renewed vigor. They had been shaking since that black-haired behemoth had punched Ailig.

Fury had engulfed her. She had fought the urge to attack the MacDonell, rip his eyes out, tear his hair from his evil head, kick him where he'd really know her feelings.

But she hadn't done any of that. Ailig could take care of himself. He was a MacLeod son, well used to sorting arguments out with his fists . . . wasn't he?

And now Tamas had sent her to see to Ailig, quelling all her arguments for why someone else should do the seeing to. He was so logical she wanted to scream. Of course he needed to keep watch over the MacDonells. She knew that. Though if the chief would simply rescind his hospitality they would have to leave and that headache would be solved. But he wouldn't, stubborn auld man, so here she was. Tamas said he trusted her alone not to gossip about Ailig's injuries. She had tried to argue, desperately tried to find some way out of coming to his chamber, without telling Tamas the truth—she did not trust her reactions to the warrior.

She stopped just outside Ailig's chamber door, took a deep breath and tried once more to steady her hands. She would leave the tray with him. In and out, just long enough to make sure 'twas nothing more serious than a bloodied lip. She'd call for the healer if 'twas something worse.

She balanced the heavy tray on one hand and tentatively knocked on the door. There was no answer. She reached up to knock again and the door flew open, startling her so much the tray overbalanced. She grabbed for it just as

Ailig reached out and steadied it, his large callused hands covering hers.

"I did not expect to see you again," Ailig said, blocking the door and glowering at her.

She was surprised he directed his anger at her. "Why not?" She brushed past him into his lair, searching for a place to set the tray. "Did you think I would take the side of your father? Of Baltair?"

"I did."

"Do not lump me in with those who cannot see what you are trying to do here." She set the tray down upon the only surface available, the bed, and turned back to face him, her arms folded across her stomach. There was anger in his eyes, and more, something deeper, darker that called out to her to soothe it. She needed to leave. "Tamas trusts you. 'Tis enough for me," she said, moving toward the door as she spoke.

"Really?" he said as she passed him. "Do you trust me?"

'Twas a poorly worded question but it stopped her. The better question was did she trust herself, and the answer was a resounding no. But did she trust him?

"Is everything the chief said true?"

"You would take my word over your chief's?" His voice was dangerously soft, brushing across her tired mind like silk.

She pushed away the seduction his voice promised and considered his question. "I would," she said. "The chief has been less and less of a leader in the last year or more. He is often closed up in his chambers for days at a time, completely unaware of how Broc was running things."

"'Tis true."

She watched the anger simmer in his eyes as her mind replayed all that she had learned this night.

"If he had been stronger," she asked, "would Broc and Duff have gotten us into the trouble we are now in?"

"They would not have been able to. But I should have . . ." He stalked to the fire, his back to her.

She watched him for a moment, then reached for the door.

"What did you bring?" he asked without turning around, stopping her with her hand on the latch.

"Tamas thought you could use a wee dram, and the healer sent a salve. Giorsal said 'twould take the sting out of anything that louse-infected MacDonell did to you. Those are her exact words."

He actually laughed, and she caught herself smiling at the sound, wondering what else she could say to make him laugh again, to send that smooth rolling sound over her skin again. She wondered if his mouth was as sensual as his voice.

She really was tired and her defenses were weaker than she'd thought if a man's rueful laugh could make her think of more sensual pursuits. She really must leave now.

She lifted the latch, but before she could open the door enough to slip out, he was there, his hand a velvet vise about her wrist.

"I have not thanked you for the tray," he said.

She should have been afraid, should have insisted he release her, should have done many things, but his voice was rich and husky, rumbling like thunder over the bens, but soft as a summer rain, holding her prisoner to her own fantasies.

His eyes held her as captive as his voice did, as his hand

did. He pulled her gently away from the door and into his arms. Shock coursed through her at the touch of his lips, firm, insistent, yet incredibly soft. She gasped and he took the opportunity to deepen the kiss, nibbling at her lips, delving deeply with his tongue. His arms held her against the hard plane of his chest, so close she could feel the pounding of his heart, feel the heat of him pour into her, igniting desires she had buried long ago.

*A*ilig *feasted on her full lips, reveled in her silky mouth,* celebrated the feel of her, the heat and softness of her pressed against him. All the anger, the betrayal, the disappointment drained from him in the moment his lips touched hers. Victory was his in the wake of so much defeat. He nuzzled her neck and was gratified when she tilted her head. A small sound of womanly satisfaction slipped from her lips. Her lips . . . He kissed her again.

"Stay the night with me, Morainn." He meant it as a question, but it must have sounded more of a command, for the lass stiffened and pulled herself free of his embrace.

She pressed her hands to her flushed cheeks and he could see the glaze of desire erased by something else—fear?

"I did not mean—"

She shook her head, then turned and fled.

He was a fool. A stupid fool.

He pivoted and made for the flask of whiskey she had brought. He ignored the cup and took a long swig directly from the heavy glass bottle. The smoky-sharp flavor of the chief's favored drink burned all the way down. It did naught to dampen the fire Morainn's touch had kindled, that her kisses had fanned to flame.

He stared at the tapestry of St. George and the dragon, and for the first time in a long while he noticed the princess standing on the ramparts of a castle in the distance, watching for the outcome of the battle. He did not know what dragon he must battle to win more kisses from Morainn, but he would do his best to discover it.

*S*everal days later Ailig stormed out of the chief's tower and into the gloomy bailey, coming to an abrupt halt amidst the normal flurry of activity there. For three days he had been shadowing his father in everything the man did . . . which wasn't much. He mostly let others come to him, reporting what needed doing, then scurrying off to get it done.

Something wasn't right.

His father used to stride through the castle, a constant presence when Ailig was a child, and yet he could not remember when that had begun to change. It had been Broc thumping about the castle these last couple of years, at least when Ailig had been home. He rubbed a knot in his left shoulder. Between reading the law with his uncle in Edinburgh, a tedious job at best, and spending as much time as possible in his beloved bens, he hadn't thought much about how things were being run, nor who was doing the running.

But now he was thinking about it, and he wasn't happy with the conclusions he was drawing. He rolled his shoulders, but the knots wouldn't loosen. If it had aught to do with the guard, or the warriors, 'twas Baltair who brought it to the chief's attention, and Baltair who handled whatever decision the chief came to. Neill never even bothered stirring himself to actually speak to the men involved, nor to watch how his men were performing at their work.

If it had aught to do with the maintenance of the castle, it seemed no one was charged with reporting to the chief. Ailig suspected that was why his sister had taken on more and more of that responsibility, and now he had thrown Morainn into that role, at least the part that focused on the kitchen.

Ailig clenched his teeth and felt a tiny muscle jump beneath his right ear. Pain zinged through his jaw and he tried to relax, tried to unclench his teeth, though he suspected 'twould take a stout stick to do so or more kisses from Morainn.

Frustration rolled through him. He'd been so consumed by the troubles of the clan, he'd not had the opportunity to corner Tamas yet. He figured if anyone knew what had scared Morainn, 'twould be him. Ailig wanted more kisses but had fought the urge to seek her out until he understood the fear that had made her pull away from him.

As if the mere thought of her summoned her before him, he found Morainn standing outside the kitchen larder, an undercroft used for storage of foodstuffs, her voice lowered as she argued with another lass who looked to be close to Morainn's age.

"'Tis a waste of time, and 'tis not my job," the other lass said. Ailig recognized her as one of the women who worked in the kitchen plucking birds.

Morainn wiped her hair out of her eyes, then rested her fists upon her hips. Ailig tried not to smile. She looked like a woman who would brook no more arguments. He wondered briefly if 'twould work upon his father, but he could not see himself carrying it off as Morainn did.

"Sorcha, 'tis not a waste of time to arrange the larder so we can find what we need without lifting every cask and basket out of the way every time. Now come. It won't take long with both of us working on it."

She caught sight of Ailig suddenly and a funny look came over her face, half irritation and half . . . The flames licked to life within him. 'Twas desire he saw, plain and clear on her face, no matter how hard she tried to mask it. She had been afraid of something, but she had not been unmoved by what they had shared. Hope warmed within him as she gave him a quick nod, then swung around and scurried into the dark opening of the larder.

He had intended to apologize to her as soon as he found a moment, not for kissing her, but for scaring her. But she was obviously avoiding him. He sighed. He was an idiot for giving in to the need to taste her so soon. He had more control than that, more finesse. Usually.

He headed over to the storage chamber where Sorcha still stood, staring after Morainn, arms crossed over her ample bosom and her chin jutting out so far he thought it must pain her more than his own did. The woman's obstinate stance over such a simple request for help irritated him.

"Do you not think 'twould work better if you were inside?" he asked, causing Sorcha to jump.

Her chin jutted out even more, giving her a sharp, belligerent look that was at odds with her plump physique. "'Tis not my job to haul about things."

Ailig studied her for a moment in silence. Her chin slowly lowered.

"And whose job might it be?"

"That's none of my concern. 'Tisn't mine and she can't make me do it."

"Fine." He spied Tamas just entering the bailey from the gate and motioned to the man to join him. "Tamas, there was that one job that you said needed doing, only the lads had managed to disappear?"

Tamas looked from Ailig to Sorcha and back, raised his eyebrows and said, "Aye, 'tis a smelly problem, that."

"Perhaps Sorcha here would prefer that task to the one Morainn has asked her to help with."

A grunt came from inside the larder followed by the sound of something heavy being dragged across the stone floor.

Tamas grinned. "'Twould be perfect. The privy chutes are in need of a thorough cleaning. Sorcha here might find it a wee bit tight but her reach would be longer than the lads."

Sorcha had gone pale and her chin, so sharp moments before, began to tremble.

Ailig took no pity on the lazy chit. "What say you, Sorcha? The privy chutes or working with Morainn?"

Sorcha aimed a glowering look at him. "You are not making me do anything," she said as she quickly disappeared into the dark maw of the storage room.

Tamas laughed and Ailig couldn't help but smile as Morainn's quiet murmur drifted out of the darkness.

"I guess she had not thought what other tasks could be found for her," Tamas said.

"Hmm? Och, aye. 'Tis always important to keep things in perspective." He wished to speak to Morainn but now was not the time. He turned his attention to Tamas. "Have you found the privy lads?"

"Aye. They are hard at work. 'Twas where I was coming from when you called me over. They are none too happy with their job, but I"—he gave Ailig a lopsided grin—"put it in perspective for them."

Perspective was a useful thing.

"Morainn has done wonders with the food," Ailig said, steering the conversation to a topic he was more interested in. "Is all well in the kitchen?"

"There are spats here and there, but she seems to have it well in hand. Why do you not ask her yourself?" There was a suspicious glint in Tamas's eye as he considered Ailig. "She has been asking me about you."

Pleasure thrummed through him. "She has?"

"Aye. I told you she would be perfect for you."

"It seems more a question of me suiting her."

Tamas nodded. "She claims she will never marry again."

"Never marry again? Why? Do you believe her?" He did not care for the tinge of worry that threaded through him at Tamas's words.

"Ask her. Get to know her. She does not trust . . . something. I cannot say I know what, but there is something that keeps her separate."

"'Tis an apt description." Ailig looked about and realized a steady stream of people were heading for the Great Hall. 'Twas time to go.

"I thank you for your counsel and your help in setting things to rights." He clapped him on the shoulder. "I still wish to discuss the guard with Baltair but my father has forbidden me to do so."

Tamas's grin faded. "Where is the chief? Does he not have to sit judgment today?"

Ailig glared up at the chief's tower. "He is keeping to his chambers, as he does so much lately. He sent me to hear the complaints today, though I doubt not that he will have someone there to keep watch over me, lest I get above myself and actually make a decision."

" 'Tis odd the way he keeps to his rooms," Tamas said, following Ailig as he made his way up the stairs to the Great Hall. "You do not think someone is forcing him to stay there, do you?"

"I do not think anyone has ever forced my father to do anything he did not want to. He claims he is fatigued and sometimes, when he is lecturing me on my faults, his eyes go unfocused and he seems to forget what he was saying for a moment. Then he acts as if it never happened. Something is not right." Ailig shook his head. "Perhaps 'tis only grief over Broc's death."

They reached the top of the stair and pushed the door open.

"In the meantime, I am doing what I can to see that his job gets done, even if he does not wish me to do it."

Relative warmth greeted them as they stepped inside, along with the sound of many gabbling voices.

"There you are, lads!" Angus Mhór waved at them from the entryway. He stepped toward them and motioned them close. "Baltair is within," he said, inclining his head towards the gathering. "He will try to cause you difficulties, Ailig. Do not rise to his bait."

chapter 6

Morainn couldn't help but grin at Ailig and Tamas's tactics as she hurried away from the open doorway. Sorcha stomped into the undercroft muttering under her breath about braw idiots who thought they could order a body about. Ailig had made an impression upon the girl. Ailig had made an impression upon everyone. Morainn could still feel the impression he'd made upon her body, her traitorous body.

"I'm here," Sorcha said as if 'twas not plainly evident.

"Good. Begin with those baskets by the far wall. We need to find out what is in each, then move the baskets so that there is some order to them. See?" She pointed to the neatly lined up baskets closest to her.

Sorcha mumbled something Morainn was sure she did not want to hear and went to work.

The quiet rumble of Ailig and Tamas's voices drifted in from the bailey but she dared not eavesdrop more than she already had. The mere sight of Ailig, striding across the bailey, had set her heart to hammering. Heat had spread through her so fast she was sure her face was flushed. She had fled. Fled. She had never fled anything nor anyone in her life, yet this man who had awakened a depth of desire in her that she had never known before . . . She shook her head at her own cowardice and yanked a basket of turnips into line.

"I do not ken why that one thinks he can order us about," Sorcha was saying, as if she had been speaking for some time.

Morainn blinked, trying to clear the haze of wanting that just thinking about Ailig drew forth in her. 'Twas a weakness she need not indulge.

"What?"

"He thinks he can order any of us about as if he were chief. 'Tis not his place." If Sorcha had been a wee lass Morainn would have said she was pouting. As she was a grown woman, it sounded like unnecessary complaining.

"Whose place is it then?" she said, wishing her repeated prayers for patience would get answered. "The chief does not lead and Broc is gone. Ailig seeks only to keep the clan safe from the king's vengeance. He must become chief, so it is only fitting that he behave as a chief."

"But the clan does not want him." Sorcha picked up a small basket and set it roughly atop another.

"Do you think Broc would have been a better chief than Ailig?"

"*He* at least liked the folk here. Ailig thinks he is better than the rest of us."

Surprise shoved away her impatience with the chit. If any of the brothers thought they were better than the rest of the clan she would have said 'twas Broc. "I can think of nothing Ailig has done to look down upon anyone, except perhaps Baltair, but that is only because the man vexes him so."

"You are blind then." Sorcha turned to face her, her hands upon her hips and her eyes narrowed. "Or perhaps you are besotted by his bonny face and fine form. 'Tis tempting, is it not?"

"I am not besotted!" Morainn said. The handle ripped off the basket she was pulling, sending her onto her backside. She closed her eyes for a moment, willing herself to calmness. "I can see the others for what they are," she said, rising to her feet and brushing off her skirts, "and for what they are not. A big, blustering bag of wind, that's what Broc was—"

"Wheesht!" Sorcha hissed, crossing herself and glancing quickly about as if she expected Broc's ghost to appear in the shadowy undercroft. "You should not speak of the dead so."

"I speak but the truth," Morainn said.

"Still, 'tis dangerous." She crossed herself again. "You could draw his spirit here with words like that."

"Admit it, Sorcha, his ghost would be no worse than he was in life. Besides, 'twould give the other three brothers something to bleat around after, like the sheep they are called."

"I will admit nothing," Sorcha said. "The man was to be our chief. Now Ailig claims the king wishes *him* to be chief or we will suffer the consequences. When has a MacLeod ever stood by and let another bully him in such a way?"

"Every time Broc demanded something."

Sorcha rolled her eyes. "You would truly rather have a chief the king commands over a chief who will only do what is best for this clan?"

"Ailig *is* doing what is best for this clan. And I, for one, would far rather have a man in charge who is thoughtful about the clan's future than one who thinks threatening the king's life is what is needed."

Sorcha shrugged. "'Twill take a lot to convince anyone that Ailig should be chief. It goes against custom and the chief's wishes. But if the chief is won over, then so goes the clan. But if he is not, no argument from you, or Tamas, or even the king himself, will convince this lot otherwise."

"Ailig is an honorable man," Morainn said, uncomfortable with her own vehemence, but sure of what she said. "You will change your mind, Sorcha. All of you will—if you give him a chance."

"'Tis he who will have to take that chance, is it not? We will not give it to him."

Morainn stared at the plump woman for a moment. "Just so," she finally said and turned back to her work, tired of arguing, tired of fighting her own feelings.

She'd been avoiding Ailig for three days, afraid of what she would do should she find herself alone with him again, and yet she knew in her bones that he was an honorable man. He had released her from his searing kisses though she knew he did not wish to stop. He had not pursued her these three days past. She tried to make herself believe that his chivalrous behavior did not disappoint her. 'Twas not his fault that he made her feel alive just by looking at her, made her feel desirable, wanted, just by saying her name in his quiet rumbling voice. 'Twas not his problem that her traitorous body yearned for more of his caresses, nor that she relived those kisses in her dreams each night.

'Twas not his problem.

'Twas hers.

*A*ilig sat at the high table trying to concentrate on the sixth complaint of the morning. His mind kept wandering to Morainn. He couldn't stop thinking about the way she had felt in his arms and the flushed look on her face just before she disappeared into the storage chamber. Someone coughed, and he forced his attention back to the man standing before him. Short Ian droned on and on about how he had stolen a cow from his brother last summer, but had returned it when his wife made him, only now it turned out the cow was with calf. Short Ian claimed that since the cow got the calf off of his bull he should be the owner of the calf.

Rory, the brother, argued just as strongly that his brother owed him another cow to make up for the loss of milk he and his family endured from last summer right up to Hogmanay, last month, when the heifer was finally returned. To strengthen his case he had brought his wife and their five weans, including one who even now was enjoying his mother's obviously abundant milk.

Ailig worked hard not to roll his eyes at the mournful tones both brothers employed. All of the complaints this morn had been like this. Ridiculous. 'Twas no wonder his father ducked this particular duty. 'Twas a colossal waste of time.

"Stop!" he finally cried, standing so abruptly he had to grab at his chair to keep it from toppling over backwards.

The crowd, for there had been a crowd the entire morning, was, wonder of wonders, completely hushed.

"Do you truly wish for me to decide who is right and who is wrong in this matter?"

Both brothers bobbed their heads and all Rory's weans and wife did, too.

"Very well. Here is what I have decided. You"—he pointed at Short Ian—"will give one pail of milk to your brother's family every day for the same number of months you held Rory's cow. And you"—he pointed at Rory now—"shall pay to your brother one half the meat from the calf at whatever time you butcher it."

They both began to complain and the crowd buzzed with comment.

"Wait, there is more." Ailig was practically bellowing to make himself heard. "If anyone ever brings such a frivolous, time-wasting, irritating, useless complaint before me or my father again, all property under dispute shall become the property of the chief."

The buzzing rose to a roar of complaint. Ailig banged his fist against the table, once more drawing a hush over the crowd.

"I sit here as my father's proxy. My judgment shall stand, no matter how much you dislike it. Now," he said, surveying his audience, "is there anyone else who wishes to be heard?"

He waited, but no one stepped forward. No one would meet his eye except for three at the back of the hall: Tamas, who was looking pleasantly surprised; Angus Mhór, who had a very thoughtful look upon his wrinkled visage; and Baltair, whose expression was clearly meant to disconcert Ailig, only Ailig did not let it.

"I thought not. We are finished here then."

"Nay, we are not."

Impatience spiked through him as Ailig glanced around the hall to see who had spoken. Gofraig separated himself from the crowd and approached the dais with a confident stride and a thunderous scowl.

Ailig stifled a sigh and slowly took his seat. He pulled the chair close to the table again, never taking his eyes off Gofraig. He did not trust the man, but he was stuck with him biding at Castle Assynt at least for a little longer. He poured himself a cup of ale and sat back in the ornate chief's chair just as Gofraig arrived at the front of the hall.

"You may speak." Ailig took a secret pleasure in the scowl that deepened on the man's face.

"There is a tocher owed my clan." Gofraig crossed his arms and managed to raise his chin enough to look down his nose at Ailig. "'Twas your sister who broke the betrothal. 'Tis my clan who should be repaid for our wasted time and the shame heaped upon our chief."

"The only shame heaped upon your chief is the shame of being a traitor. As for the betrothal, it was never formally announced. The banns were not called. My sister could not break what had not been made."

"Your sister's tocher was to be six wagon-loads of food, weapons and goods."

Ailig blinked. "Did you say six?"

"I did."

Six wagon-loads . . . 'twould beggar the castle and the clan. Surely the man lied.

"'Tis impossible."

"You will not honor the contract?" Gofraig sneered at him, raising Ailig's hackles.

"There is no contract. There is no marriage to be made between Catriona and Duff. 'Tis a ridiculous amount of goods. We could not spare so much and insure the well-being of our own."

"What kind of man are you that you do not stand by your word?"

"I always stand by my word, but 'twas not my word that you had. No doubt 'twas Broc's and 'tis clear by the sheer absurd amounts that he never intended to make good on it—but then that does not surprise me."

"And you are too daft to honor the word of your own brother?" A new voice came from deep in the hall.

Baltair.

Just what he needed. One of his own kinsmen joining forces against him with the MacDonells . . . again. A dull pulsing ache at the base of his skull started, picking up speed with each step Baltair took, until it beat a battle charge against his temples.

"What do you want, Baltair?" Ailig asked, unable to keep his irritation out of his voice. A man could only be pushed so far before he snapped. And he feared he was at the edge of this particular precipice and all his careful self-control was going to go flying into the abyss.

"Mostly, I want to beat you to a bloody pulp until you beg me to stop."

Ailig's skin crawled at the hatred so clear, not only in the other man's words, but also in his voice.

"And you will get a chance to try," he said, slowly rising from his seat. He could feel his pulse rise to battle readiness, his muscles bunched in anticipation. Ailig speared a glare at Gofraig, who took a step away from the table. He could only deal with one of them at a time and clearly Baltair needed to be dealt with right now. "But not here. I do not need your . . . help with this issue. Our"—he wanted to speak his mind but that way definitely led over the edge and into the deep darkness—"guest is quite capable of negotiating on his clan's behalf without your getting in the way."

"I am not in the way. I am defending Broc's good name as is my right. You are not chief. You cannot say what we will or will not honor. You are only the least of the chief's offspring. Even your sister had more strength than you."

The crowd was rising to their feet, nodding their heads with each statement Baltair bit out.

"Then take this to the chief." Ailig leaned forward, resting his palms on the table. He tilted his head toward Gofraig. "And take that one with you."

"I will, but first I make formal challenge."

The hall went absolutely still, absolutely silent. Ailig's mind flashed through all his possible responses, knowing that he could not duck this, but also that he was not likely to best Baltair in a straight fight. The man was half again as big as Ailig and did nothing but practice in the training yard when he was not eating—or bedding the lasses. His brute strength would eventually overcome any intellectual advantage Ailig might have.

He stood up straight, arms akimbo, fists on his hips and notched his chin up in the most dominant pose he could devise. "You are challenging me to . . . ?" He stalled for time.

"To combat. The winner will be the next chief."

The gathering shouted their approval and Ailig felt a trickle of sweat run down his back. He felt the edge begin to crumble beneath his feet, but he would not allow himself to be pitched into the pit. Not if he could help it.

"Has the chief agreed to this?" He rose slowly and made his way around the table. "Nay? And the king? Think you this will satisfy his command?" He stood face-to-face with Baltair, raising his voice with each question, determined that all there gathered would understand the ramifications of such a challenge. He could not allow the man to think he could intimidate him. He'd not allow anyone to think they could intimidate the next chief of Clan Leod of Assynt. "Think you defeating me will keep the clan safe from the king's wrath? Would you put your own aspirations ahead of the safety of the entire clan?"

Baltair said nothing, but continued to glower at Ailig, though he could tell the pointed questions had penetrated.

"If you wish to challenge me, I will face you, but think first if it is what is best for your clan."

The two of them glared at each other for a long moment, each ready to do battle there, though Ailig hoped it would not come to that.

"He is right Baltair." Angus Mhór startled everyone with his loud voice. He pushed his way through the crowd and joined the two men in front of the dais.

Ailig allowed himself one deep, slow breath. Perhaps the old man could pull them back from the precipice's edge.

"'Tis as Ailig has said. You must think what is best for the clan."

"I always do what is best for the clan," Baltair growled, keeping his eyes firmly fixed on Ailig.

"You ken as well as I," Angus Mhór said, "that 'twill be for your own conceit, not for the good of the clan, if you . . . how did you put it? Beat him to a bloody pulp?

Och, that was it. If you insist, then you may challenge him before the gathered clan once he is declared chief."

"I do not care to wait," Baltair said, though there wasn't quite the force behind the words of a moment ago.

"Then you do not care for this clan." Ailig took a chance baiting him, hoping he might reveal something of use. "Do you care only for your own glory? 'Tis hardly a worthy goal for a champion."

"I am champion. What I do not care for is a wee nasty like yourself shiting on your brother's good name."

"Did you not hear what happened? Are you deaf as well as dumb?" Ailig knew he was courting a beating but he needed to know what was driving Baltair.

Angus Mhór clucked his tongue like an auld woman with misbehaving children. "Stop acting like a couple of weans squabbling over a sweetmeat. The clan's future is much more important than your wounded pride—the both of you. Baltair, if you truly are the clan's champion, act like one. And you, Ailig, if you are to be chief you must learn not to bait those whose job it is to keep you and yours safe." Angus looked pointedly at Ailig, as if there was more to his chastisement than just the words.

Suddenly Ailig understood. The odd gravelly undertone in Baltair's voice, 'twas guilt. Guilt and shame. He was champion. 'Twas his duty to keep his chief, and the future chief, safe, and he had not. Broc, his friend and his charge, was dead and Baltair had been nowhere about to prevent it.

Ailig stepped back, no longer needing to goad the man and using Angus Mhór's timely chastisement as an excuse to back down. He would not force Baltair to reveal his shame before the hall full of people, but he would make sure that Baltair knew Ailig had discovered it.

A movement caught Ailig's eye. Gofraig was trying to hide a grin behind his fist.

"You need not be so happy, MacDonell," Angus Mhór said, following the direction of Ailig's attention. "You are acting just as poorly as these two. You are a guest in this place, yet you would assault Ailig, then impugn his reputation by accusing him of breaking a word he did not give. I am amazed that Ailig has restrained himself from beating *you* to a bloody pulp. He has had provocation enough—"

"I am protected by the chief's—"

"Think you the chief gives a rat's arse about your protection right now? He has lost a son, four really. His daughter has forged an alliance with a clan he does not know." He cast a quick glance at Ailig to keep him quiet. "And the king of Scotland is threatening us with banishment and damnation. What makes you think the chief even remembers that you are here?"

Gofraig's face burned red with anger and Ailig could see a small tic jumping by his right eye.

"He has given us the protection of his word. Anything done against us would shame him and this clan."

"Do you really think there is more shame than a son, a future chief, who was killed while conspiring to harm the king?" Ailig asked, teeth clenched against his once more rising anger.

"Aye, I do, wee Ailig." Gofraig glanced around the crowd gathered about them. "And you will, too, when Duff returns and we learn the truth."

Ailig shook his head.

Angus Mhór laid a hand on the table in front of Ailig and glanced at the three men. "I suggest . . . strongly suggest . . . that you all take time to think." He pinned Ailig with his brilliant blue gaze. "Skaeth awaits you in the yard." He turned his gaze to Baltair, gracing him with a scowl. "The guard needs tending. I caught a man asleep at the gate this morn." He then shifted his ire to Gofraig. "You might keep close to your quarters for a while, or better yet leave as you have been asked to. Your continued presence here does not endear you to any." He turned to the rest of the gathering. "Don't you all have work awaiting you?" A murmur answered his question but no one made to leave the hall.

"Go!" At Ailig's bellowed order they began to move towards the exit. He felt a momentary satisfaction that at least in this they obeyed him.

Baltair glared at Ailig but also turned to go.

"This isn't over," Gofraig said under his breath as he passed Ailig. He did not look at Angus Mhór.

After the place was empty, save for Ailig and the auld man, Ailig grabbed two goblets and filled them with ale, then joined Angus Mhór again.

"I would rather have whiskey just now," he said as he handed one of the goblets to Angus Mhór. "But this is here and I do not want to be stared at by yet another set of eyes."

Angus chuckled and drank.

"Thank you," Ailig said, swallowing his pride and staring into the amber depths of his cup. "I should have been prepared for all of that."

"Aye, you should have. 'Tis why you should have a council, people to help you see the trips and traps that will be set for you."

"I have Tamas MacRailt and the mercenary, Skaeth. He is more observant than most."

"But do you ask their opinions? Request their ideas? Tamas was here. He did not seem as surprised by the events that just unfolded as you were."

"I am not used to asking for opinions," Ailig said.

"And yet that is a skill needed by a chief."

Ailig nodded. "I know I have much to learn."

"You do. 'Tis admirable that you recognize that. 'Twas not something Broc understood. Information is a valuable weapon, Ailig, both gathered and given. 'Tis worth your while to cultivate good sources. Other than Tamas, do you have any sources?"

"Skaeth has keen eyes."

Angus pursed his lips and stared into the distance. "Anyone else? Anyone who can move about the castle without drawing so much attention as those two? The council is used to servants in the chamber and they pay little heed." He looked at Ailig and winked. "Is there not a lass or a wean who would tell you what goes on within these walls?"

His thoughts went immediately to Morainn. She was in a position to hear many things. All gossip made its way to the kitchen sooner or later, and if he were to convince her to expand her responsibilities—

"There is one, Morainn MacRailt. She has taken on the kitchen," he said quietly, "but I do not think she will welcome any more responsibilities, not from me."

Angus Mhór's face lit with a knowing smile that made his eyes crinkle up until Ailig almost couldn't see them any longer. He put a time-weathered hand on Ailig's forearm.

"Talk to her, lad. Charm her if you must. She'll know more than even she realizes. But also talk to Tamas. He is a good man and kens the workings of this clan better than he lets on. He has little ambition, so he keeps to the fringes of things. Pull him into the center. With Skaeth you have a formidable trio on your side. Use their knowledge."

"Why are you telling me all this?"

"'Tis in my interest to see you become chief, lad, though the chief resists, and the council has their doubts. I have lived through banishment and its aftermath when I was young." His eyes misted over and he seemed very far away for a moment. "'Tis not a fate I could ever wish upon anyone," he said quietly. "And I do not plan to spend my last years hiding in the bens when I could sit near a comfortable fire with a full belly and be entertained of a winter's night with music and tales."

They were quiet for a moment as Ailig considered the trio of confidants Angus recommended. Skaeth had already proven useful and willing in that area. Tamas, too, showed his willingness to share his information and concerns with Ailig. So that left Morainn. Her own concern for the clan and its future was evidenced by her taking on the work of organizing the kitchen, but would she be willing to expand her responsibilities so that 'twould not appear unusual for her to move about the castle wherever and whenever she wished?

Angus put down his cup. "Go and train with Skaeth, for Baltair is sure to challenge you again soon. Gofraig may snap even sooner."

"We can only hope," Ailig said.

Angus laughed. "Aye, we can only hope. 'Twould be a joy to meet him with swords drawn I'm thinking. I'd like to . . ." He clapped Ailig on the back surprisingly hard. "But I must leave such fun to you. Go. Skaeth awaits, then seek ye out Morainn and Tamas."

Ailig nodded. "My thanks for your good council, Angus," he said, his thoughts already turning to Morainn.

Ailig had been so preoccupied with plans on how to approach Morainn about expanding her duties . . . and spending more time with him . . . that Skaeth had nearly beaten him to a pulp, if not Baltair's preferred bloody pulp. Right now Ailig wanted nothing more than to get the grit out of his eyes and teeth, the aches from his muscles and perhaps an unripped tunic to replace the one that now had several slices in it from Skaeth's skillful parries. He would have to remember to wear this tunic the next time he trained. He groaned out loud. That would be tomorrow. And now that Baltair had openly challenged him, Ailig had all the motivation he needed to heed Skaeth's schedule.

Ailig headed for the well. Drawing up a bucket, he plunged his hands into it and splashed his face with the icy water. Rivulets ran down his chest. Droplets hung on his eyelashes and dripped from his hair. He plunged his hands in again, scrubbing at his face this time and realized 'twould take more than a quick rinse to rid him of the dirt that seemed to have found its way even beneath his clothes.

He needed a good, hot bath—a soak-the-aches-out-of-you, lift-the-grit-off-you bath. He pushed his wet hair out of his face and headed for the kitchen. 'Twould be as good an opportunity as any to speak to Morainn.

He took the steps two at a time, the prospect of seeing her making him forget how much his muscles complained. The kitchen was buzzing with activity, but it seemed to be a contented, well-ordered buzzing. He stood in the door and watched as Morainn moved through the workers like a ship sailing in calm seas. Her hair was bound tightly in her accustomed braid and he found himself itching to loosen the tie and run his fingers through it, letting the silky . . .

"Ailig?" Morainn's concerned voice came from across the room. "What happened? Who did this?"

"Who did what?" he asked as she came closer.

"You look as if you have been fighting, and you did not win."

He laughed. "'Tis an apt description. I have been sparring with Skaeth." He reached for her hand, unable to resist touching her. He could feel her tremble, but she allowed him to run his thumb over the back of it. "I am afraid my mind was not on my swordplay today," he said, just loud enough for her to hear. He gave her hand a squeeze and released her, afraid he'd pull her into him for another kiss right here in front of everyone if he did not.

A blush stole up her face, casting a rosy glow to her creamy complexion and making the freckles that danced across the bridge of her nose and over those cheeks stand out. She clasped her hands together, but he noticed she rubbed her own thumb over the spot he had caressed. He suppressed the urge to grin at her. She was not as cool as she was trying to be.

"What do you need?" she asked.

You. 'Twas what he most wanted to say, but he did not. "A bath," he said, instead. "Can you have one brought to my room. I would not bother you, but . . . well, you can see 'tis needed."

"I can," she said, gracing him with a shy smile. "Alasdair," she called over her shoulder. "See that a tub is prepared for Ailig."

A lad, with adoration clear in his eyes, bobbed his head at her and grabbed a bucket, then two other lads, and disappeared through the door on the opposite wall.

"I see you have made a conquest," he teased. Her brow furrowed and he realized she had no idea the effect she had on any of the men around her. "Young Alasdair. 'Twas adoration on his face, clear as a summer's day."

"Nay, he simply likes to be useful," she said, turning her back to him and surveying her new domain.

"'Tis easy to be useful when 'tis such a bonny woman asking."

"I'll have them bring the tub to your chamber as soon as they set the water to heating," she said, as if he had not said anything about Alasdair.

"My thanks," he said. "I did not mean to make you nervous around me, Morainn. 'Tis the last thing I want," he said.

"It has been a long time since anyone kissed me. It does not matter. We cannot let it happen again." She gave him a rueful smile over her shoulder.

His heart was hammering. Not kiss again? His body remembered how soft her lips had been, how hungry he was to taste her again.

"Were things different . . ." She shrugged and Ailig touched her shoulder, turning her with a light touch to face him again. The pleasure that washed through him just by touching her bemused him.

"What, Morainn?"

She swallowed, her eyes wide. The gold flecks against the deep brown seemed to sparkle. Her own struggle against the pull between them was palpable and his body fairly hummed in acknowledgment.

"It does not matter," she finally said.

The kiss had hit her as hard as it had him. Pleasure rolled through him. He had not been able to get the memory of her rounded body pressed up against him, nor her hungry mouth and soft lips, out of his mind these past days. She had been equally affected. He was sure of it. Ailig struggled not to pull her into his embrace right then and there.

"I need to ask you something, but I cannot do it here. Is there someplace private we can talk?"

She looked at him for a long moment, as if deciding whether to chance being alone with him again. He could not blame her for her caution. He had every intention of kissing her again. He had no doubt she could see it in his eyes. At last she looked about.

"The larder," she said. "There is a stair down to it from here." She pointed to a door in the corner of the kitchen nearest the wash pots.

"That will do," he said and motioned for her to lead the way.

Everyone in the kitchen was diligently working, but Ailig noticed heads turning as they passed and knew everything he had said to Morainn would be discussed throughout the castle by dinnertime. He supposed he should expect a visit of some sort from Baltair this night. He sighed as he passed through the larder doorway, pulling it firmly shut behind him, then following Morainn down the stairs into the darkness.

chapter 7

❧

Morainn stood in a wavery circle of light cast by a single torch as she waited for Ailig to join her at the bottom of the larder's stair. She was curious and uneasy. An uncomfortable restlessness nearly had her pacing the confines of the undercroft, but she did not. She waited, as patiently as she was able, while he slowly descended the dark stairway.

He stepped off the bottom stair and into the circle of light and she knew, before she could draw another breath, he was going to kiss her again. She also knew she would let him.

He cupped her face in his hands and stepped so close their bodies almost touched. Heat pooled between them as his lips touched hers, gently, softly, giving this time instead of taking. Asking instead of demanding. This kiss was nothing like the last one.

She leaned into his strength, answering his question.

The brush of his chest against her sensitive breasts stole her breath and she found herself gripping his waist, deepening the kiss, allowing herself to indulge in the feelings that poured forth—passion, desire, longing—at least for a few moments.

Ailig pulled back just enough so that she could see the question in his eyes. "Three days ago you ran from my chamber. Only a few minutes ago you wished me to believe I would never kiss you again. Now you draw me closer and let me kiss you." He took her mouth again and she could taste his frustration, his confusion, his passion.

'Twas the last that scared her and yet she did not want the kiss to end. 'Twas sweet with longing, dark with desire, and she felt wonderfully alive, awakened as if from a sleep of many years. Why had she fled this?

She stepped away from him, not far, just enough so that he could not distract her with another kiss. Not yet. She needed to understand what she was doing. She needed him to understand.

She looked at him carefully, taking in every nuance of his face. The stubble that shadowed his chin. The lines at the corners of his compelling eyes. The way one corner of his mouth quirked higher than the other. What was she doing here?

"I . . . I had not been kissed in a long time. I was not prepared . . ."

"Prepared? You need to prepare for a kiss?"

She laughed and that, too, felt wonderful and alive. It did sound ridiculous. "I was surprised, by the kiss, and by the feelings that came with it."

"And this time you were prepared?"

"In truth? I have been able to think of little else."

"And yet you just told me—"

"I know. You must think me a fickle beast."

"I do not."

"You must know that this . . ." She searched for a word to describe what she was feeling.

"Attraction?"

'Twas good enough. "Aye, this attraction, there is no future in it. I can give you no more than kisses."

"I did not mean to ask you—the other night—I was not thinking clearly when I asked you to stay the night with me." He ran his hands through his hair, pushing it away from his face as he began to pace. "I did not mean to imply that you were—"

"Wheesht. 'Twas what startled me but 'tis not why I left . . . fled. I want to be honest with you, Ailig."

"And I with you, Mora."

The name made her look at him. "Why did you call me that?"

"It seems right for you. I will call you Morainn if you do not like it."

She shook her head. "You may call me what you like. 'Tis only that my mother used to call me Mora. No one else ever has."

They were silent for a moment as she gathered her thoughts. "I cannot offer you more than kisses because I will not marry again." She did not look at him as she said the words. She needed to remember 'twas Hamish who had first made her feel alive this way. 'Twas Hamish who had taught her 'twas not a feeling that lasted. She'd not suffer that kind of pain again. She'd never allow herself to cherish feelings and the man who caused them when both would disappear all too soon.

When he said nothing she glanced at him.

"I did not mean you meant to marry me," she stammered, feeling her cheeks heat as she realized what she had said. "I only meant—"

"I know what you meant." His voice was neutral but his eyes gleamed, and she wondered if 'twas hurt he hid or relief. "I am in no position to take a wife, at least not until 'tis clear that I will be named chief and the clan will be safe from the king's threat. In the meantime, kisses will hurt no one, will they?"

"I suppose they will not," she said, surprised at the wisp of disappointment she felt when he did not try to convince her to give him more.

They sat down, and he took her hand in his, lifting it to his lips and pressing a kiss to her knuckles. "You distract me from my purpose. I did not mean to kiss you when I asked to speak with you privately, but I cannot regret it. I could kiss you again. Will. But there is something I need to ask you—something that has nothing to do with kissing," he added quickly, smiling at her. "I need your help, again. More. What do you know of Baltair?"

She was surprised by the change of subject. "He trains much, eats much, drinks much and brags much. He thinks if he bothers me enough I will give in and marry him." Ailig's hand flinched in hers. "Which I will never do. He is not a complicated man, but he is very loyal to your brother and your father. It seems he wishes to take Broc's place, to be another son to your father."

"What makes you say that?"

"He spends a lot of time with the chief—when you are not there, or so I have heard."

Angus Mhór was right. Morainn knew much. "Have you heard what he does when he is with the chief?"

Morainn cocked her head at him as a slow smile spread on her rosy lips. His stomach, and parts lower, tightened.

"Did you think you needed to seduce me with your kisses to gain my help as your spy?"

He shook his head. "The kissing was purely selfish. The spying is for the clan. I would not confuse the two. I hope you do not. Would you mind spying for me?"

She considered what he was asking. "I would not mind. I like you, Ailig. I did not expect to." Did not want to was the more honest answer, but she kept that to herself. "If I can help you save the clan, then that is what I must do."

"Will you consider becoming chatelaine, keeper of the castle, as Catriona was?"

Chatelaine? She stared at him, eyes widening. 'Twas a huge thing he asked. 'Twas one thing to see to the kitchen, another completely to be in charge of running the entire castle.

"You need not take it all on at once," he said. "I know the kitchen requires much of your time, but if you are chatelaine, then you can come and go wherever you need to within the castle . . . wherever I need you to."

He ran his thumb over the back of her hand again, sending delicious sensations swirling through her, distracting her from what he asked.

"You ask a lot, Ailig. I do not know if I can see to the whole castle."

"Just take the keys for now. Familiarize yourself with the storerooms and those folk who tend the chambers. Your friend Una is bound to know what needs doing in the rest of the castle. Please?"

" 'Tis a word you use too often on me."

"Aye, but it seems to work. Will you do it?"

"I will."

He kissed her, sweetly, chastely, caressing her cheek with his callused hand.

"Mora . . ." He cupped his hand at the back of her neck and rested his forehead on hers. "I must go." His voice was low, husky, as if he struggled to get the words out. She nodded and watched him leave, still feeling the heat of his hand upon her skin and the taste of his lips upon hers.

Morainn *wandered out of the dark larder and into the* late afternoon daylight of the bailey still in a daze from Ailig's kisses. What was she thinking to kiss him again . . . and again . . . and again. She rubbed the spot between her eyebrows that had begun to pound and wondered where her resolve had gone.

Ailig's kisses had opened up something inside her, a door to a deep black empty pit in her heart that she had spent years ignoring. That pit held such yearning to be touched, to be held, to be cherished. It held a deep need to share all of those feelings with someone. Kissing him had stirred up yearnings she didn't want to acknowledge, desires she wasn't sure she'd ever felt before.

She wrenched herself back to reality, chiding herself for acting like a lovelorn lass. She was happy with her life just the way it was. She didn't need a man's affections. They were nice, to be sure, but not necessary. And yet she knew the next time she was alone with him she would likely be the one to kiss him.

She pushed her hair out of her face and remembered the

feel of his heated palm upon her cheek, his fevered lips upon hers. Heat pooled deep within her. She closed her eyes and realized that she was finding it increasingly difficult to say no to this man about anything. She feared if he asked for more than kisses, she'd have no strength to deny him. She would have to shore up her defenses, protect her heart, before he found his way there. For if he ever did break through those defenses, 'twould be a disaster.

She took a shaky breath and tried to focus on why she had followed him out of the undercroft and into the bailey. He had a bath awaiting him in his chamber, but she resolutely refused to let her mind follow him there. Casting about for something to remind her of what she was supposed to be doing, she locked her eyes on Una tending her huge wash kettle set over a smoky fire.

She was going to ask Una about Catriona's keys. Aye, that was it. She grabbed hold of that idea like a drowning woman scrabbling for a rope to pull her free. She all but sprinted across the bailey. 'Twas only as she skidded to a halt beside the cauldron that she realized Tamas stood beside Una, their heads bent in conversation. They smiled at her simultaneously, and she had the distinct feeling they had been speaking about her.

"Where was Ailig bound for?" Tamas asked her, the smile turning to a grin.

Morainn's normally calm temper crackled. "Are you two conspiring together now? Do you not think you've pushed me enough of late, Tamas? 'Tis because of you . . ." But she did not want to tell them what had passed between herself and Ailig. She put her fists upon her hips and glowered at the two of them. "Do not think you can get Una to push me any harder than she already does."

"Good day to you, too, Morainn," Una said, the smile disappearing and reprimand thick in her voice.

Tamas looked at Morainn quizzically. "I do not speak of you in every conversation I have, lass," he said. "Though any advice Una has for you I would suggest you take." He turned a dazzling smile on Una. "She is an uncommonly wise woman. Not all of us enjoy loneliness like you do." He pecked Una on the cheek, gave Morainn a wide-eyed so-there look and took off across the bailey. His off-key whistle drifted back to them.

"He is in a good mood today," Morainn said, watching him go.

"Despite a certain good sister's waspish greeting." Una gave the clothes a fierce stir. "You've no cause to treat him so, Morainn."

Morainn felt like a wee lass, though the scolding was well earned. Tamas had always wanted Morainn to be happy. 'Twas just that he pushed, and she was already feeling off-balance when she spied the two of them with their heads together.

"I am sorry, Una. You are right. I shall apologize to him later. Why was he here?" she asked.

Una stopped her stirring and gave Morainn a look usually reserved for misbehaving weans. "Cannot the man wish to share my company?"

"Of course he can. I only meant . . ." She shook her head, not sure what she meant. This would never do. She had let herself get so addled by Ailig and the uncomfortable feelings he raised in her that she had all but attacked both Una and Tamas. She took a deep breath and dropped her shoulders which had somehow crept up about her ears. "Can we start over? I did not mean to be so cross."

Una looked at her for a moment, then returned to stirring the clothes.

"Did Tamas tell you that you will be getting a new roof?"

"He did, several days ago." A dreamy look lit Una's face as if the moon glowed from within her. "He says 'twas your doing. Thank you." She laid a hand on Morainn's arm. "You did not need to do that.

"I saw no reason not to ask for something in return for my help in the kitchen."

"Tamas says you are a wonder with the kitchen workers."

"They just needed someone to lead them."

"'Tis not unlike this clan, is it?" Una said, giving the kettle a vigorous stir. "Do you think Ailig will become chief?"

Morainn narrowed her eyes at her friend. "Why would I know? Tamas, he would know. Did you ask him?"

Una's glow turned pink. "Do not be angry," she said, still stirring the kettle. "We were speaking of you, Tamas and me. He says Ailig is much taken with you, and that you . . . Tamas thinks you might be softening towards the man."

"I do not want to soften towards the man."

"But are you?"

"Perhaps . . ."

Una squealed and did a little jig, sloshing the boiling water over the sides of the pot.

"Wheesht. I only said perhaps. I do not know what my feelings are, except that they are confused."

"He is a braw man and Tamas says he is a good man, not like his brothers at all."

" 'Twould seem to be true," Morainn said.

"So you do think he will become chief," Una said.

Morainn shook her head. "Truly, I do not know, but I am doing what I can to help him. Which reminds me why I came to see you. He has asked me to act as chatelaine. Do you know where Catriona kept the keys to the castle?"

Una stopped her stirring and stared at Morainn, her mouth open in a silent *O*. Morainn chuckled. 'Twasn't often one could make Una speechless.

"He has asked you to wed him?"

"Nay!"

"But chatelaine, 'tis mistress of the castle. 'Tis for the chief's wife to mind the castle."

"But there is no wife, nor sister. 'Tis only temporary. Once he becomes chief he can take a wife and I will gladly turn the keys over and return to my own life." She said the words lightly, but they sat, heavy as stones, in her stomach. He had said he could not marry until he became chief. 'Twas only logical that he would find a wife once that was accomplished. And she had said she would not marry. Anyone. Ever.

And yet, the idea of him kissing someone else, bedding someone else. She stared into the bubbling water and held her suddenly cold hands out to warm in the heat of the fire.

"Is it possible to want someone without falling in love with him?" she asked, her voice barely above a whisper. "I cannot get him out of my mind, Una." Her voice wobbled and she feared tears were not far behind. The things he made her feel were wonderful, and yet they frightened her.

"Lass," Una said, folding her into a motherly hug. "Do not fret. Love comes when it will and there is little you can do to force it or prevent it. 'Tis a lesson I have learned twice over. All you can do is to open your heart to it and see what happens."

"You make it sound so simple."

"'Tis . . ." Her voice trailed off and her attention focused across the bailey.

Morainn turned to see what Una was transfixed by, but all she saw was Tamas heading into the gate tunnel.

"I promise I will apologize to him before the day is out," she said.

"Och, that man will forgive you anything. He loves you as if you were his real sister. You know that, don't you?" Una said, giving her another quick hug before turning back to her kettle. "I'm thinking he may not be the only one with feelings for you."

"Keys, Una. I need to find a set of keys," Morainn said, unready to delve any deeper into her feelings for Ailig.

Una grinned. "We are not done with the topic of Ailig MacLeod, but I will let it go for now. The chief must have a set of keys and Catriona had the other. I do not know if she thought to leave them behind when she fled, but 'tis possible. If 'twere me, I would have left them in my chamber. Perhaps you should look there?"

"I knew you would have a good suggestion for me. And I am sorry I snapped at Tamas, but I was not wrong, was I?"

"Nay, you were not. Go along now. I've got work to do here."

Morainn pecked her friend on the cheek as Tamas had done and headed for the chief's tower. She closed the tower door behind her and stared at the steps ascending before her. Damn. She'd forgotten that both Catriona's chamber and the chief's were on the same floor as Ailig's.

But she was being silly. She needed the keys in order to take stock of the castle and its supplies, and besides, his bath would be arriving any minute. 'Twasn't as if he'd be lurking in the hallway, waiting to whisk her into his room for another kiss, or more. He was probably stepping into his tub this very moment. An image of Ailig naked, submerging his leanly muscled body in a tub, swept every other thought from her mind. As clearly as if she were in the room with him she could see water dripping from his tangle of golden blond hair, running down his muscled back . . .

Her breath was coming in short bursts and she was not even climbing the stairs. What was wrong with her? He was a braw man, aye, and his kisses . . . he was a brilliant kisser, but she had to get her wayward, wanton thoughts under control. This was what came of setting her own life aside. If she had kept to her own cottage, kept to her spinning and weaving, she'd not be having these unwelcome thoughts, these unwelcome feelings. Working with the wool always calmed her, focused her, kept her out of trouble. But there was no time for that right now. She'd just have to get herself under control—and stay away from Ailig. Aye, 'twas the only way she was going to keep her heart safe. If only she had the willpower necessary to do so.

She made her way quietly past Ailig's door, overcoming the urge to stop and listen for the sound of water, and was pleased to find that Catriona was a very organized person, or at least her chamber was. She had left her keys in the third place Morainn had looked—under the woman's pillow. Now all she had to do was pass Ailig's chamber door once more without stopping. She could do it. Really she could.

At last Ailig's father, Neill, and the elders left the high table, signaling to the gathering that the evening's meal was at an end. Ailig waited until the elders had filed out of the hall with most of the castle folk following them. The days were more difficult even than he had anticipated. Except for those shining moments when he held Morainn in his arms.

He had watched for her tonight, but she had never entered the Great Hall. Was she avoiding him again? She had seemed calmer when he left her in the undercroft. Surprised, aye, as he had been by their conversation. But calmer than when he had first spoken to her in the kitchen.

He had been anything but calm, leaving her with that simple kiss before he lost all control and dragged her into the darkness and had his way with more than her sensuous mouth. She had said kisses were all she could give him, but he wanted more. Much more.

He waited until everyone had cleared the entryway. Those few who were left were busy taking down the trestle tables and pulling out pallets for those who slept here in the hall. A large, gray dog snuffled the rushes, weaving amongst the workers, looking for a meal, no doubt. The fire burned low and someone threw a log onto it, sending a shower of sparks up the chimney.

Slowly, Ailig rose from his seat at the high table and left, skirting the edge of the cavernous hall, careful not to make eye contact with anyone still there. He was in no mood to speak to anyone, except perhaps Mora.

As he passed the serving vestibule, he found the kitchen was dark, save for the faint glow of the banked fire. Mora must have returned to her cottage and found the comfort of her bed already. 'Twas good that she was well away from him. At least that's what he kept telling himself.

He peered out the door at the stair down to the bailey, which was thankfully deserted. Quickly, because 'twas cold and he did not have his cloak, he crossed the snow-covered courtyard and opened the door to the chief's tower. He had barely stepped into the tower when he sensed someone standing in the shadows. He drew his dagger as the wind caught the door and slammed it behind him.

"Who's there?" He kept his back to the wall and circled toward the stairs.

"You will not take Neill's place as chief, wee Ailig, nor Broc's." A familiar raspy voice spoke.

"Are you such a coward you cannot face me in the light, Baltair?"

The champion stepped into the weak light cast from the torch halfway up the stairs. A huge shadow cast by his bulk loomed upon the wall. "I am no coward, whelp. If Broc is truly dead, his death will be avenged, of that you can be sure. But whether he is or is not, *you* will never be chief of this clan."

"Are you threatening me?" Ailig kept his dagger at the ready.

"I am."

"'Twould seem you are no longer interested in being champion."

"I am champion. Broc and Neill have declared it so."

"And when I am chief I will make sure you are not, for

no champion can be such a coward as to threaten the life of one of his own clan, the son of his chief, no less."

"You are no son to Neill."

"He may not like it, but I am."

"Nay, you are not. 'Tis why he will not have you as chief."

Not Neill's son? His knees threatened to buckle but he could not let his guard down. "Do you wish to make me angry with your lies?" he said, glaring at Baltair.

The horse's arse had the nerve to grin at him. "You are not the chief's son. Broc figured it out long ago, but Neill forbade him to speak of it."

"Then how do you come by this dubious news?"

"A champion needs to know certain things. You will not be chief."

Not Neill's son? Distantly, he felt his fingernails bite into his fists as he remembered his eldest brother's constant derision, his father's unprovoked disdain, his mother's overbearing protection, until he got old enough to push her away. A muscle ticked in his jaw. He'd always been the different one, slighter than his brothers, fairer, and the only one with gray eyes. It seemed so obvious, he was surprised he had not realized it himself, and he wondered, if Broc had figured it out, how many others had, too. His heart thudded. His blood roared in his ears as humiliation and anger surged through him.

"You must leave Assynt," Baltair was saying, pulling him out of his tangled memories. "Leave now and Neill can explain why you cannot be chief to the king, if it comes to that, without having to reveal his shame before the entire clan. Go back to your uncle in Edinburgh or to your sister's new home. Neill does not want you here." Baltair stepped closer so that Ailig could see the dark centers of his eyes even in the dim light. "*I* do not want you here."

"What do you gain from this, Baltair? Why tell me this if you are so determined to protect the chief's honor?"

"'Tis simple, whelp. If I get rid of you, then I have saved Neill from the shame of seeing the results of his wife's unfaithfulness take his place. Neill will deal with the king and his ridiculous edict and he and I will both be heroes in the eyes of the clan."

A suspicion formed, hard and black in his gut. "And Morainn?"

"Morainn will be mine. Despite your interference and despite her maidenly protests, she will be mine."

Anger pushed away all the hurt, the questions, the humiliation, exploding the hard, black rock in his gut. "I am not leaving, Baltair, but I shall tell the chief that myself," he said, his voice hard and flat. "As for Morainn, the lass does not want you. Leave her alone." He turned his back to the growling man and took the steps three at a time.

'Twas past time Neill faced the truth. Apparently, 'twas past time for Ailig, too.

Moments later he banged on the chief's door but did not wait for an answer. He barged in, only to find the outer chamber deserted, a lone candle burning in the stand near the door to the inner chamber. He crossed the room in four strides and banged on that door, again not waiting for an answer before he swung it inward and stepped into the bedchamber.

Neill sat on the edge of his bed looking startled and disoriented. Suddenly he seemed to focus on Ailig.

"What do *you* want?"

"Is it true? Did my mother cuckold you?" Ailig hoped

to startle the man with his blunt words, but Neill just looked at him blankly for a moment then scrubbed at his face with his hands before leveling a glare at Ailig.

"And if 'twas?"

"'Twould change nothing and explain everything." Ailig watched the chief, but there was no remorse, no anger even, only resignation.

Neill rose and faced Ailig across the room. "So why would I bother to spread the news of my shame? Who did you hear this from?"

"Baltair. He claims Broc knew and told him when he was made champion. He wants me gone from here and thinks this will drive me from these walls."

"And will it?"

Ailig clenched his fists and glared back at the man he had thought was his father. "It will not."

"More's the pity." Neill pulled a blanket off the bed and wrapped it around his shoulders as Ailig stared at Neill, taking in the hurtful words one by one. But one question refused to remain silent.

"You would truly rather see this clan banished from this castle than see me become chief?" He hated the hurt he felt, the anger, the pain. He was a man grown and had long tried to set aside any need for this man's approval. At least his voice did not betray him.

"The MacLeods are warriors, Highlanders. We care naught for Lowland laws and the politics of the kings. I will not bend to Robert the Bruce. Not now, not ever."

Ailig couldn't believe the words coming from Neill's mouth. "There will be no clan left to be chief of," he said, wincing inwardly at the strident edge that cut through his voice.

Neill wouldn't look at Ailig. "Go back to Edinburgh," he said as he shuffled toward the door. "Serve the king if you must, but you will not be the chief of this clan so long as I have any say in the matter."

Ailig crossed to the door where Neill waited, a hand on the latch, his eyes still cast downward.

"You are a blind auld man if you cannot see the future that lies in front of you. I shall be chief here. I will not do it to spite you. I will not do it to please the king. I will do it so that my children will have a home, so that their children will have a future. I shall be chief because it is the one sure way to keep this clan safe as the tides of change sweep through Scotland. I will not have the blood of this clan on my hands as you seem so determined to do." He fisted his hands and struggled to keep his voice calm, even. 'Twas a losing struggle. "What kind of chief does that make you? What kind?"

Neill stared at Ailig, fear and hatred clear in his eyes. "I am the only chief this clan has."

"Not for long," Ailig said as he strode to the outer door and slammed it behind him.

chapter 8

Instead of heading down the corridor to his own chamber, Ailig took the steps upward, two at a time, until he reached the top. He slipped through the door and out onto the wall walk. His stomach was knotted. His mind was alternately filled with disjointed thoughts and completely empty, numb. His body was as unsettled as his mind, so he paced the wall.

The few guards on watch ignored him, which was fine with Ailig. He needed to clear his mind of the jumble his fath . . . Neill's words had created. Ailig couldn't quite make sense of what he'd learned, and yet, in an odd sort of way, it made perfect sense. He was not Neill MacLeod's son. He was someone else's son, someone his mother had sought out. But who? He had the strangest sense of being set loose, like a leaf blown before a stiff wind, separated from everything he had been connected to, his family, himself. Did he even belong here? How could he make a claim to become chief if he was not even blood kin to Neill? And yet, how could he not? 'Twas nothing more than habit and pride that said a chief's son should take his place. His own father . . . nay, Neill . . . had been chosen over the previous chief's son.

'Twas not how he wished to become chief, but the clan's future was at stake and he could not afford to let his own pride come between what he wanted and what he must do. 'Twas clear Neill would never willingly make Ailig chief, so Ailig would simply have to figure out how to force him to it.

He'd made it all the way around the perimeter of the castle once and started on his second circuit, still shaken by the change in his life that had occurred in the space of only a few moments. Passing the first guard post, he glanced up into the darkness and realized that the faintest glimmer of firelight shone in the distance. He stopped and oriented himself. 'Twas Morainn's cottage, no doubt, but why was her fire showing? She should be abed by now, her cottage shut up snugly against the winter's long, cold night. Was she ill? Had Baltair decided to push his attentions on her again?

Concern and sudden anger shoved aside all thoughts save getting to Morainn. He sped toward the nearest tower, down the stairs and raced for the gate, slowing down only long enough to grab a torch by the door to the guard's chamber and be grumbled at when he demanded the small portal be opened for him. Once outside, he raced towards Morainn's home, the wind of his passing nearly extinguishing the flame that lit his way along the rocky and icy path.

•　　•　　•

Morainn lugged the heavy buckets from the spring back towards her cottage. She was so tired she could cry, but it had been several days since she'd fetched water to the cottage and 'twould not wait for morning. Her fire had been nearly dead when she had arrived home after seeing that the meal was served and all was cleaned up. That, too, had nearly brought her to tears, but she had set to building the fire up again and, after what seemed an eon of patiently feeding the remaining embers from her banked fire, she had been satisfied with a blaze.

Maybe she had been wrong about insisting on staying in her own cottage instead of moving into the castle. If she took a chamber there, someone else would haul her water and tend her fire. She wouldn't have to go out in the bitter cold before the sun had even thought about rising to get to the kitchen, nor would she have to brave the biting cold, dark night when she was done for the day.

But that would mean giving up her quiet refuge. It would mean putting herself in Ailig's path even more than she already was. She was confused enough about the feelings he brought forth in her. She could live without the small comforts of castle life.

She rounded the corner of her cottage to find her door wide open, the cold wind whistling inside and whipping the fire into a dance. Just as the fairy fire danced on the path . . . Fairy fire?

She was truly exhausted for her mind to make up such a thing, but as she watched the bobbing fire drew nearer. She stepped inside her cottage, set down the buckets and reached for the door to draw it closed when she stopped.

Was that her name she heard? But the fairy folk didn't bother themselves with the names of humans.

"Mora?"

There it was again.

She rubbed her eyes, gritty from fatigue and squinted into the darkness as the fire drew nearer and at last she could see 'twas a torch held aloft by a man.

"Ailig? What are you doing here?" she demanded.
Relief nearly made him giddy even though she sounded tired, cross, but she was safe. He wanted to pull her into his arms, tell her all that had happened, but something in her eyes stilled him.

"I saw your fire," he said. "I thought something was wrong."

"You were watching for my fire?" She picked up the buckets by her feet and lugged them across the small room. He followed her in, closing the door behind him.

"Nay. I was on the ramparts. I just happened to look out and your fire . . . Why was your door open?"

She looked at the buckets she had once more set down, then back at him, one eyebrow raised. "The castle is not my only responsibility, Ailig."

Shame slammed into him. She was out getting water, tending to her own chores after spending a long day tending to the clan's.

"Of course. I did not think. But the door?"

"The wind must have blown it open. The hinge is loose so it does not latch well."

Ailig looked at the door. 'Twas an easy thing to fix. "I'll see it fixed on the morrow," he said, looking about the cottage to see if aught else needed fixing. 'Twas neat, cozy, even though 'twas cold. Dried herbs and smoked meats hung from the rafters. Baskets marched along the floor near one wall, wool of different colors spilling from several of them. A loom sat in a corner, looking lonely and forlorn, as if it had been abandoned. And it had been, he realized. She had given up her own pursuits, set aside her own work, to help him, and he had not so much as thanked her.

"You have enough to worry about. I'll see to the hinge when I have time," she said. The slosh of water flowing into a basin stopped his inventory of her home.

"Let me," he said, taking up the other bucket before she could lift it. She pointed at a ewer and he emptied the bucket into it. "Do you need more water?"

"Nay. Go back to the castle, Ailig. You need not worry about me. I have lived alone here long enough to tend to everything myself."

"Do you ever ask for help?" he asked, noticing now the dark circles under her eyes. "Do you ever let anyone help you?"

"Tamas, sometimes." She looked up at the rafters. "He makes sure I have meat. Other than that?" She looked about her cottage. "Nay. I do not need help."

Ailig felt like a heel. He had asked so much of Morainn, expected so much. He had been selfish, thinking only what was best for himself, what would help him accomplish what the king had commanded.

"I am sorry," he said. "I did not think about what you would have to give up to help me in the castle. I did not mean to make your life harder."

"You do not make mine harder," she said, hiding a yawn behind her hand.

"Ah, so you enjoy hauling water in the middle of the night?" His sarcasm earned him a glare.

"'Tis not the middle of the night," she said. "I would have to haul water to the cottage whether you were here or not, so you need not make me out to be a martyr for Saint Ailig."

He watched her for a moment, the desire to make her life easier, softer, better gripping him. "I did not mean to make you out that way. I am grateful for all that you have done at the castle. I forgot you would have tasks here, too, that could not be ignored."

He stepped towards her, taking her hand and leading her towards her bed. She stopped and he shook his head.

"I'll not deny that the idea of you in that bed appeals to me." He tugged on her hand but she did not budge. "But for now I wish only to see you safely in your bed . . . alone."

'Twas most definitely not what he wanted to see, but for now she needed caring, not desire. "Come. I will not look while you prepare for bed. I'll get your fire going better." He moved away from her, keeping his back to her. "'Tis too cold in here."

He heard rustling behind him and it took all his self-control not to turn and watch her undress, though his mind was not so circumspect. He could well imagine what she looked like shedding her gown, perhaps loosing her hair from its tight braid. His body begged him to turn around but he resolutely tended the now roaring fire.

"Are you going to tell me what sent you to the ramparts

on a cold, dark night?" she asked, her sleepy voice drifting over him like the softest of caresses.

"'Twas nothing," he answered. He'd not burden her with more of his problems.

"You just needed some air?"

The rustling had stopped, so he turned and found her lying on her side, her hair loose on her pillow, the blankets pulled up under her chin.

"Aye," he said, slowly moving to her side. "I needed some air." As he needed air now, cold, biting air that would quell the desire that raced through him. He knelt beside the bed and allowed himself to smooth her heavy hair away from her silky cheek. "Sleep now. Do not worry about the castle, or me. I will wait here awhile," he gestured toward the hearth, "to tend the fire."

"'Tisn't necessary," she said, starting to sit up.

Gently, he pushed her back down and tucked the blankets back over her shoulders. "I know 'tisn't, but I'm going to do so anyway. Let me take care of you, Morainn, at least for a little while."

She started to speak again and he quieted her with a kiss. "Wheesht," he whispered. "Go to sleep. I will not linger long."

Her eyes were big but she gave no further protest.

"Close your eyes, lass," he said, as he settled on the stool near the hearth. "I will see you on the morrow."

At last she did as he suggested. Within moments of her eyes closing he saw her body go soft. He could hear her deep, rhythmic breathing, so at odds with the pounding of his own heart. Fiery desire tormented him even as he forced himself to simply sit and watch over her. With effort, he slowed his own breathing until it matched hers breath for breath, until a sense of peace he'd never known drifted down on him. The clutter in his mind yielded to a quiet he had been searching for for weeks.

'Twas a long time later that Ailig finally slipped out of Morainn's cottage and made his way back to the castle by the pale light cast from a thin sliver of the moon. He had had lots of time to think while he watched Morainn sleep, yet the only thing he was sure of was that he wanted this woman more than he had ever wanted anyone or anything before. She intrigued him with her strength, her determination, her good humor and her vulnerability. She nearly drove him mad with wanting her body. She made him feel protective, strong, able. And he wanted to be all those things for her.

But the future was still too uncertain. He had nothing to offer her, nothing to make her life better, easier, sweeter. Not yet. Once he was chief, then he would have a life to offer her.

He was more determined than ever to see that he became chief of this clan. What he had once planned to do for the good of Scotland and his clan now also offered him a future he'd never dared imagine for himself, for Morainn. A future he desperately wanted.

M orainn woke the next morning more rested than she had been in a very long time. She rose to find a pot of water, already warmed, hanging over the banked fire. Oatcakes, cheese and a cup with a flagon of ale sat awaiting her on the table, a sprig of dried heather, laid across the cakes. Tears sprang to her eyes. She blinked rapidly, chiding herself for being foolish. 'Twas only that she could not remember the last time someone had taken care of her as Ailig had done last night. The memory of his hand on her cheek, the sweet kiss he had given her and the sight of him keeping watch over her made her feel soft, cared for and inexplicably aroused.

She wiped the errant moisture from her lashes and scooped warm water out of the kettle to wash in. She smiled at the thought of warm water. 'Twas a luxury she hadn't expected this morn.

He was so unexpected, so unlike the brothers she had always lumped him in with. He was kind, thoughtful. She'd almost asked him to stay with her last night, and not across the room, tending the fire. She'd almost asked him to climb into bed with her, to hold her until she fell asleep. She shook her head and laughed. She must have been truly exhausted, for if they ever ended up in a bed together she doubted very much they would simply sleep.

What was she thinking? Did she want to go to bed with the man? Aye, if she was honest with herself, she did. He was an intriguing combination of strength and tenderness, crushing her to him with heart-stopping kisses one moment and gently tucking the blankets around her and tenderly smoothing her hair another. She could as easily imagine his hands rough and demanding on her, driving her need quickly and explosively, as she could imagine them soft, coaxing, driving her mad slowly and sensually. He was a contradiction that she found hard to resist exploring.

But did she dare risk exploring that contradiction? The man had already barged into her life, whisking her along in his quest, turning her world inside out without so much as a thank-you . . . until last night.

She stared at the stool where he had been sitting when she finally gave up and went to sleep. He should not have come to her cottage. Should not have been so kind, so thoughtful. She did not want to admire him, did not want to desire him, did not want to let him into her life.

But it seemed 'twas too late. Somehow he had cracked open the wall she had built about her heart and she could not decide whether 'twas safe to let him inside. She'd let Hamish into her heart and he had not known what to do with it, bruising it without ever knowing he had.

But this was Ailig. Could she trust him with her heart? Could she keep it safe from him when she desired him so much? Did she dare take the chance that he would be more gentle with her feelings than Hamish had been?

She wanted to believe he would be, wanted to find out, in spite of the shimmer of fear that clutched at her stomach. She was tired of being a coward, hiding in her cottage away from life, away from feelings. Ailig was a different man and she was not the girl she had been when she married Hamish.

A weight she had not been aware of lifted from her as she quickly ate the meal Ailig had left for her. She dressed and carefully threaded the heather sprig into the brooch that held her arisaid in place, then gathered her cloak and set out for the castle, anxious to find Ailig.

Ailig paced the ramparts as he had the night before. He had no idea what to say to Neill. What could he say? So he kept watch for Morainn. He needed to know that she was all right this morning, that she had slept well. He wanted to make sure the hollows under her eyes were gone, that she had eaten the meager meal he had left out for her. 'Twas uncomfortable, this feeling of protectiveness that had come over him, and yet, 'twas a comfort, too. So much of his life had been spent following after his brothers or his sister, cleaning up the messes they left in their wake when no one else did. Catriona had let him watch over her some, less and less as she had taken on more and more responsibilities around the castle and he had spent more and more time in Edinburgh. But Morainn, she had let him take care of her last night. She had not wanted to, but she'd let him and in that acceptance, he had found a deep sense of peace he'd always missed.

"Ailig!" The bellow from the bailey caught his attention.

"Here," he called, leaning over the wall to see who called for him. Too late, he realized he should have kept quiet. 'Twas Baltair. The champion looked none too happy, but then, that was no surprise.

Ailig waited, keeping his watch for Morainn as Baltair climbed the tower steps and came to him. He had just spied her walking quickly down the path when Baltair burst out of the doorway onto the wall walk.

"Stay away from Morainn." His voice was a threatening growl. "She is to be *my* wife!" he said, slapping himself on the chest.

Anger burst to life within Ailig's gut. The gate guard must have told Baltair of his late-night foray. Just once he'd like to see the loyalty of this clan on his side.

"She has said quite plainly she will not be your wife," Ailig said. "If she wishes my company, she shall have it."

"Why would she wish for the company of a bastard?

Why would she wish for the company of a man who does not even belong here?"

Ailig looked about, but no one appeared to be close enough to hear. "Why would she wish for the company of a man who will have no place in this clan once I am chief, for I will be chief, Baltair."

"You will not." The man stepped forward, hand on his dagger hilt, but then he seemed to realize where he was and backed off, glowering at Ailig.

"I will. Neill may not be my father, but I am a member of this clan and 'twould not be the first time someone other than a chief's son took his place. I will be chief. You may want to remember that before you threaten me again."

"Baltair!"

That bellow Ailig recognized.

"Neill calls you," he said, tipping his head toward the bailey. "You should go while you still have a chief to serve."

"Baltair!"

"Stay away from her."

"Nay."

The champion spat at Ailig's feet, then left at a run. Ailig watched as the two men met up below. He caught the mutter of their voices on the wind, then saw them look up to where he stood. He stared back until they turned and made for the Hall. As soon as they had disappeared inside he followed them.

A steady stream of petty complaints took up most of the morning. At first Ailig stood at the back of the hall, watching. At one point Neill seemed to rock forward, almost as if he had fallen asleep. The man presenting his grievance paused, and after a moment the chief sat up straight and yelled at the man, "Continue! We haven't all day." The petitioner looked around, shrugged and continued.

Ailig made his way to the front to watch more closely. Once more his father seemed to . . . disappear? His attention did, anyway. Physically he was there, but there was a moment where everything in his face went lax and his eyes seemed to stare at something in the middle distance. He did not blink; he did not even seem to breath. And then he was yelling again, as if nothing had happened.

Ailig spied Tamas on the far side of the hall. His attention was fixed on the chief. His eyebrows were drawn down, and he stroked his chin as if he had a beard, though his face was smooth-shaven. Ailig made his way over to Tamas when his father abruptly paused the proceedings and demanded wine.

"How often does that happen?" he asked without preamble.

"You noticed, too?"

"Is there anyone who did not?"

Tamas shook his head. "'Tisn't likely to go unnoticed."

"How often?"

Tamas looked about and drew Ailig into an alcove near the hearth. "I noticed it a fortnight ago for the first time, but when I asked him if he was well, he acted as if he did not know of what I spoke. A sennight later it happened again, and since then I've seen it perhaps every second day. This is the first time it has happened twice in one day, at least as far as I know."

Ailig ran a hand through his hair; it was a worry he did not want.

"So whatever 'tis, 'tis coming more frequently."

"Aye. 'Twould seem there is a more pressing need to

have you made chief than just the mere whim of a king."
Tamas smiled at him.

"'Tis no whim—"

"'Twas a joke, Ailig. Well, the whim part was. 'Tis no
joke that there is something ailing your da, and I do not
think it bodes well for the clan."

"I fear you are right." Ailig sighed. "I suppose I shall
have to speak with him again."

"He does not want you for chief, does he?"

"He has little choice in the matter," Ailig said quietly.
Not wishing to discuss this here where everything could be
overheard, he sought to change the subject. "Have you
seen Morainn this morning?"

The mere thought of Morainn raised Ailig's pulse. He'd
been scanning the crowd all morning, hoping for a glimpse
of her.

"Aye, she had a smile on her face this morn," he said,
suddenly turning to look at Ailig. "And a sprig of heather
in her brooch."

Ailig couldn't help but smile back. "I think I shall see if
there is aught she needs for the kitchen," he said. Some-
time during the course of the morning, the protective feelings he'd been harboring since late last night had finally
given way to the desire to see her again, touch her again.
Perhaps she would need some help in the larder. He smiled
to himself as he hurried from the hall.

chapter 9

*M*orainn wiped the sweat from her forehead with the back of her wrist. What had started out as such a bright, hopeful day had rapidly deteriorated into a morass of trouble. She had only just started planning the meals this morning when one of the cooks had come to her screaming that there was no one to prepare the vegetables or clean and pluck the doves. A precious hour had been lost trying to locate the missing helpers. Each had begged off his or her duty, claiming exactly the same stomach cramps and odd malaise. She had gathered up what helpers she could and set to getting the kitchen running.

Now she was up to her elbows in hot water, scrubbing all the things the kitchen staff had managed to dirty this morning. Alasdair stood nearby, drying as fast as he could in an attempt to keep up with her furious pace. The slosh of water, and the relative quiet as the kitchen seemed to pause before the flurry began to get the next meal served, lulled Morainn into a momentary peace. She let her mind drift away from the myriad needs of the clan to the man who had taken care of her last night.

The flicker of firelight had softened the hard planes of his face, making him look younger, almost vulnerable, as he sat watch over her. He was nothing like what she had imagined, nothing like his brothers. Where they were loud, he was quiet. Where they demanded, he asked. Where they barreled through life scattering all in their way, he was thoughtful, considerate, kind. Softness uncurled within her. He was nothing like his brothers.

"Mistress?" Alasdair nudged her elbow, jarring her from her thoughts. "'Tis a visitor for you," the boy said, glancing at the doorway.

As if summoned from her daydreams, Ailig stood there, filling the doorway. His hair gleamed a rich gold in the mix of weak sunlight and dancing firelight. He dazzled her with his brilliant smile as he strode through the tangle of people towards her.

Nervous tingles danced over her skin as she quickly dried her hands and sent Alasdair for more hot water. The lad looked from Ailig to Morainn and grinned, then disappeared.

Ailig stood in front of her, not saying a word, though his eyes asked questions. Morainn smiled, unsure what to say.

"Did you sleep well?" he finally asked. The concern in his voice sent a fresh wave of tingles through her.

"Aye. Thank you." She kept her voice quiet as she glanced around to see who might be listening.

Everyone.

Everyone in the kitchen had suddenly become very absorbed in whatever task they were working on, quietly, alertly absorbed. She rolled her eyes. This would never do.

"Is there aught I can do for you?" she asked, trying to alert him to their audience with her eyes, but he was not looking at her eyes.

He reached out and touched the heather she wore in her brooch. Heat rushed through her, radiating from that whisper-light touch. Before she could stop herself she leaned, ever so slightly, into him, her body begging for more.

A pleased smile played on his inviting lips. "Aye," he said.

Someone snickered and she felt her face flame, but she could not bring herself to move away from him. She had so much she wanted to say to Ailig, but she had no wish to say it in front of an audience, but neither did she trust herself alone with him. Not yet. Not when even his slightest touch woke feelings in her she'd never known. Not when his smile clouded her mind with thoughts of his lips and the havoc they played on her senses.

"I did not want to leave you last night," he said, his voice an intimate whisper.

"I—"

A crash made Morainn jump, reminding her of where she was. Violent cursing came from one of the chambermaids impressed into kitchen service this morn, as the contents of a large kettle oozed onto the floor.

Morainn sighed and Ailig ran a shaky hand through his hair.

"Are you sure Catriona is not coming back?" Morainn asked him, only half joking.

"We should continue this later . . . in private," he said.

She wanted to say no, not in private, but her body had gone taut with wanting at his words. She could only nod.

He touched the heather again. "I shall find you later, then."

She watched speculative glances follow him as he wove his way back across the kitchen and out the door.

A ilig left the kitchen in a storm of need. The lass was happy to see him. He could see the quickened pulse at the base of her slender throat when he touched her, could see desire in her eyes. 'Twas lucky the kettle had spilled, lest he might have forgotten all about the crowd in there and taken her in his arms or dragged her off to the darkness of the larder.

His elbow was snagged by someone, pulling him out of his thoughts of Morainn with a jolt. Tamas nudged him away from the steady stream of clanfolk leaving the Great Hall.

"What has happened?" Ailig asked.

Tamas shrugged. "'Twas odd. In the midst of Tall Davy explaining himself, the chief said he was done. He'd hear no more complaints this day. Baltair helped him from his chair and hastened him from the Hall. The chief did not look right, Ailig."

"Right?"

"Aye, I cannot say why exactly, but something was not right."

"I think I shall pay the chief a visit," Ailig said. Tamas agreed as Ailig followed the last of the gathering outside.

When he knocked on the chief's chamber door, it

opened almost immediately and Ailig found himself standing nose to nose with Baltair.

"What do you want?" the champion demanded, deliberately blocking the door so Ailig could not see inside.

Anger roared through him that this man would try to keep him from the chief, but he bit back his sister's favorite epithet. Instead, he glared at the man who narrowed his eyes, but finally stepped back from the doorway, allowing Ailig inside.

The chamber was empty, the sleeping room door closed. Ailig rounded on Baltair, determined to get an answer, sure that the man must know what was happening to the chief.

"What is wrong with him?"

"What do you mean?"

"The lapses, the blankness, you escorting him abruptly from the Hall. 'Tis clear he is not well, yet no one thought to mention it to me."

"If you had been more observant you might have seen it for yourself," Baltair snapped, spreading his feet and crossing his arms in an obstinate stance, but there was an odd note in his voice. If Ailig had not known the man so well, he would have thought 'twas worry or, at the very least, concern, but he did not think Baltair capable of such feelings, at least not for others.

"So there is something wrong."

"The healer says 'tis nothing but fatigue and age. She bade him drink a cup of herbed wine before bed and again on rising. She thinks leeching him might be of help, but she does not have any leeches and he forbade her to bleed him otherwise."

"Yet Tamas says his . . . episodes . . . are happening more and more often."

"Tamas should keep his gob shut." Baltair's chin rose a notch. "Neill is fine. 'Tis but a moment now and then."

"'Tis a load of horse manure," Neill said from the door behind Ailig. He shoved his son out of his way and made for the table where a pewter goblet and a pottery flagon sat. "I am not ill. 'Tis a tale born of long winter nights and that is all. If 'tis all you are here to discuss, you should leave."

Baltair crossed to the table and poured wine into the goblet, then handed it to the chief.

Neill shook his head. "I do not want that bitter potion."

Ailig could see Baltair start to argue, but when Neill closed his eyes and put his head in his hand, Baltair set the goblet on the table.

"You are ill," Ailig said. "I saw it for myself this morning, and now you leave the petitioners before all have been heard? What has happened? And do not tell me all is well with you and expect me to believe you."

Neill's forehead wrinkled with deep furrows. "Nothing happened. I am fine. I only wish all of you would quit worrying over my health," he said with a pointed glare at Ailig. "Now both of you, leave me. I do not wish to be hovered over like some helpless bairn!"

"Da." All three of them went still at the name Ailig had called this man for all of his years. Ailig huffed out his breath. What to call this man was another problem for another day; there was a much more pressing issue to be dealt with now. "You *are* ill," he continued. Ailig wanted to shout at the man. Of all the things Neill could do to thwart him, denying this illness was the most perverse. But long experience had taught him to be calm, even in the face of pure stubbornness. "You must name your successor now, just in case—"

"I. Will. Not!" Neill surged to his feet, knocking his chair over backwards. "I'll not give over my position to you." He pounded his fist upon the table making the wine slosh in the goblet and the flagon rattle. "'Tis for *my* son to become chief!"

A stricken look rushed over Neill's face and he collapsed behind the table.

Ailig raced to his side, relieved to find him still breathing, but ashen, his eyes open, but unseeing. "Da? Da! Baltair, help me get him to his bed."

The champion seemed frozen to the floor. His eyes held the same shocked surprise Ailig was feeling, but at least he was acting. "Baltair!" He banged a fist on the table to jar the man out of his immobility. "Help me now!"

In moments, they had the chief in his bed. "Summon the healer," Ailig said as he stirred up the fire and added several peats to it.

"The healer?"

"Aye, Giorsal. Go! He is not dead. Fetch the healer!"

"Dead . . . nay, not dead." The man moved as if through deep water until he reached the door, then 'twas as if tethers were released and he flew out of the chamber.

Ailig checked Neill again to make sure he still breathed. He touched the auld man's cold hand, then covered him with a heavy blanket. What had happened? He could not believe the man who had been bellowing at him only moments before now lay here still and cold, as if death had snuck up behind him and tried to snatch him away.

Everything that had passed between them in the last day

scious. Perhaps 'tis apoplexy. Giorsal does not know when . . . or if . . . he will awaken."

"I am so sorry. Is there anything I can do to help?"

"I am afraid there is little that will help this situation." His gaze drifted to the door where Baltair had disappeared. "I should speak to the council with him."

"I think you must leave that to him. There is someone here to see you," she said. "A messenger from the king arrived just after Baltair returned here. He is asking for the chief. I had the cook serve him a meal, but I doubt he will wait much longer to see Neill."

His shoulders hitched up a notch again and tension etched lines about his mouth. He scrubbed at his face with his hands. "Perhaps Tamas should speak with him."

"Ailig! You will be chief. 'Tis you he wishes to see."

"Do not fash yourself, Mora." He sighed. "'Twas just a thought. Where is he now?"

"In the Great Hall. Skaeth is keeping him company," she said.

"'Twas a canny thing to do." He took her hand and ran his thumb over her palm.

The intimate gesture warmed her. There was still much to say to this man, but now was not the time.

"No one will dare try to pry news from him while Skaeth is there," Ailig said.

"I wish 'twas my cunning that devised it." She slowly pulled her hand free of his. "But 'twas Skaeth's. He seemed to know 'twas a king's man before anyone else did. 'Twas he who bid me find you and tell you the news quietly."

Their eyes met and for a moment time stopped. She could see the need in him, the worry, and knew they were mirrored in her own eyes. She stepped into him, wrapping her arms around his waist as he pulled her close. She could feel the weight of his cheek as he rested it against her hair. She could feel him take a long, deep breath, just as she could feel the tension coiled within him.

"We should go," she said after a few minutes. "I am needed in the kitchen and he is waiting for you."

Ailig released her but made no move to leave.

"Giorsal will tell us if there is aught she needs. I'll send Alasdair up here to be her messenger. He is a loyal lad and he will like an excuse to get out of the kitchen today. I will tell him to find you the moment there is any change in the chief."

Ailig gave her a brief smile that didn't make it to his eyes and nodded. "'Twould ease my mind, a little anyway."

"Then it shall be done," she said, taking his hand and pulling him towards the door. "I would do more, if I could."

chapter 10

❧

Ailig entered the hall slowly, still reeling from Neill's untimely collapse, yet he had no time to dwell on that turn of events, not with the sudden arrival of the king's man. He could see the messenger and Skaeth sitting at a table near the dais, their heads bent close in conversation, the remains of a meal shoved to one side. There was a swath of unoccupied space about them, but there were many more people in the room than was normal for this time of the day, and all of them seemed to have found some task to busy themselves with that kept them close at hand.

As Ailig strode through the hall, he sent people scattering out of his way.

"On behalf of the chief of Clan Leod of Assynt, I welcome you," he said, his voice pitched carefully so none would guess the strain he experienced. He had no official right to speak for the chief and yet someone must. "I hope you have enjoyed your meal." He nodded to Skaeth, who raised his chin slightly in greeting.

Ailig slid into the seat next to Skaeth, across from their guest. "You have a message for the chief?"

"Aye. Are you Ailig?"

"I am."

The man nodded. "I am directed to speak to you and if you are not yet chief, your father as well."

"Neill, chief of this clan, has taken ill just this morning. Perhaps you should speak with the council."

Skaeth looked at him askance. "He'll speak with you, Ailig," he said, turning an enigmatic look at the newcomer as he rose from the table. "I have training to see to." He gave a little bow to their guest, then left.

Ailig noted the sign of respect, something he had not seen before in Skaeth, and he bent his attention more fully to the man across from him.

"You are a friend of Skaeth's?"

"Nay, but we found we had much in common," the man said, rising.

Ailig puzzled over this. "You have much in common? I have not found Skaeth willing to reveal anything about himself, beyond his skills as a mercenary."

The messenger shrugged. "Perhaps he was of a mind for a good blether this day."

"Perhaps." He did not have time to worry over Skaeth revealing himself to this stranger. There was nothing damaging he would disclose, for Skaeth was not yet privy to the latest news.

"Is the chief well enough to receive His Majesty's missive?"

"I fear not. If you wish, you may convey the message to me and I shall see it delivered when he is well enough."

"The king bade me give it directly to the chief. He said you should be present, if you were not yet chief, but I was to give it to the chief."

Ailig took a deep breath. There would be no hiding Neill's collapse from the king. 'Twas just as well. 'Twould help nothing to hide the circumstances from the king.

"Very well," he said to the messenger, as he rose from the table. "Follow me."

As they entered the chief's antechamber Ailig stopped.

"I do not know how the chief fares at the moment. He collapsed a short while ago."

Ailig quietly knocked on the inner door. Freya, the apprentice healer, opened it, took one look at Ailig's face then stepped back, swinging the door wide enough for the men to pass into the darkened bedchamber.

Giorsal stood near the bed, chanting quietly. A sickly sweet smoke hung in the air like a gauzy curtain. A small pot was suspended above the fire, bubbling away. The healer looked over her shoulder and motioned them closer, though she did not stop her sing-song chant.

"This is Neill, chief of Clan Leod of Assynt."

The messenger looked at Neill, then up at Giorsal. "Can he hear us?"

Giorsal ceased her chanting, thrust out her lower lip and shook her head. "I do not know. He has not moved since I came into the chamber, except to sigh every now and again, as if he is having trouble filling his lungs." She shook her head again. "I am doing all that I can for him."

Ailig looked to the messenger. "We have not told the

clan yet. I would ask that you say nothing to anyone save the king."

"I understand. Can we be alone with him for a few moments?"

Ailig glanced at Giorsal and she consented. "Freya will be in the outer chamber should he need us. I shall go to the still room for more supplies. Do not try to wake him."

They waited until the door closed behind the women.

"What is your message, then?" Ailig asked, crossing his arms and readying himself for he knew not what.

The man wandered over to the fire and held out his hands for a moment, then faced Ailig, his hands clasped behind him.

"Duff MacDonell, chief of Clan Donell, known as Dogface, escaped the king's guard over a fortnight ago."

Disbelief slammed into him and he reached out for the bedpost to steady himself. "How? Have they recaptured him?"

"Nay. It is believed that he was bound either for here or for his home at Dun Donell."

"But that makes no sense. Dun Donell is the obvious place for the king's men to look for him and why would he come here? There is no welcome for him here and he well knows it."

"The king does not think he is looking for a welcome place to hide away. The king sends warning that the man is out for vengeance. He blames you and yours for his downfall and he was heard to swear he would get vengeance against you all."

"Where is my sister, Catriona?"

"She is well guarded by her husband's family and a company of the king's own guard. 'Tis you the king is concerned for." He walked to the bedside and stared down at the stricken chief. "'Twould seem his concerns are not unfounded, even before the MacDonell escaped."

The man had no idea.

Ailig paced the chamber. If Duff showed up at Assynt, he might very well find allies even from within the MacLeods, especially once it was known that Ailig was not a true son of the chief. Never mind the MacDonells who still resided here. They were a weakness in any defense they might mount against Duff. And any aid given Duff would bode ill for Ailig and his clan, for any aid to an enemy of the king would be seen as treason. The king would not wait to see if Ailig could bring the clan around to his cause, for there would be no reason to do so if they were found to be traitors.

Determination filled Ailig. He could not allow such a fate for the clan. He desperately wanted to explore that future he had glimpsed with Morainn. So Duff must be stopped. Or captured.

"We have MacDonells biding here. They were awaiting the return of Duff and my sister. They refused to leave until they had verified that Duff was indeed culpable and a captive." Ailig shook his head and ran his fingers through his tangled hair. "Perhaps you could convince them?"

"Who gave them leave to remain?" the messenger asked.

"My father."

"And now, who is in charge?"

Ailig scowled. "This happened not an hour past. The council of elders is being told now. The king bade me become chief, but Neill . . . I am not his choice." He looked toward the door, worried that Baltair would burst in at any moment and reveal the weakness in his claim to the position.

"Did you not tell him of the king's command?"

"I did, but this is the Highlands. Highlanders do not do what they are told unless it suits their purposes. Making me chief does not suit the chief's purposes."

"And yet you are here, speaking with me."

Ailig narrowed his eyes at the man, but he kept a tight rein on his rising irritation. "I will not allow this clan to be run out of our homes and off our lands just because Neill MacLeod is too rooted in the past to see what the future is bringing. The king will have our fealty. He has commanded it and there is naught to gain and much to lose if we go against that command."

"And yet you say Highlanders do not do what they are told unless it suits their purposes, so what purpose does it suit for you, Ailig MacLeod?"

There was something about the man's tone that put Ailig on guard. It had an icy, sharp edge to it, in spite of the casual way the man stood with his back to the fire, his hands held behind him as if to warm them. And yet, Ailig could swear the man was coiled, ready to strike should he say the wrong thing. 'Twas eerily similar to his impression of Skaeth, calm and relaxed to the casual observer, yet with a core of steel, poised to strike at any moment. Perhaps the messenger did have much in common with the mercenary.

"My purpose is to protect my clan, to see them safe from Duff and Broc's ill-conceived plot." And to keep Morainn safe, he added silently. If he had also once hoped that Neill would at last see him as worthy of such a position, well, 'twas time to give up that. He had no more time for such childish needs. Right now he must buy some time to sort out the tangled mess. He must keep the king's confidence that all would go as he commanded. The future depended on it.

"And you will protect your clan by becoming chief even if no one but the king wishes you to?"

"I will. Were you sent here to test my resolve?"

"Aye, amongst other things. The king knew you would not have an easy time of this."

"Will you be staying then, to make sure my resolve stays firm?"

"Nay. I am here to deliver the warning and to return to the king with a report. 'Twould do you no good to have a king's man at your elbow."

"You speak the truth. It would never sit well with this clan, nor any other Highlanders."

"'Tis true. Will you tell the MacDonells that Duff has escaped?"

Ailig considered the idea for a moment. If he told them, would it change their belief that Duff was an innocent in this mess? Probably not. If the messenger verified his story, would it change anyone's mind? He doubted it. Would it embolden the MacDonells to know their chief was likely on his way to Assynt Castle? Probably.

"I think we shall keep it from them for a while," he said at last. "At least until I can assure myself they will not be able to assist him should he turn up here."

"Very well, then I shall not linger to speak to them. 'Twill be better if I am gone quickly."

"And what will you tell the king?"

The messenger took a long look at Neill, lying upon his bed, his breathing shallow. Ailig thought the man looked as if death lingered nearby, awaiting just the right moment to sweep in and finish him.

"I will tell him that your resolve is firm but that there is much fighting against you becoming chief. I do not think he will be surprised by either piece of information."

"Will you stay the night?"

"Nay. Though I will not speak to those MacDonells here, I must travel to Dun Donell as fast as possible. They must know that if any give succor or shelter to Duff, they will all be counted as traitors to the crown. Their lands and their lives will be forfeit—as will yours."

Ailig looked to the chief.

"You can tell the king I will do all I can to secure Assynt against Duff. The only shelter he will find here is in the oubliette."

"Good luck, Ailig. The king wishes you to succeed in this task."

"You may assure him that I am doing everything within my power to do so." 'Twas a pity his power was nonexistent.

With that, the messenger left the chamber, leaving Ailig to stare at Neill's pale face for another moment, waiting for some sign that he had heard what had passed here. But there was nothing from the chief but the quiet whistling of his labored breath.

Morainn had been searching for a moment all afternoon when she could slip away and locate Ailig, find out what had happened, for there was no doubt that something had occurred. The messenger had appeared in the kitchen requesting supplies. He had left without revealing anything more than an appealing smile and a polite manner in spite of her subtle, and not so subtle, questions. Worry had her looking for Ailig, but every time she found a moment to search for him she would find him deep in conversation with Tamas or Skaeth or the guard or the elders or . . . the man seemed to do nothing but talk today, and to everyone but her. Twice she had caught his eye but he had given no indication as to his mood nor to what was going on.

She wiped her hands on her barmcloth and took a swift look around the kitchen. Everything was well in hand. The evening meal was done. She would find him now and wait until he had a moment, then he would tell her what the messenger had been about even if she had to pry the information out of him!

She whipped off the apron, flung it towards the pile of dirty linens and strode out of the kitchen. Torchlight flickered as she made for the archway that led into the Great Hall. Automatically she looked back at the torches to make sure they were not guttering and, while her attention was elsewhere, she crashed into someone.

Large hands gripped her shoulders. "Mora?"

She looked up into Ailig's silvery-gray eyes. Stormcloud eyes, she thought. "I was just coming to find you."

"And I was coming to find you. You cannot leave the castle."

"What?" The feel of his hands upon her drained away all the irritation she had been harboring and she found herself watching his lips, the memory of his kisses momentarily stealing her will.

"Where is your cloak?"

The question seemed odd, particularly on the heels of

his first comment. She pointed over her shoulder back towards the kitchen.

"Stay here," he said as he disappeared into the kitchen and swiftly reappeared with her fur-lined cloak.

He settled it over her shoulders then took the ties and fastened it for her, the backs of his fingers tickling the sensitive skin under her chin, sending shivers over her. A yearning for those hands to do more than brush her chin arrowed through her. Desire. She could not deny it. She had worried about Ailig most of the day, but even more, she had wanted him since she awoke this morning. She wanted him as she had not wanted any man in a very long time.

He finished tying her laces then ran a finger down her cheek.

"Come with me," he said, reaching for her hand.

She linked her fingers through his, relishing the way his hand enveloped hers. "Where?"

"The wall walk."

She nodded and followed him. She was starting to think the wall walk was where he escaped to when he was disturbed or angry.

She followed him up the stairs to the doorway that let out onto the top of the castle walls. Neither said a word. When they stepped outside, Ailig took a moment to look around. 'Twas dark now, and the night sky was thick with stars as he pulled her around the caphouse into the lee of the wind. He turned to her and took both her hands in his. Morainn's breath hitched at the intensity in his eyes, at the strength in his grip.

"What disturbs you so?"

"Too much . . ."

She could see him weighing what to tell her. He had

brought her here to tell her something important, yet he hesitated.

"What did the messenger tell you that has had you closeted with the council today. What is it that has you so worried? Why do you want me to stay in the castle?"

"You do not really want me to answer that last question, do you?" He smiled at her then, a sad smile with just enough of a leer in it to reassure her that his humor was intact, though clearly weighed down by whatever had happened. He squeezed her hands. "Duff MacDonell has escaped the king's guard," he said. "It is believed he is headed here to find his revenge against us for the troubles he brought upon himself."

He raised her hands to his chest and let them rest lightly there, still clasped in his. "If I ask you to stay here, in the castle, just for now, will you?"

Her stomach lurched at his quiet question, her old fears momentarily gripping her, before she pushed them away. She would not be a coward anymore. She'd not hide any longer.

"Mora? If you insist on returning to your cottage I shall be forced to spend each night with you . . . on your cold, hard floor."

Her heart stopped at the thought of him, not on her floor but in her bed.

"There are things I will need from my home," she managed to stammer out.

Relief eased the furrows in his brow. "And on the morrow, I will escort you there, but for tonight, please, stay here." He touched her face and she leaned her cheek into his palm. "I could not bear it if something happened to you," he whispered, almost too quiet to hear, but she did.

"I would not add to your worries, if I could help it."

She gave in to the need to comfort him, to comfort herself. She stretched up and met his lips with hers in a tender kiss. Closing her eyes, she reveled in the feel of his lips against hers, the strength of his arms around her, the warmth that filled her every time he touched her. 'Twas exactly where she had wanted to be all day.

"I keep asking you to give up things," he said at last. "Someday I will repay you, Mora. Somehow."

"Do not fash." She looked up into his eyes. "I do not do anything I'm not willing to."

"Why were we not friends before now?" he asked.

"'Tis my fault, I fear," she said. "I thought you were like your brothers and I wanted nothing to do with any of you."

"But Hamish, he was Broc's friend. He was much like my brothers."

"Aye. But he worked hard to prove that he was not like them, until . . ."

"Until?"

"Until after we were wed. He hid his true self from me until 'twas too late."

"And me? Do you think I hide my true self from you?"

"Nay, I think you hide your true self from many, but not from me."

He sighed. "There is one thing you do not know about me that you should, though I would prefer it went no farther, at least for now."

Fear crowded her, but she pushed it away once more.

"I have not hidden it from you," he said. "I only learned it myself yesterday. Neill is not my true father."

She heard the words, saw the confusion and concern swirl through his eyes.

"Morainn?"

"It explains much," she said. "'Tis why you are not like him, like them." She reached up and touched his stubbled cheek, suddenly realizing that this was what had driven him to these heights last night, which had led him to her cottage. "Why did you not tell me last night?"

"I did not want to burden you with more of my problems," he said. "But I did not want any secrets from you either."

She smiled, moved even more by his care last night, knowing that he had more on his mind than an exhausted lass. He was truly nothing like his wild, selfish brothers. He was a man with honor. A man who could easily steal her heart.

He ran his fingers over her smile, and Morainn couldn't breath, couldn't move beneath the intense longing she saw in his eyes, a longing that she knew was matched in her own.

Ailig leaned down just as Morainn stretched up on her toes. Their lips met and the world melted away in the heat that coursed between them.

Morainn reveled in the feel of Ailig's hard chest pressed against her soft curves. She wanted to lose herself in that kiss, in the passion that flowed from him, fueling her own overwhelming desire.

She threaded her fingers into his hair, drawing him closer still. His hands skimmed under her cloak and over her back, leaving trails of heat wherever he touched her. He hesitated, his hands upon her ribs, tantalizingly close. She shifted slightly, moaning softly when he hesitated no longer and cupped her breast. She pressed into him, and he smiled against her mouth.

"Mora, love, I fear I do not want to stop this."

She kissed him, letting all the desire she felt for him flow into it. "Nor do I," she said.

"I can offer you nothing, not yet," he said, "not until all is settled with the clan."

"I am not asking for anything but this," she said, kissing him again. "Well, maybe I'm asking for more than that." She felt giddy, powerful. "I am no maid, Ailig."

"I know that, lass."

"And there is no fear of bairns." She swallowed, looking down. If he could share all his secrets with her, she could do no less with him. "Hamish . . . we tried, but never was there a bairn. I am barren."

He tipped her face up so she looked into those pale gray eyes. "I am sorry to hear that, Mora. You would be a good mother." He looked as if he wanted to say more, but instead he kissed her again, lingering over it, seducing her with it.

chapter 11

Ailig lost himself in that kiss. Everything else in his life was in danger of falling apart, but this, this one moment, was perfection. He murmured her name as he spread little kisses over her freckled cheeks. He nuzzled her neck, unable to get enough of her scent: peat smoke, heather and Morainn. A thrill of victory rushed through him when she arched her neck for him and a tiny sound of feminine satisfaction escaped her.

"Come to my chamber, Mora," he whispered. "Come to my bed."

She nodded.

He kissed her hard, then grabbed her hand and raced around the wall past surprised guards, toward the chief's tower and the stair that would lead to his chamber. As they hurried down the stair, rapid footsteps echoed up to meet them. He put a finger to his lips as they reached the landing but 'twas no good. Alasdair, taking the steps at least three at a time, ran into Ailig and would have tumbled backwards down the stair he'd just climbed if Ailig and Morainn hadn't both reached out to steady the boy.

"What's happened?" Morainn asked.

Alasdair's chest heaved as he caught his breath. "The chief. He is awake. Giorsal said to get him." He cocked a thumb at Ailig but never took his eyes off Morainn.

Anger, knotted with frustration, pierced his gut, followed swiftly by regret and resignation as he looked at Morainn's flushed face. Never had duty interfered with desire as it did at this moment.

She squeezed his hand and swallowed. "You must go," she said. "Your father." She paused. "Neill is awake," she said, her voice strained. "You must go immediately. This may be your last opportunity to gain his blessing."

"I do not want to leave you."

She looked from him to the boy, still standing before them. "Alasdair, go back and tell Giorsal that Ailig will be there soon."

"Aye, Morainn."

"Just go a bit more carefully this time," she called after him as he barreled down the stairs, leaving them alone once more.

"I'm sorry," Ailig said. "I do not know how long I will be." He laid his hand against her cheek and stroked a thumb over her milky skin. Wanting sizzled through him just from touching her face. "Take Catriona's chamber. I will come to you when I am finished," he said, drawing her to him for one last kiss, allowing himself one more moment to concentrate wholly on Morainn.

"You must go, Ailig." The regret he felt at leaving

showed brightly in her eyes, too, limned by desire so vivid
he swore he could feel the heat of it.

The last thing he wanted was to leave her there, alone
on the cold landing, but he would not leave her alone long.
Without another word he turned and left.

A ilig had calmed his body, if not his mind, by the time
he entered the chief's darkened chamber. Neill sat up
in his bed, pillows heaped behind him, blankets piled over
him. Freya sat on the edge, her back to the door, feeding
him spoonfuls of broth. Ailig thought her a particularly
brave lass, considering the thundering anger that was so
evident on the chief's face . . . on the left side of his face.
Freya dabbed at the drooping right corner of his mouth
where broth had dribbled into his beard.

"How is he?" Ailig asked.

"I am fine," Neill answered, though his speech was
slurred and strangely run together. "Leave."

Ailig reminded himself that this was not his sire. He
was chief, to be sure, but he was no longer fit for that position. 'Twas only a matter of deciding who would take his
place. He was surprised to see the elders of the council fil-
ing into the room, followed by Baltair. The champion
glanced at Ailig, a calculating look, then turned his attention to the chief, positioning himself near the head of the
bed, facing everyone else. 'Twas a very effective reminder
of where the man's loyalties lay.

Neill growled at Freya and waved her away.

"What is this?" he asked, though 'twas more of a demand.

Nigel Hunchback, eldest of the council, shuffled to the

bedside. "You are much recovered?" His voice rumbled in the dim room, like thunder over the mountains.

"I am fine. Giorsal makes much of nothing." The words were forceful, but the effect was less than it once was when half his mouth did not move.

"You collapsed, Neill," Shamus Crooked-Nose, another elder, said. His nose rivaled Baltair's for the bumps and turns in it.

"'Twas nothing."

"You collapsed and have not woken for most of a day," Ailig said, pleased that his voice was firm. "You cannot make light of it, nor can you deny that you are ill."

"I can deny whatever I wish, boy," Neill said, his eyes full of hate. "You have no right to be here. Leave."

"He has every right to be here," Angus Mhór said, stepping up to Ailig's side and resting his weathered hand on his shoulder. "And well you know it."

"He is no son of mine. He will not be chief." When no one reacted, Neill narrowed his eyes at Ailig. "You have no shame? You told them?"

"Baltair told the council," Angus Mhór said. "The shame is not Ailig's. Do not take out your hatred for your wife on him."

"'Tis not my wife I hated," Neill said. A deep wracking cough overtook him, yet no one moved.

"'Tis time, Neill," Nigel Hunchback said. "Too much is at stake for you to chance another spell, for the clan to be without a strong leader."

"I do not dispute that," Neill said. "But I will not see him"—he pointed a trembling finger at Ailig—"as chief. He has no respect for tradition, for custom. Tell the king to send home my other sons. Calum will make an adequate chief."

"We do not need an *adequate* chief," Shamus Crooked-Nose said, his nasal voice loud in the crowded room. "We need a strong leader. Someone who has the ear of the king would be a boon. Someone your daughter's new clan trusts to keep an alliance would be a boon. 'Tis not Ailig's fault the king laid this at his feet. Ailig is the logical choice." He sent a quelling look in Baltair's direction. "Ailig has already begun seeing to the well-being of this castle and its people, even before your spell, even in the face of your stubborn opposition, and the opposition of others. Set aside your hatred for the lad's real father and name him your successor."

"If you do not," Nigel Hunchback said, "the council is prepared to do so. I do not think the clan would go against our choice."

Ailig was stunned by Shamus's speech and Nigel's ultimatum. Baltair appeared to be stunned, too. Ailig looked about at the elders and each gave him a single nod. When he looked at Angus Mhór, still standing at his side, he could swear the auld man was struggling to hide a grin. His sky blue eyes sparkled, and one corner of his mouth twitched. He winked at Ailig but said nothing.

Neill's face was bright red, his left hand fisted in his lap while his right sat limp beside him. "I will not see him take my place!"

Ailig thought the chief was glaring at him, but suddenly he realized 'twas Angus Mhór who now claimed his hatred. Ailig looked from the ailing chief to the smug counselor and back. His scalp prickled as all the kindnesses the elder had shown him in his life flew through his memory.

Angus Mhór had ever been a supporter of Ailig, a friend in his own way, yet it had never occurred to Ailig to question the behavior. He had taken it gladly, but without curiosity. Now his suspicions ran wild.

"Very well, Neill," Nigel Hunchback rumbled. "We will give you a few days to change your mind. But whether you do or not, Ailig MacLeod will be given the chief's oath at the Saint Bride's Day celebration. He will be our next chief. 'Tis up to you whether 'tis by your acceptance or the council's decree."

Baltair stood rigidly, glaring at everyone and no one.

The chief spluttered but could not seem to voice his rage.

Ailig looked to Angus Mhór to verify Nigel's ultimatum. The twinkle in the man's eyes told him the outcome had been decided before they had even set foot in this chamber. Relief was tempered with wariness. He glanced back at the seething men: Neill, arguing between racking coughs with anyone who would make eye contact with him, and Baltair, silent. Somehow his silence was the more ominous reaction.

There would be trouble from this. How could there not be?

Angus Mhór used his grip on Ailig's shoulder to push him toward the door.

"Fetch in the healer, lad," he said quietly.

Ailig obeyed despite the questions flying through his head. Questions he suspected only Angus Mhór could answer, but that would have to wait for privacy. He thought longingly of Morainn but knew 'twould be a long night of arguing before he could slip away to make her his own.

• • •

Morainn *rolled over in the soft bed and opened her* eyes to the strange room. Dawn had not yet banished the night, but the graying sky visible through a small window told her 'twould be daylight soon. Disappointment twined around her heart. He had not come to her. She pushed hair out of her face and tried to clear the cobwebs from her head as she sorted out what had been dreams and what had been real.

She had kissed Ailig. He had kissed her, wanted her in his bed. That part was real. But she was here, alone, her chemise wrapped about her, covers tangled, and no sign of Ailig having joined her in that bed, and yet her body knew . . .

He had been in her dreams, driving her mad with want. His hands—everywhere. His mouth—nothing was more sensual in all her memory. His body—firm, supple, slid along her, over her, in her.

She leapt from the bed, unable to get a deep breath. Her hands shook, her skin tingled as if he still trailed kisses over her face and down her neck. Her breasts felt hot and tender and swollen. They ached for his touch.

She ached for his touch.

Folly. How had she let herself get to this place? Was she truly willing to risk her heart, lose herself in the attraction that overwhelmed her? Was she willing to risk the peace and the life she had made for herself, safely separated from everything in her little cottage? Her lonely, little cottage. Would she risk everything by giving in to sensual pleasure, by giving in to that delicious feeling when he wrapped his arms around her and crushed her to him? Would she risk everything to touch him, make him smile, make him lose himself in her?

She had known the answer on the ramparts last night as well as she knew it now. She would. She wanted him as much as he seemed to want her.

Her thoughts tangled over each other, twisting and twining with the need Ailig had brought to life deep within her, making her feel tense, scattered. She needed her loom. She needed the quiet calm that came over her when she worked on a complicated pattern, focused on the slide of the shuttle, the rhythm of the shafts shifting up and down, one after another. She needed the feel of the treadles beneath her feet, with that one smooth-soft place on each, where generations of the women in her family had rested their feet as they threaded a shuttle or untangled a knot, or simply contemplated their work.

She couldn't seek her loom. She'd promised Ailig she would not go to the cottage alone, but she could seek out Ailig. She rushed to get dressed. There were things here she must tend to before going to the cottage. She wanted to know how the chief fared, and if the healers needed anything beyond a meal and perhaps an opportunity to find their own beds for a few hours. The kitchen required her attention, and there was the Saint Bride's Day celebration to arrange. She sighed. If she hurried, perhaps she could be finished by midday. Perhaps, if Ailig could get away, they could go to her cottage ... She stopped as the image of him in her bed sent heat flowing through her, taking her breath away once more.

She closed her eyes and tried to find a steady place inside her, a place that wasn't roiling with emotions and desires gone almost out of control, a place that was calm,

practical. She pictured herself sitting at her loom and
pulled that quiet feeling of being in control, of orchestrat-
ing the pattern of her own life into her, letting the peace
she always found in her work wash over her, calm her.
Steady her. Slowly, she found she could breath easily
again, as long as she didn't think about her bed.

There was no water in the chamber to wash her face
with, but then no one had expected her to stay in the castle. Perhaps she would see to her own needs. It wouldn't be
a secret that she was staying in Catriona's chamber, next to
Ailig's, but neither did she want those that kept the chambers clean and the fires stoked to feel they could pry into
her comings and goings. She was used to the privacy of her
own solitary cottage. She'd not give that up entirely.

She opened the door and stepped into the freezing corridor. A muffled, but clearly angry voice came from behind
Ailig's door. Baltair's voice. Stepping closer, she listened
for another moment. There was Tamas, yelling almost as
loudly as Baltair.

If they were started this early, had Ailig slept at all?
Concern pushed aside her plans to get him to her cottage.
There was no telling what had happened with the chief last
night. Ailig was no doubt tired and distracted by more important things than her. She ignored the hollowness that
opened up inside her at that thought and spun on her heel.
She hurried down the hall, distracting herself from
thoughts of the silent man in that room with the list of
things she must accomplish that day.

Ailig leaned back in the large chair, closed his eyes and
sighed as Baltair and Tamas shouted at each other.

What had he ever done to deserve this fate? All he wanted to do this morning was to find Morainn, hold her in his arms again and lose himself in the passion that kept bursting to life between them. When he held her, he was able to forget the chaos that grew greater about him every day.

"Ailig, 'tis pure folly! You cannot agree with Baltair." Tamas stood before him, his fists clenched and a deep burning frustration etched on every inch of his normally unruffled face.

Ailig had listened to Tamas and Baltair argue over how to best defend the castle for the last hour and still they agreed on nothing, except that the castle did indeed need to be defensible.

"We must defend the gates first. They are the weak points." Baltair bellowed at Tamas. He had been shouting since first he set foot in Ailig's chamber, not more than a handful of moments after Ailig had found his bed, Tamas and Skaeth seemingly pulled along by the force of his rancor.

"You're a wee daft eedjit." Baltair pointed a stubby finger towards Tamas. "And Ailig is just daft enough to agree with you and put the whole lot of us in mortal danger."

Ailig almost smiled. The council had bid them both keep their silence about the chief, and Ailig's parentage, at least until the chief had made his decision. They had told Baltair to obey Ailig's orders, though he did not think the champion was of a mind to do so.

"Just because you cannot think beyond hacking and slashing to the strategy required to defend this castle does not mean I am the daft one," Tamas ground out.

Their voices rose still louder, complete with creative name calling and threats of violence. Ailig glanced across his chamber to where Skaeth sat. He had his back propped against the wall, his stool kicked back on two legs and his own legs stretched out in front of him, crossed at the ankles as if he were completely relaxed—except he wasn't.

Ailig had taken to studying the mercenary and while he still could not put his finger on what gave the man away, at least to him, he could tell when Skaeth was only feigning relaxation. As he was now. Ailig had no doubt if the other two came to blows, Skaeth would break it up almost before the blows could start. He'd seen the man do it more than once in the Great Hall when the ale flowed a bit too freely and tempers rose between the MacDonells and anyone close enough to gain their attention.

'Twas odd, the way the mercenary had appointed himself the peacekeeper of the clan and Ailig's personal guard as well. What was he after? 'Twasn't the first time Ailig had wondered about Skaeth's motives. Lord knew why but the man seemed to have made Ailig his personal project, beating him up daily in the training yard, grilling him with strategy talk over the evening meal. Whenever Baltair or Gofraig or the MacDonells were near, Skaeth would appear as if from nowhere, always silent, always making his presence felt.

And yet last night Skaeth had been blessedly absent when Ailig had gone with Morainn to walk upon the wall, when he had kissed her, molded her body to his . . . Ailig's body surged at the memory.

"Ailig!"

"What?!" He raised his own voice in irritation as he was yanked from his reverie back to the angry men standing before him.

"I said either I'm in charge of the defense of this castle

or he is," Baltair said. "Send him away and let me *do* something!"

Ailig glared at the champion. "Nay. I need someone who is calm to advise me." He raised his eyebrows at the seething man. "I need an advisor who is loyal to *me*."

Baltair started to protest, but Ailig held up his hand to stop the man. He was sick of this.

"It matters not," he said, scrubbing his face with his hand and shoving his hair back. "You both ken the needs and the challenges of defending this castle. Go you both away and come back when you can agree on how best to do so.

"I do not trust the MacDonells," Ailig continued, "and I fear there is not much time before Duff appears. We cannot expect the rules of hospitality to overcome loyalty to their chief, no matter how much of a blackguard he is. We must each serve the clan with our strengths. Baltair, you know the men in the guard better than the rest of us, save perhaps Skaeth. Tamas kens strategy. Use your strengths."

Baltair grumbled and Tamas glared.

"Perhaps if your other advisor dared open his mouth," Tamas said, "and offered up his own opinion, we could establish which plan is the best."·

"'Tis only bickering over your own prides, not over what might be best for the clan," Skaeth said, never shifting from his relaxed position. "I've naught to add to that discussion." He glanced over at Ailig and raised one white blond eyebrow but said no more.

"Go," Ailig said, waving the two posturing men away. "We all have much to do today."

Baltair reached the door first only to have it burst open, sending him stumbling backward into Tamas, who uttered an oath about lumbering kine as he also stumbled backward. As the two men struggled to keep their feet and regain their dignity, Ailig noticed Skaeth chuckling, though he quickly covered it with a cough.

So, the man did have a sense of humor after all. Wonders never ceased.

"I kent you were a liar and now I have proof!" Gofraig stalked past Baltair and Tamas and made for Ailig. Ailig and Skaeth were both immediately on their feet. Gofraig's anger crackled in the air like lightning. Ailig readied himself to do battle right here in his own bedchamber. Skaeth stood behind Gofraig, and Tamas and Baltair stood on either side of the uninvited guest, effectively boxing him in. If he did draw on Ailig, he'd not be standing long enough to do anything about it.

"I do not lie," Ailig said calmly, his entire attention now focused on the man before him. "Perhaps you would like to take that back?"

"I would not, liar," Gofraig roared.

Ailig tensed, then remembered Skaeth's lessons. He took a deep breath, shifted his weight slightly to the balls of his feet and waited.

"What has angered you now, Gofraig?" he asked.

"Duff has escaped his false imprisonment."

How had he found out so soon? Suspicion chased through him. "And how is it you come by this notion?"

"'Tis no notion. Duff is free and he'll be here soon to collect what belongs to him."

"Ah, he's finally coming to get the refuse he left behind," Tamas said.

Gofraig ground his teeth but did not take his attention

from Ailig. "He will be here soon, with many warriors, and he will have what is due him."

"And that would be?" Ailig couldn't imagine what the man might think was owed him after what he had done.

"A wife. A tocher. And justice."

"There is no wife, and therefore no tocher, no bride price. As for justice—"

"He will see you dead."

"I think not, lad," Tamas said. "There is a wee flaw in your logic."

Still Gofraig stared at Ailig, and Ailig was content to stare back. Tamas and Skaeth and he had discussed this possibility. Now 'twas time to put the MacDonells in their place.

"What is the flaw?" Gofraig finally demanded when the silence had gone on for longer than he could stand.

Ailig crossed his arms over his chest and allowed himself a small smile. He'd been suffering these MacDonell fools for too long and at last the time had come to put them in their place, or at least to move them along towards it.

"The flaw is that you and your kin are guests within my clan's castle. You cannot raise a hand against us lest you breach the rules of hospitality. And if you do that—and I do wish you would—then you and yours will become prisoners and continue your guesting in our oubliette. You can rest assured that Duff will never be allowed through our gates.

"If you wish to remain here you will behave according to custom, else you will be joined in the oubliette by Duff, if he should find his way here. The king's men will be here in the spring. I am sure you will find our dungeon quite . . . uncomfortable . . . until then.

"So you see, you can leave and help Duff all you want from outside our walls in the thick of winter, or you can maintain your status as my father's guests. You cannot have it both ways. Though, as I said, I do wish you would try."

A wicked grin spread across Gofraig's face. "So, you do not think Duff can enter this castle unseen?"

Ailig flicked a glance at Skaeth who nodded imperceptibly. He shifted his eyes to Tamas who also nodded ever so slightly.

"Are you threatening me and this clan?" he asked quietly.

Gofraig grinned even wider. "Nay, for I am a guest and I would never . . . give you what you so desire. I am but asking a question."

"Hmph." Ailig sat back down in his chair but Skaeth, Tamas and the scowling Baltair continued to box Gofraig in. "How is it you came by this amazing information that Duff was free?"

Gofraig crossed his arms over his chest as Ailig had done earlier and assumed a relaxed and confident stance. "A messenger came."

"I would question this messenger. Tamas, have someone fetch him here. Surely, he is in the kitchen filling his belly."

"Nay," Gofraig said. A strange gleam shone from his eyes. "You'll not find him there, nor anywhere else within these drafty walls. He has already left."

"Where has he gone?" Tamas asked. "'Tis a storm blowing up out there. No one would venture out until it passes—except perhaps for a daft MacDonell."

Gofraig pushed past Baltair and Skaeth. As he reached

the door, Tamas's words hit Ailig and he suddenly understood the gleam in Gofraig's eyes. Every hair on his body
stood to attention. It could not be . . .

"Gofraig," he said, standing slowly. The man stopped
but did not turn back to him. "*Who* was the messenger?"

Gofraig faced him. "That is the first intelligent question
you've asked, wee Ailig." His face was ruined by the sneer
that twisted his mouth. "'Twas Duff, and your own lads
delivered him right to the Great Hall."

Tamas and Skaeth had their hands on their dirks and a
mixture of disbelief and anger etched across their faces.
Baltair's back was to Ailig, but he seemed as tense as the
rest of them were.

Ailig held perfectly still, his mind racing. The castle
must be searched. They could not trust that Gofraig spoke
the truth when he said Duff had left the castle. Duff must
be found and quickly.

"Is there aught else I can tell you, wee lairdie?" Gofraig
said.

"Nay, but you can be assured Duff will never again
enter this castle. Baltair." The champion edged sideways to
acknowledge Ailig's summons but he did not take his eyes
from Gofraig. "Escort our guest back to his quarters and
see that a guard is posted there. If any of his kinsmen complain of his absence, they are free to keep him company."

Baltair only inclined his head and Ailig shared a surprised glance with Skaeth. Baltair taking orders from Ailig
without so much as a scowl?

"Are you imprisoning me?" Gofraig demanded.

"Nay, I am only protecting my guest from a known traitor. 'Twould not do to have you charged with treason
against the king while you are biding in our hall. As your

host, it is my duty to see to your safety. Baltair." He motioned for the champion to escort Gofraig away.

There was silence in the chamber for a long moment after Baltair closed the door.

"Skaeth, find the imbecile who allowed Duff within these walls. He guested here not so very long ago. There is no reason why any of the guard should not recognize him enough to keep him out. Then see that every inch of this castle is searched. Go!" Skaeth gave him a wry nod and hurried from the chamber.

"And what of our earlier discussion?" Tamas asked when they were alone. "'Twould appear the time for debate is over and a decision must be made."

Ailig furrowed his brows but could not think of what had gone before Gofraig's sudden revelation. 'Twas one revelation after another of late—and he was having a hard time keeping track of all of them.

"'Tis suddenly clear that the gate is our weakest place, though I hate to give Baltair that point. 'Tis clear Duff means us ill and he is near. We will devise a plan immediately to keep him out of the castle or to rid him from it if necessary. You do not think he would deliver such a missive then slink back to Dun Donell, do you?"

"Nay, the man cannot return to Dun Donell. 'Tis the first place the king's men will search for him and 'twill not be long after that that they will come here. At least we need not wonder any longer when he will arrive."

Ailig strummed his fingers on the arm of his chair as his mind raced over all the implications of Duff's return. If he was not found within the castle, trackers would have to be sent out to find him. In any event, the defenses would have to be strengthened, and the clanfolk who lived scattered up the glen would have to be warned. Suddenly, he was very glad he had convinced Morainn to stay in the castle last night. At least he knew she was safe, once the castle was searched, anyway.

"Before you speak with Baltair," he said to the patiently waiting Tamas, "I want only our most trusted guards on the main gate. Men *you* would personally trust with your life," Ailig said at last. "And the postern gate. Have the others keep watch over the walls, especially for a lone man, for I doubt Duff has any others with him, despite what Gofraig claims, or he would not have bothered to sneak into the castle to alert his men that he was here. Somehow we will have to make sure that all is kept watch over. I'll not have that man within these gates!"

"I'll see to the guards. You ken Baltair will not like me giving the orders."

"I confess I do not care what Baltair likes. He has other responsibilities at the moment and the castle must be sealed." He paced across the room and back. "I must speak with the council. We can wait no longer for Neill's decision. We must have a new chief named before we all perish from this folly."

Fleetingly, he thought of finding Morainn and convincing her to leave this place with him, now, today, to escape the growing madness of the situation. But he could not. Someone had to take charge. The king had chosen him and the council had decided to support him. For good or ill, despite his lack of a true claim to the position, he had given his word. And the future of everyone, the future he wanted to give Morainn, depended upon him keeping it.

Tamas shut the door as he left and Ailig took a moment to compose his arguments for the council. The time for prevarication was past. The chief was incapacitated and a traitor with vengeance in his blood had breached their gate. The king would not take it well if warfare broke out between the MacLeods and the MacDonells, for such would distract from turning the Highlanders to help with the greater travails of Scotland as a country.

He knew he looked as power-grasping as Broc ever had, that he looked unfeeling for his ailing . . . chief, that he looked uncaring for the opinions of the clan. None of those were true, but he had no time to convince anyone otherwise. He had little choice if he did not want to see his people run out of their homes and a price set upon their heads.

He wished Morainn was here now so he could hold her, just for a moment, draw on her calm reassurances that what he was doing was right, was necessary. He shook off the melancholy hovering near his shoulder and focused on the task at hand.

The time was past for playing Neill's game. His decision must be made, and the only reasonable choice was to make Ailig chief now. The rest could be sorted out once the clan's future was secured.

chapter 12

❦

Shortly after dawn the kitchen staff was busy enough for Morainn to slip away to the larder. She needed her loom, but she had promised to wait for Ailig to go with her to her cottage. With him there, the loom could hardly work its magic on her thoughts. So the quiet of the larder would have to serve. She scanned the cavernous chamber, touching each basket of vegetables, savoring their earthy smells and even the sharp smell of the salted meats hanging from hooks in the ceiling. The pungent aroma of the dried herbs hung from pegs along the walls greeted her, mixing with the subtle tang of the ale kegs settling along the opposite wall. Odors and aromas poured down the stairs into the space from the adjacent kitchen. Her mouth watered and she realized she was hungry.

She pulled out her eating knife from its sheath at her waist and reached up, slicing off a thin piece of the smoked venison that hung above her. It was tough, and dry, and the

flavor was only a hint of the fresh venison it had once
been. Fresh venison . . . 'twould be a treat to have fresh
meat for the Saint Bride's day feast. A venison haunch,
slow roasted over a peat fire, was Ailig's favorite. She
shook her head, surprised she knew that, but she did.
Somewhere along the line she had tucked away that bit of
information about him.

Saint Bride's Day was only a few nights away. On that
night she would gift Ailig with a feast of his favorite foods,
with music and dancing and everything joyful she could
arrange. She was beginning to realize his life was no easier than hers, despite the impression she'd always held of
the favored MacLeod brothers. She'd like to give him a
taste of that favored life she'd imagined. She'd like to
dance with him, see him laugh, slip away into the darkness
with him.

Venison. With effort she pulled her thoughts back to the
feast. Slow roasting took time, and deer were scarce and
hard to find this time of year. If they were to have Ailig's
favorite, she must send out a hunting party right away. Perhaps they could find other game as well. Yes, that would
be good, but she'd have to wait to see what they came back
with before she could plan much more. She didn't know
who the best hunters were in the clan. She should, but she
didn't.

Who would know who the best stalkers were? Tamas
came immediately to mind. He would know. She'd find
him and leave the hunting party up to him.

A basket of dried figs caught her eye. She picked up a
piece of the slightly sticky fruit, closed her eyes and lifted
it to her nose, letting her memory show her the best thing
to make with these . . . Figs in cream would be good . . . a

stuffing, perhaps in a goose or a duck . . . aye, she would ask Tamas to see if they could find any for her, then she'd have a fine feast for Ailig, and for the rest of the clan, she reminded herself.

But mostly for Ailig.

Her mouth watered at the thought of fresh venison or hare, perhaps a fat goose or two. She left the quiet of the larder by the bailey door and ventured out to find Tamas. She checked the training yard first and though Skaeth was there putting several men through the intricate, almost dancelike moves he favored, Tamas was nowhere in sight.

And neither was Ailig. She should be ashamed of herself for the way she searched every room for him, held her breath as she rounded corners in the corridors. An odd sense of hope permeated her spirit at the mere possibility of seeing him.

But he wasn't here. He was probably closeted with the council, or with his father . . . nay, not his father, she reminded herself, the chief. Concern skimmed through her mind. But she had to find Tamas and dispatch her request for a hunt to him, before she could ease her worries over Ailig this morning.

Perhaps one of the castle guards would know where Tamas was. She passed back through the postern gate and was surprised at the groups of people entering the castle. Many were folk who lived in cottages scattered up the glen, as she did. She was glad she was not the only one who was taking refuge in the castle, at least until they caught Duff MacDonell. She crossed the snowy bailey, greeting folk as she passed them, and entered the gate tunnel.

The guards' chamber was just this side of the iron gate.

A small room set into the tunnel wall provided a place for them to warm themselves by a fire, or to protect themselves if the castle was attacked.

Arrow loops lined the tunnel and she could see the flicker of the guardroom fire through the last two of them. Three guards stood in the weak sunlight just beyond the gate, technically outside the wall, watching everyone that entered. She could not blame them for seeking out what warmth and light as could be found instead of lurking in the bone-chilling shadows of the tunnel.

"Have you seen Tamas this morn?" she asked the nearest guard, jolting him out of his concentration.

"Aye. He was here but a moment ago," the man said.

"He said something about checking on the laundress," a second guard said, waggling his eyebrows and grinning at the other two guards.

Una? Why would he be checking on Una? "My thanks," she said, turning back towards the castle just as the guardroom door opened.

"I thought 'twas your voice," Baltair said, crossing his arms across his chest and leaning against the jamb. A slow smile spread over his face and it seemed to pull his nose even further out of alignment than it usually was. "I would speak to you," Baltair said, stepping back and motioning her inside. "'Tis warmer in here."

"I'd rather speak out here," she said, wary of the man since her last run-in with him.

"I do not think you wish everyone passing through here to be privy to this conversation, Morainn."

She did not want to step into the tiny room with him, but there were others close by and a shout would easily be heard through the open arrow loops. She passed into the guardroom and was not surprised when she felt like a trapped hare.

He moved next to her and gazed down. She tried to ignore the frisson that ran over her skin. 'Twas not from cold, and 'twas nothing like the heat that Ailig caused when he stepped near. This was a warning. The man was a threat. She took a half-step away from him, needing more distance than he had allowed.

"What did you want?" she asked.

"I want to know why you align yourself with Ailig? Why do you go against the chief?"

"How have I gone against the chief? I have seen that the kitchen is working properly again. The rest of the castle is doing so as well. How is that going against the chief?"

"You have been seen in Ailig's company."

"As have you," she said, wondering what his purpose was in making her angry.

"You have been seen in his arms, kissing him. My own guards have told me."

"First, they are not *your* guards, they are the clan's guards. Second, I do not see where 'tis any of your business who I kiss."

'Twas time to leave, but he blocked the way to the door, which wasn't hard for such a large man to do in such a small chamber. Fear joined anger in her gut, standing every hair on her body on end, setting off alarms in her chest.

"Let me pass."

"Why do you choose him over me?" His voice was a low, barely controlled growl.

She struggled for a deep breath and gripped her skirts with cold, clammy hands. "I did not choose him over you, just as I did not choose him over the chief. What passes between me and Ailig is personal. I'll not speak of it with you."

"Is it so impossible to consider me as your husband?" he asked. There was no softness in his voice. 'Twas accusation, anger, that gave the hard edge to his words.

"Aye, 'tis." She tried to step around him, but he grabbed her upper arms and held her still in front of him.

"Did he tell you he is a bastard? That he has no right to be chief?"

"He told me, but it has no bearing on whether he should be chief or not. Except that both you and Neill would hold it against him, he who had no say in the matter of his birth. Perhaps Neill did have something to do with it, though. Perhaps Neill seeks to punish Ailig for his own shortcomings in keeping his wife?"

"He is not worthy to follow Neill!"

"Then who is? Is it you, Baltair, you who wishes to be the next chief?"

"I would be a better chief than Ailig."

She shook his hands free of her arms and stared at him. "Nay, you would not. You think only what is best for Neill and for yourself. Ailig does what is best for the clan and for Scotland."

"And you?" Baltair said, still blocking the door. "Does he do what is best for you or is he simply playing with your feelings, playing with your future to spite me?"

"He wouldn't."

"Are you sure or are you so blinded by him that you cannot see that he has only been interested in keeping you from me?"

"You are wrong. He is an honorable man." He had to be,

yet the parallels to Hamish and his courtship of her were strong. Hamish had only been interested in her once Broc had started pursuing her, and once she had pledged herself to Hamish, his interest had waned rapidly. But Ailig was different, wasn't he?

"'Tis clear you are not thinking clearly where the wee eedjit is concerned. He will be a nobody soon. I doubt not that he will be driven from these walls by his own kin. He cares nothing for our traditions, seeking to set himself above the rest by wooing the favor of the king."

"You know nothing about Ailig, or what he will do to keep this clan safe," she said, her anger so great she shook. "You are blind to what is happening all around us."

Baltair's face looked like a fierce winter storm. "You *will* see the error of your judgment," he said, finally letting her pass. "He does not deserve your loyalty."

"He does, Baltair. And he deserves yours, too. Time will tell which of us has the better judgment," she said, opening the door. "I do not think it will be you." She desperately hoped it would not be him. Morainn hurried away from the guard house, anger and doubt turning her mood sour.

Morainn crossed through the crowded bailey to Una's bothy. Anger at Baltair vied with anger at herself. The man had made her question herself and Ailig, question her feelings, and she didn't like where those questions had taken her. Ailig stirred up feelings that she didn't want to have in the first place. She hadn't allowed herself to be seduced into opening her heart only to have it trampled again, had she?

"Una," she called as she opened the door. A gasp drew her attention to a dark corner at the back. Una was there, partially hidden by drying bed linens. She was straightening her gown. Her veil had dropped to the ground and her blond hair looked as if someone had been running fingers through it . . . a man.

"Tamas?"

Her brother-in-law gave her a sheepish grin, his cheeks a suspicious pink. He gave Una a tender kiss. "You will stay within the castle?"

"Aye," Una said.

"And Lili."

"She will be fine, Tamas. Go and do not fash. We will stay within these walls until you say 'tis safe again to go out."

"You, too, Morainn," he said to her, then left them staring after him.

"Una?" She was dumbfounded. She looked from the door to Una and back, as if Tamas was still there. "What . . ."

Una's face was glowing. Her eyes looked dreamy. Her lips looked swollen, and Morainn couldn't help but remember how her own had felt that way last night . . . after Ailig kissed her.

"Are you dallying with Tamas?" she asked.

Una smiled. "Perhaps 'tis how it started, but 'tis no dalliance now."

Morainn tried to understand what Una meant. She could hear the words but they made no sense. Una had twice been widowed. Twice she had been left to raise her child on her own. Twice Morainn had held her as she cried and raged at fate, at her husbands, at all men for being so daft as to put themselves in harm's way when their women and children depended on them, loved them. Una had sworn she was done with men. They had been of one mind about that, and yet here was Tamas, kissing her, as Ailig had kissed Moriann.

Morainn blushed as she thought about the rapid straightening of clothes that had occurred. More than kissing had been taking place.

"Do not look like that, Morainn," Una said, her voice quiet and soothing as if she spoke to a frightened kitten who might turn teeth and claws upon her at any moment.

"Like what?"

"Like you've swallowed something sour," she said, smoothing a hand over her tousled hair.

"I am only confused. You swore you'd never let another man hurt you. You raged and swore, yet here you are in Tamas's arms, and now you tell me 'tis no passing fancy? What are you thinking?"

"Perhaps I am not thinking," Una said, moving silently through the drying wash. "Sometimes just feeling is better than thinking." She smiled, her focus clearly not on the laundry in front of her. "It started as simple friendship. I think Tamas could tell I was lonely, so he would come and sit by the fire with me and let me prattle away about Lili, or, well, whatever I wanted to say. He listened, he asked questions, told me stories, made me laugh."

"Tamas would make a fine friend. Friends do not rip out your heart when they leave, when they die."

"Do you think I would not grieve if something happened to you? Would you not grieve for me? Friends hold your heart in their hands, too. Perhaps not as deeply, but you cannot wall yourself off from all hurt, Morainn. Tamas has shown me that."

"I do not wall myself off."

Una raised an eyebrow. "Life is hard enough without denying yourself whatever solace you can find, whatever joy. I cannot embrace loneliness the way you do, my friend. He lightens my heart. He is sweet to my child. He cares for me and about me."

"Do you love him?"

Una nodded. "Can you be happy for me?"

Morainn took a deep breath and realized that the feeling that burned in her chest wasn't concern for her friend. 'Twas jealousy. Jealousy that Una had found the courage to love again, that her friend was smiling, glowing. And that she did not question Tamas's motives for loving her.

Fresh anger that Baltair could manipulate her so easily, make her doubt not only Ailig but herself, had her pacing. But she did not have to let him. If Una could take another chance with her heart, Morainn could, too.

She stopped and embraced Una. "Of course I can be happy for you. I *am* happy for you!"

"Thank the saints," Una said stepping back but keeping her hands on Morainn's shoulders. "I've been so worried about telling you, yet I've been bursting to share my happiness. Tamas has asked me to marry him! We thought to announce it to the clan at the Saint Bride's Day celebration."

"I think 'tis a wonderful idea. I have just come from planning the feast. Damn."

Concern washed all the color from Una's face and she squeezed Morainn's shoulders. "What?"

Morainn smiled. "Nothing. 'Tis only that I was looking for Tamas, but I was so flustered finding you two together that I forgot 'twas what I came for."

"Are you sure 'tis all right with you?"

"Of course." She hugged Una. "I can think of nothing better than two people I love finding happiness with each other."

Una nodded. "Aye, 'twould be wonderful for you, too. Ailig is a fine man. I heard he was seen kissing you just last night."

The memory of his kisses washed through her with all the force of the original one. She paced again amongst the hanging wash.

"'Twas a kiss between friends."

"Umm hmm. Then why do you blush at the mention of it?"

"I do not."

"Aye, you do. Do you love him?"

"I do not know. I care for him. I want him." She rolled her eyes at Una's snicker.

"If you did not want him, I would worry you had died," her friend said, a grin on her face.

"But . . ."

"But you fear he will be like Hamish?"

"Am I so obvious? I know he is not like Hamish. I do, but my heart, it is not so sure. I gave my whole heart to Hamish, and I thought he had done the same, but I was a prize to him, something to be won, something to be kept away from Broc particularly. I was blinded by his attentions. I swore I'd never allow that to happen again."

"You were young, Morainn, and grieving when Hamish started courting you. You are not the same woman you were then. Ailig is not the same man."

Morainn hugged herself. "I felt so lost, so alone after Mum died, and Hamish, he made me feel as if I was his whole world. But it turned out that I was only a small piece of his world, as I would be with Ailig."

"Would you? He will have many responsibilities when he is chief, but do you truly think he would forsake you as Hamish did?"

"He might have no choice."

"I do not believe that. I have seen him watch you. I have seen the hunger in his eyes, the desire. Hamish's attention was calculated. Ailig's heats the air between you."

"Truly?"

Una smiled and shook her head. She hooked an arm around Morainn's waist as they stood between the drying linens. "How do you feel when he is near?"

Morainn felt her cheeks heat and she could not look Una in the eye.

"'Tis as I thought. Do you find yourself looking for him whenever you enter a room or cross the bailey? Do you think about him as you lie in bed at night? Can his smile lift your spirits? And perhaps most important, when he kisses you, do you tremble and burn? Can you imagine your life without him in it?"

"Is that how it is for you and Tamas?"

"It is. I love the man, enough to chance my heart breaking if I lose him. But, Morainn, he makes me so happy. Why would I give up that because of some pain I might have to endure in the future. Life is too short and too hard not to take what happiness comes your way."

Morainn's vision blurred as tears threatened to spill from her eyes. If she stopped thinking, stopped listening to the doubt and just let herself feel the true answers to each of Una's questions, the truth was clear. Her heart was already forfeit.

"I am lost," she whispered.

"Nay, sweetling, you are found. Can you not feel it? Do you not feel more alive just because he is in the world? Tell him how you feel. He deserves to know."

Morainn closed her eyes and tried to focus on the joy and desire Ailig created deep inside her with just a look.

"You are too wise, my friend. I will tell him, when the time is right," she said, if that time ever came. She hugged Una. "I promise. But for now I must find Tamas again. I must congratulate him on his excellent choice of a wife before I send him out hunting for the feast. We shall have much to celebrate on Saint Bride's day."

chapter 13

Ailig burst into the bailey, *finally free of the council,* and the chief. 'Twas the first opportunity he had had all day to find Morainn. He needed to share the astounding news of the council's support and ultimatum. He needed to explain why he hadn't come to her chamber last night. He raced for the kitchens, but didn't find her there. She wasn't in the Great Hall. She wasn't with Una, though that lass gave him the oddest look as he left her hanging the never-ending laundry.

He stood outside Una's bothy unsure where to look next when he caught a movement across the bailey. Morainn strode out of the deep shadows of the smith's shed. Their eyes met and joy at simply seeing her cascaded through him.

"Morainn!" he called, jogging to meet her.

She stopped, ran a hand over her hair. An unsure smile

made her look like a lost wee lassie. The need to banish whatever made her unsure hurried his feet.

"How fares the chief?" she asked.

"He has recovered his temper. As for the rest, Giorsal says we shall have to wait and see."

"Did he give you his blessing?"

"I will tell you all, but not here." He needed to get her alone, he needed to touch her, to kiss her, to continue what had been interrupted last night. He needed to celebrate the future with her, for now that the council had made their intentions clear, there was a future for them.

"I could take you to your cottage now, to gather what things you need to have here with you, if you wish. We would not be overheard there." He took her hand, unable to wait any longer to touch her, and pulled her through the many people working in the weak winter sunlight. Baltair stalked out of the gate tunnel shadows. He glowered at the two of them as they passed, but he kept going.

"What about Duff?" Morainn asked as they neared the gate. "Is it not dangerous to be outside the walls? Tamas said—"

"There is a contingent of warriors scouring the area for the man. As long as we are vigilant, 'twill be safe enough." He pulled her along so fast she almost had to jog to keep up with him, but he could not contain himself. He needed to be alone with her. Now.

They hurried through the gate tunnel, into the outer bailey and through the palisade in silence. The frozen loch stretched beside them as they made their way down the path to her cottage.

• • •

Morainn was already out of breath when they rounded the bend in the path and her cottage came into view. Ailig had not slowed his pace the whole way there and she found herself pleased at his impatience to get her alone. The moment she had spied him in the bailey the rest of the world had faded away and she could think of nothing but him. When he stood before her, close enough to feel the heat of him, she thought she would cry if he did not touch her. And then he had taken her hand and her world had focused on that moment, that touch, and all other worries and doubts had vanished.

And now they had arrived at her cottage, her wee lonely cottage, set away from the castle and the prying eyes of the people that lived there. 'Twas what she had wished for this morning, what she still wished for, in spite of the quivering in her stomach.

Ailig closed the door behind them, checking the latch to make sure 'twas secure, then taking her hands in his he pulled her to him. His kiss was searing, filled with desire that fueled a need deep within her that she could not deny.

"My mind goes fuzzy when you touch me, Ailig. 'Tis as if every part of me yearns for you, overwhelming all logical thought."

"'Tis the same for me."

What started as a quiet kiss this time, filled with wanting, quickly turned hungry, aching. Desire licked sweet heat through her veins, though her gut was in knots. She wanted him . . . oh, how she wanted him!

He ran his hands over her back, caressing her bottom, then sliding them back up to bury his hands in her hair as he rained kisses down her neck. She wanted his hands on her breasts, between her legs.

'Twas not seemly to have such thoughts about a man she was not married to, but she did not care. All desire had not fled her flesh when Hamish died. It had hidden for a while but lately . . .

Ailig returned to her lips, kissing her deeply, their tongues dancing over each other as desire burned away the knots, leaving a deep, insistent ache that only Ailig could ease.

"I want you, Mora, as I've never wanted anyone before."

She closed her eyes, savoring the words. She remembered what such desire led to, things most pleasant, most satisfying. Things she could easily imagine doing with Ailig.

He framed her face with his hands and tilted her head up. "Look at me, Mora."

She opened her eyes and found desire and something deeper, something that tugged at her heart.

"If you do not . . ." he said.

"I do." She placed her hands over his and tried to show him the truth with her eyes. "I want you so desperately you cannot imagine." Her voice was low, just barely above a whisper.

She could swear the man growled as he crushed her to him. She reveled in the feel of his large hands sliding over her back, tangling in her hair, skimming down her sides, tantalizingly close to her breasts, making her ache for him to touch her there, to lift the weight of them in his hands, to suckle them. He nuzzled just below her ear and along her neck, sending delicious waves of longing through her, heating her, driving a whimper from her.

"Ah, Mora." His breath was coming nearly as fast as her own.

She knew what she wanted above all else at this moment. Her body was shouting its need to her even as another part of her tried to pull back. She needed to guard her heart, but her heart was already given and all the logical arguments for denying him fled in the face of the truth. She wanted him. He wanted her.

"We do not have to stand here," she said quietly when she thought her legs could hold her up no longer.

He looked at her and she could see myriad emotions flash through his eyes, desire, disbelief, questioning, hope.

He caught a stray curl in his fingers and raised it, tickling her cheek with it. "Are you sure?"

"I am." Her voice was husky, breathless. "Is it so wrong that I want your hands on me, your mouth? I want you in me, Ailig."

He went absolutely still. Even his breath stilled. She had shocked him. She had shocked herself, but 'twas only the truth. She wanted him inside her and nothing less would still the neediness his kisses had stirred, nothing less would chase away the ache that filled the hollow place inside her. She tried to let all the desire that was coursing through her show in her face.

"I am selfish enough to want you in my bed, to share that with you."

He took a long breath and she saw his hand shake as he released the curl and caressed her cheek with the backs of his fingers.

"Then we are well-matched."

Ailig kissed her, slowly, sensuously, letting his lips play over hers, nipping at the corner of her mouth, now dipping his tongue deep inside to dance with hers. His hands roamed, as did hers, as if they learned the form of the other with only their touch. Hunger exploded within her. She needed to touch *him*, not his clothing. She ached to touch his skin, to feel his skin against her own.

"Stop." Her voice was husky. At the stricken look on his face she giggled. "Just for a moment."

Confusion.

"You are wearing too many clothes," she said, reaching for the pewter brooch that held his plaid in place. Understanding and relief flooded his eyes. Deftly, she released the pin, but there was nowhere near to set it down. Ailig took it from her hand and with a grin, tossed it over his shoulder.

She reached for the belt that circled his narrow hips but sudden shyness made her fumble.

"Let me." He quickly released the buckle and the heavy plaid dropped to the floor. He stood in his tunic, and the evidence of his desire was plain, though hidden beneath the pale saffron fabric. His legs were still wrapped in wool and his brogues were still on his feet.

She reached for his tunic, almost desperate to see him. She pulled it over his head, then simply looked at him. The golden hair that often peeked from the V of his tunic covered his chest and his flat stomach, finally narrowing down to frame . . . She wrenched her gaze up to meet his. He had been watching her. The fire in his eyes told her that she could look her fill.

She reached out and touched his chest, indulging her curiosity. The muscles, honed by years of wielding Highland weapons, were taut, the hair surprisingly coarse and curly. She ran her hands up and over his shoulders, down his arms. She stepped closer to him, trailing kisses across his chest while she ran her hands over his back, down over his buttocks and back up to his waist. Still kissing him, she let her hand slide over his hard stomach and down. She wasn't sure who stilled this time, but she knew they both concentrated on the same thing. Lightly, she ran her hand down the length of him, around him, then down to lift the weight of him in her hand.

"Now 'tis you who are wearing too many clothes," he whispered against her lips. His breath was coming faster than it had a few moments before and that made her smile. It had been a long time since she had made a man struggle for breath.

Ailig reached for her belt, releasing it with well-practiced ease. She raised a brow at his skill, but he just continued to grin at her as he pushed her arisaid off her shoulders, then reached for her gown, removing it easily and leaving her in her woolen hose, her chemise and her shoes.

They both bent to remove their shoes, laughing in their rush. Before she was done he scooped her up in his arms. One shoe still dangled from her toes. She kicked it off as he gently laid her on the heather-filled mattress.

The grin disappeared from his face, replaced by a look she could not interpret, as he looked down upon her.

"I would never do anything to hurt you, Mora."

She reached for his hand and pulled him down to sit next to her. "I know that."

He hooked his free hand around her neck and drew her close into a kiss that filled her with bittersweet joy, and a longing she hadn't known she harbored. She wanted this man. She wanted him body and soul, but mostly she wanted his heart.

"I don't ever want to stop," he said. "I want you with me always. The future is still uncertain. I cannot promise—"

"The future is not now," she said, taking his face in her hands and looking deep into his eyes. She tried to show him just how much this moment meant to her lonely heart, to her battered soul. "Neither of us meant for this to happen, but it has, and all we have is right now. The future is always uncertain. I am here, now, because I cannot imagine being anywhere else. We should not miss this moment because of a future that is uncertain at best." She looked away for a moment, then back at him. "I did not want to give you my heart, Ailig," she said, laying her hand over her heart, "but my heart has a mind of its own."

He smiled and she kissed him, letting all her emotions flow through her kiss into him. He groaned and pulled her into his lap.

"I always liked your mind," he whispered between desperate kisses. "And yet there are other parts of you I am less familiar with." He cupped her chemise-covered breast in his hand, lifting its weight, running his thumb over the tight nipple, sending slashes of heat through her. A moan of satisfaction escaped her and she could feel his satisfied smile against her lips.

He laid her back on the bed again, following her down until his weight rested on her and between her legs. He kissed her, starting with her eyelids, her nose. Her mouth he lingered over, then moved to her earlobes, trailing sensual kisses down her neck. The laces holding her chemise closed seemed to vanish and he tugged it off her shoulder, exposing one breast. He stopped, holding himself completely still before he groaned and dipped his head to taste her.

Need tore through her, arrowing from where his lips brushed her breast straight to the core of her. She writhed beneath him, a sudden need to move against him overwhelming her. Once more she could feel his satisfied smile, even as he lightly ran his teeth over the sensitive skin at the side of her breast. She felt the heat and the weight of his hand on the breast that remained covered and the difference between his hot mouth against her skin and his warm hand over her garment made her whimper. She needed. She needed, but before she could do anything about that need, he was gone. She opened her eyes and found he was on his knees, at her feet, staring at her. Suddenly, she felt shy and he must have seen it.

"You are beautiful, Mora. More beautiful than I ever knew."

Gently he placed his large, clever hands on her ankles, then began slowly running them up her legs, pushing the hem of her chemise higher and higher. When her thighs were exposed, he paused and lightly ran his fingers over her skin there. He leaned down and kissed her thighs, never stopping the play of his fingers across her skin. She couldn't keep a small groan of frustration from escaping. She reached for him, threading her fingers through his golden hair, trying to bring him back up to her mouth.

But he wasn't through tormenting her, and it was such an exquisite torment that she acquiesced.

Gently, he kissed one thigh, then the other, pushing her chemise higher, until it bunched at her waist and she was completely exposed to him. Again, she tried to pull him to her. She needed him inside her. Now.

But he was in control. He chuckled at her whimper.

"You are an evil man," she said, though the only heat in the words was from her desire.

"I am not done exploring you, love." But he did cease his kisses on her thighs and slid himself up her body to kiss her mouth once more.

Mora wrapped her legs about his waist, cradling him between her thighs. She kissed him with all the desire and need he had raised within her, increasing her own hunger even as she inspired his own.

"Now, Ailig. Now."

"I cannot deny you longer," he said and stroked into her.

For a moment, he was motionless, giving her time to adjust to the feel of him within her, but she wanted to move, needed to move. She rocked her hips beneath him, drawing a moan from him. He kissed her, hard and full of passion, then locking her hands in his, he held her to the bed as he pulled away, then stroked into her again, deeper and harder, again and again, pushing her closer and closer.

Need built in her until it was almost painful, until it shut out everything but the exquisite feel of this man moving over her, in her, pushing her closer and closer until at last, when 'twas almost more than she could bear, the world shattered about her, casting away the darkness and surrounding her with a brilliant white radiance that cleansed the hurts from her soul and filled her with such joy as she had never imagined.

And Ailig was there, holding on to her, shattering with her.

•   •   •

A long time later Morainn lay curled up against Ailig, her head resting on his chest and her glorious hair spread out around her. More than ever he knew he must see that he became chief. If he did not . . . the future was too bleak if he did not. He'd have nothing to offer Morainn but a lifetime of running, hiding. He closed his eyes against the pain that thought caused. He could not give her up. 'Twould be like cutting off his arm, or ripping out his heart, and he could not even contemplate what she would endure. He could not let that happen, would not.

He tightened his grip on Morainn and she snuggled closer, her mere presence calming him. Did he give her the same comfort, or did he simply make her life more difficult? He suspected the latter and he vowed to change that.

He rested his cheek against her silky hair and breathed in the scent of her, sweet heather mingled with the musk of their lovemaking . . . and smoke.

He realized he had smelled smoke for some time now, and only as the haze of lovemaking cleared from his mind did he remember that they had not stoked the fire. The crackling sound of tinder catching fire caught his attention as he looked toward the cold hearth, then upward. Two different corners of the thatch glowed and popped as licks of flame ran up the dryer inside of the roof, sending showers of embers towards the floor.

"Mora! Fire!" The intimate peace of a moment before was gone as they scrambled to find their clothes. Morainn was heading for the door, coughing from the increasing smoke, as the importance of fire in two separate parts of the roof hit him. He grabbed her arm. "Do not open the door. 'Tis a trap."

"What? Who . . . Baltair?"

Ailig threw his plaid around him and his shoulder and clamped his belt over the bulk. Morainn had her arisaid held to her face and he could see panic flirting at the edges of her eyes. "I do not think he hates me this much."

"Aye, he does," she said.

Ailig went to the one window in the back of the cottage and shoved at the shutters. They did not budge. The only way out was the door. He grabbed his sword.

"Let me go first," he said, pulling her toward the door. "Stay here until I draw whoever it is away. You must run as hard as you can for the castle, love. Do not stop until you reach the gate."

"But you—"

"I shall be fine. Skaeth has not been training me for nothing. Though he will surely skin my hide for allowing this to catch me by surprise."

"I'm sorry," Morainn said and Ailig could not help but smile through the thickening smoke.

"I'm not. I would not trade anything for the last hour here with you." He looked up at the roof, half of it already engulfed in the hungry flames. The heat was growing with each minute, and the smoke thickened. "Give me a moment or two, no more, to clear your path then, no matter what, you must run. I fear the roof will not stand much longer."

She nodded, her eyes large, as he inched open the door.

M orainn crouched by the open door, unable to see far past the smoke that billowed through it. She closed her eyes against the stinging smoke and tried not to breathe

deeply. As fast as her heart was racing, 'twas hard to
breathe at all. She heard the clang of steel against steel and
gasped.

"Now, Mora!" she heard Ailig yell. She streaked from
the cottage, sparing only one glance at the fighting men,
Ailig and one other. She gave thanks that 'twas but one
man, even as she realized it must be Duff MacDonell. Ailig
seemed to be holding the larger man off, but for how long?

Running as hard as she could, she made for the castle,
yelling as soon as she was in sight of the walls. Guards
swarmed to the top of the wall and out of the gate.

"'Tis Duff MacDonell. By my cottage. Fighting Ailig."
She pointed back the way she had come, gasping for breath
between words. "Go! Help him!"

Baltair emerged from the gate at a run, his sword
drawn, hollering instructions. One group of guards followed Baltair; others began closing the gates. For a moment she stood, catching her breath, trying to grasp what
had happened. One moment she had been lying in Ailig's
arms, satisfied in a way she could not describe. The next
they had been escaping a trap as her home burned around
them. Ailig had protected her and now Baltair was going to
his aid.

Shame washed through her as she realized Baltair had
not been responsible for the fire, even as concern for
Ailig's safety doubled. She raced back to her cottage, the
smell of smoke and the fear of disaster whipping her on.

As she came to the clearing she skidded to a stop. Ailig
was there, his sword still in his hand, but Duff was
nowhere to be seen. Her roof was completely in flames
now. An ominous snapping was quickly followed by a
thunderous boom as the roof gave way and collapsed into

the house. Smoke whooshed from the still open door and a roar rose from the house as if the fire celebrated its success.

Baltair and the others were using anything they could find to scoop up snow and throw it on the flames, but she knew 'twas futile. The stone walls might yet stand, but the cottage and everything she owned was gone. The bed that had belonged to her parents, her mother's loom that had passed down through four generations, the plaid she had gifted to Hamish on their wedding day, her dye goods, wool, everything. She wanted to sob, to rail. She wanted to rush in and save those things that connected her to those people she had lost.

But she could not. She stood as if rooted to the spot, unable to move or utter a single word. All she could do was stare as her world burned away in clouds of ash and smoke.

chapter 14

Morainn watched, *almost as if she were someone else*, as Ailig led her back to the castle. She felt like she had been caught in numbingly cold water that dragged on her limbs, blurred voices, slowed her mind. And all the while she waited to feel something. Anything.

She tried to listen as Ailig spoke to the gate guards, but she couldn't separate the sounds into words. He said something more to the guards, then pushed her down the short tunnel and into the bailey.

Ailig stood before her. Distantly, she was aware that he held her hands, gripped them, shook them as if he wanted to tell her something. If she concentrated very hard, the words came only slightly after his lips moved.

"Mora, are you okay?" He gave her a little shake and she realized he was waiting for a response. She nodded. 'Twas all she could manage. "I must find Tamas and

Skaeth." He looked about the bailey and called to someone.

Una appeared at his side, her sleeves pushed up to her
elbows. The odd thought that she should be shivering crept
past Morainn's mind, though she couldn't decide if she
thought of herself or Una.

Ailig cupped her face in his hands, but she barely felt it.
"I shall be back as soon as I can, Mora. Una will stay with
you until then." This time his words were a little easier to
pull from the air as they floated between them. Again, he
seemed to await her response, so she nodded. He said
something else to Una, kissed Morainn lightly, and disappeared.

"Morainn, sweet, come. I shall take you to your chamber. We shall warm you up."

Morainn felt her mouth turn up in a smile. So it was she
who should be feeling the cold.

She allowed Una to take her hand and lead her into the
tower; up too many stairs. At the first landing Morainn just
wanted to sit down and never move again, but Una would
not let her. At last they reached a chamber and Una pushed
her down to sit upon a soft bed.

Morainn heard the quiet hiss of a peat catching fire,
then felt the bed give as Una sat next to her and once more
took her hand. Her friend chaffed it between her own, and
Morainn felt the beginnings of warmth, a slight tingling in
her fingertips, a curious stretching sensation in her palms,
as if they had been asleep and were now being forced
awake.

She did not want to wake.

"Tell me what happened," Una said to her, switching

hands and continuing her chaffing. "Ailig said Duff set a fire."

Morainn slowly looked at Una but still could not manage to form words.

Una moved away then and Morainn noticed that it was colder without her there. She quickly returned and forced a cup into Morainn's hands.

"Drink. 'Tis only water. You've had a shock, I know, but if you do not speak to me soon I shall call for Giorsal and have her give you one of her most noxious potions."

Morainn drank. The water was icy and she could feel it flowing through her all the way down. So she could feel something. The thought was comforting. Una urged her to drink more, then took the cup from her and resumed her hand chaffing.

"Now, Morainn, tell me what happened. Really, talking about it will help. I ken you'll not believe me, but I know a thing or two about grief and keeping it in is never useful."

Morainn sighed and closed her eyes. The destruction of her home shone brightly against her lids.

"Everything," she said, her voice almost inaudible, even to herself. "Everything was destroyed." 'Twas as if those few words broke a dam within her. Tears began to flow and words demanded release. "My mother's loom, the plaid I gifted to Hamish on our wedding night, my dishes, my bed, my clothes, wool, my dye goods, everything. He burned the thatch, thatch my own father put on that cottage. 'Tis gone. They are all gone."

Una had an arm around her shoulders and pulled her close. "They?" she asked quietly. "What do you mean they are all gone?"

"Everything is gone. My past, my family, my home. Everything. Una, I have nothing now."

"Och, there is where you are wrong. You have me and Lili. Tamas dotes on you as if you were his own sister. The clan will look after you. You have this beautiful chamber . . . and you have Ailig."

"I do not have Ailig. 'Twas because of me he was there. 'Twas because of me Duff was able to trap him."

"I'll not argue with you about that. I'll let the lad convince you. All I mean to say is that there are many here who love you, who will see that you are safe from harm and will help you with your cottage, as soon as 'tis safe, so that you will have your home again. Though personally I think you belong here in the castle . . . with Ailig."

Morainn felt a tired smile tug at her lips. "Thank you," she said, hugging Una.

"Nothing has been harmed that cannot be mended."

"You did not see the fire. My mother's loom will be beyond saving."

Una nodded her head. "'Tis sorry I am about that. I ken how much that loom meant to you. 'Twill not be the same, but we will have another loom built for you. The clan has grown too fond of your beautiful work to let you be without a loom for long. We'll all spin more thread to resupply your store, and Lili and I will wander the bens with you this spring and summer to gather your plants for your dyes. 'Twill take time, but I suspect you will be well settled before winter comes again."

Morainn stared into the fire. "I'm sure you are right." She squeezed her friend's hand, finally able to feel how cold her own hands really were. "Go back to your work. I shall be fine. 'Twas a shock, 'tis all. I am going to sit here a wee bit longer, then I'm sure the kitchen wants tending."

Una looked at her for a long moment, and Morainn tried her best to stay focused on her.

"Truly. I will be fine. I just need a few moments to pull myself together. The kitchen will distract me. 'Twill be much better than sitting here thinking about what is gone, and what I could have lost today."

"Very well. But I will check on you later. When you get to the kitchen, get yourself a wee dram of the chief's finest whiskey. On second thought, get two, and do not make them wee."

Una kissed her and hurried out the door.

Morainn sat perfectly still upon the feather bed, her feet resting on the floor, her hands folded calmly in her lap, her eyes focused on the flames dancing in the fireplace.

Una had broken the dam and weathered the worst of the storm, but now there was more for Morainn to think about.

She *had* lost everything, her past, her home, even her future was uncertain. She had lost everything, yet now that the tears had passed, she had a curiously light feeling, almost a sense of relief. She could dwell no more upon the hurts of the past, for the past had been taken from her. She did not want to dwell on the uncertainty of the future.

For the first time she wanted naught but to live in this moment, now, free of both the past and the future. Free to live only in the present. 'Twas strange to think that the destruction of her home was a blessing, but in an odd way, once she accepted the loss of those things that connected her to her past, it was freeing.

Except . . . she focused for a moment on what had happened before the fire: the joy she had shared with Ailig, the passion, the laughter and the quiet peace that followed. She'd not forget that and could only pray that the present would continue to include Ailig.

Excitement had lit his face when he'd dragged her off to the cottage, but he had not told her what had happened. Curiosity pushed through the grief fog still drifting through her thoughts.

She rose and went to the basin to wash the tears from her face. She straightened her clothes, finger combed and rebraided her hair. When she thought she was recovered enough she left the chamber, determined to find Ailig, to reassure him that she was fine, and to find out what he had meant to tell her. And if he was done with her now, she would understand, or try to. She knew he could not afford to be distracted by her as he had been today, not when the future of the clan depended on him.

Hours later Morainn dashed out of the kitchen, leaving behind a cursing cook, a crying pot washer and a scowling fishwife. She didn't care. The entire kitchen staff had taken turns bemoaning her loss, then took turns blowing up at each other, and her, over trivial matters. She had been trying to get free of the kitchen for hours. She needed to find Ailig, yet she had been detained, over and over again, as if the kitchen staff conspired to either drive her mad or keep her hostage. Probably both.

But she had broken free, at last. She reached the doorway into the Hall just as the MacDonells were streaming out of it. She stepped back, lest she be trampled by the oddly quiet, glowering men. She watched them file up the stair leading to the chambers Gofraig and several of his men occupied, not a word passing amongst them.

'Twasn't a good sign. What had happened? She turned back to the door only to find it blocked by Baltair. His face was tense, and his jaw worked, as if he chewed on a tough piece of meat. Each clenching moved the tip of his crooked nose, ever so slightly.

"Thank you, for aiding Ailig and trying to save my cottage," she said.

"I am sorry about your cottage, but I regret helping that eedjit. He'll not get the support of this clan if I have anything to say about it."

Gooseflesh prickled down her arms. Worry made her stomach clench.

"What has happened?" She clenched her fists in her skirts to keep Baltair from seeing her shaking hands.

"He will not be chief," he said, shaking his head. "No matter what the council says. And you can tell him I said that."

Morainn stared after him as he stalked away. She stepped into the Hall in search of answers and found almost as much chaos as she had left behind in the kitchen. Ailig was huddled at the high table with the elders, Tamas, and the mercenary, Skaeth. He must have sensed her there, for he glanced up, over Tamas's shoulder and held her gaze for a moment, concern haunting his eyes, before he turned his attention back to the men about him.

What had happened here? She searched the crowd for someone who would tell her what had passed. She spotted Una, sitting at a table with Lili in her lap, a pool of calm in the midst of mayhem. Una waved her over and she made her way slowly to her friend, then slid into the seat next to her.

"How are you?" Una asked, examining her face.

"I am better. Thank you for earlier. I do not ken what came over me."

"'Tis called grief and despite the face you show tonight, 'twill be with you for a while. Do not try to hide it from everybody. 'Twill pass quicker if you share it with those who love you."

"Like you shared your grief with Tamas?"

Una's cheeks pinkened.

"I like Tamas," Lili chirped. "He made me a poppet to go with the one you made me." She held up the two dolls, the cloth one Morainn had made and a carved wooden one.

"'Tis beautiful, Lili," Morainn said, smiling at the little girl. "And I like Tamas, too. He's a fine man and a good friend."

Una patted Morainn's hand. "Thank you."

Morainn shook her head slowly. "You need not thank me. I think I understand what you were trying to say, about taking what joy you can from life when you can find it. I'm not very good at that, not lately anyway. 'Twas a skill I lost somewhere. Tamas is a good man and you both"—she ran a hand over Lili's silky hair—"you all three deserve to find some happiness."

The two women hugged. Lili, caught between them, squirmed out of her mother's lap and scampered away, drawing Morainn's attention back to the milling crowd.

"What has happened here?" Morainn asked.

"Nigel Hunchback declared that the chief was no longer fit to lead, that Ailig was the only logical choice to follow him and that all would be made official on Saint Bride's Day."

"'Tis what he wanted," she said, pleased that someone had finally seen fit to do as the king commanded. She reached for Una's wine and took a long draught. But what did that mean for her, for them?

"'Tis not all he wants," Una said. "The two of you belong together. I can see it in your eyes when you look at him. And when he watches you. He has a hunger in his eyes that is plain for any to see."

Morainn looked up at the high table and was caught in Ailig's glance. 'Twas almost as if he reached out and caressed her across the crowd. Memory of his touch washed through her, pushing away some of the darkness she felt inside.

"You have the same hunger in your eyes, Morainn, and a softness that comes over you when you look at him. I have not seen you so before."

Morainn watched Ailig at the head table. She could see the tension in his shoulders, even as she vividly remembered the way his skin felt there, under her hands. She wanted to go to him, care for him, see the knots in his shoulders were eased. But she could not in good conscience expect him to put her before the needs of the clan.

"I am for my bed—*alone*. There is much to do on the morrow to prepare for Saint Bride's day. 'Twould appear there is more than one reason for celebration that day."

"Aye," Una said. She reached over and gave Morainn a firm hug.

She looked back at the huddle of men on the dais. An argument was taking place, in hushed tones, but with much waving of hands and clenching of fists. 'Twas clear they were not in accord about something. Ailig would need every bit of support he could gain from that group, and from the rest of the clan, if he was to successfully lead them. She could not get in the way of that as she had this afternoon. She couldn't.

"I'll need your help on the morrow," Morainn said, trying to smile at Una.

"You have it whenever you need it. You know that."

Morainn squeezed Una's shoulder by way of thanks and left the crowded hall, avoiding the clumps of people standing about. She dared not speak to anyone, for her heart was in her throat and she would not feel sorry for herself. There was more at stake here than what she wanted, than what Ailig wanted.

H*ours later, Ailig stood before Morainn's door debating* whether to knock or to leave her in peace. He had tried to check on her this afternoon, but the council had kept him busy.

He had worried about her when she hadn't attended the evening meal, but then, she had responsibilities, tasks she had taken on at his request. Now he wished he had not asked that of her, for he would rather have had her by his side. He drew strength just from her being near.

He had wanted to break the news to her himself. Had meant to, but the opportunity had been stolen from him, first by the destruction of her cottage, then by the needs of the clan and council. He needed to know that she was recovering from her shock, that she would be well. He rested his head against her door. He should leave her be. She would have waited for him if she had wished to speak to him. He *should* leave her be, but he would never sleep worrying about her. He had not been able to break free of the bickering elders until after she had left the hall.

He knocked lightly. He did not want to wake Morainn if she was sleeping, but he needed to make sure she was all right.

The door opened just a crack. "Ailig?"

Need slammed into him so hard he could not speak. He needed to hold her in his arms, needed to feel her arms around him, needed the quiet calm that came over him and the heat that burned between them.

She swung the door wider. "What is it?" she asked, concern clear in her eyes.

He hesitated, but there was no one in the corridor to see, and he promised himself he'd only make sure she was well, then he would leave, go to his own bed, in his own chamber . . . alone, if she wanted him to.

"May I come in?"

Without hesitating, she stepped aside to let him enter and closed the door quietly behind him. For a moment they stood, trying not to stare at each other, then he stepped towards her and she flowed into his arms. Pleasure hummed over his skin and sizzled through his veins.

"I was worried about you," he said, his cheek resting against her hair.

"I'm sorry," she said.

"For what? For being shocked? For grieving over the destruction of your home?" He hugged her tightly to him. "You need not apologize. 'Tis I who am sorry. I should not have taken you there. Duff never would have thought to burn it if I had not been there. I am sorry, too, that I had to give you over to Una's care. I did not want to leave you when your heart was breaking so."

She pushed away from him, releasing his waist and taking his hands in hers. "'Tis not your fault, and I cannot regret going to the cottage with you." She smiled shyly and lifted his hands, rubbing her soft cheek against his knuckles. "I thought you would blame me."

"Never."

"But you would not have been there if it weren't for me."

"I would not have been, but as you said, I cannot regret taking you to your home. I only regret that it did not end as I would have liked. Are you sure you are well, now?"

"I am. Una is a very wise woman." She tucked a hand under his elbow and pulled him over to the fire. "I will miss the things that were destroyed, but they can be replaced in time. You are the one who has truly had a momentous day."

'Twas clear she was done talking about her cottage. He did not believe her that she was taking it so lightly, not after the way she had reacted. He wanted to make sure she never had to experience that kind of grief again and the council had finally seen fit to empower him to do that.

"I saw Baltair as he was leaving the Great Hall," she said, standing so close to him he could feel her heat. She slid her hand from his elbow to his hand, threading her fingers through his, and leaned her head on his shoulder. She stared into the flames with him.

"He was not happy," he said.

"He was not. He threatened you, Ailig. He said you would not have the support of the clan."

He nodded and squeezed her hand. "You do not need to

fash over Baltair, Mora. 'Tis no secret that he sides with Neill, but I will be careful."

"Do you know who your real father is?"

"Nay."

Her eyes narrowed and for a moment he thought she was going to scold him.

"But you have an idea." It was a statement. She knew him too well. When he did not answer, she cocked her head, her eyes narrowing further as she studied him. "'Tis hard, is it not, losing that connection to where you came from?"

He had not thought about it in that way, but he supposed that was the hardest part, not losing a father who had never cared for him, but losing that sense of belonging, of having a right to be a part of everything—and pretending like it didn't matter.

"I suppose that is why seeing my father's cottage and my mother's loom destroyed was so . . . upsetting." She pressed against his side again, looping her arm around his waist. "I think I had convinced myself that the things I connected to them were important, kept them alive somehow . . . but they aren't, they don't, not really. I have not lost my family any more now that their belongings are gone than I already had. I lost them a long time ago and all this time I have been hanging on to the past."

"No one blames you for trying to hold on to your family, Mora."

She gave a scoffing little laugh and he looked down at her, surprised by the sound. "You have not spoken to Una about this, have you, or Tamas?"

"I suppose they will lord their wisdom over you now?"

"At the very least."

"As their new chief I shall command them not to," he said, trying to suppress a chuckle at the idea of commanding either of those two to do anything of the sort.

"You have enough impossible tasks to accomplish without that," she said.

"And yet I feel I owe Una a debt. You are much improved since this afternoon and I think we have her to thank for that."

"Una has much experience with grief and she isn't afraid to use it."

"You have had your own share of grief, love. Do you miss Hamish?"

She was silent for a moment. "Nay. I think I missed the idea of Hamish, but he did not love me, and after a while, I did not love him either."

"And yet you mourned him a long time."

"At first I truly mourned. No matter what was between us, he was my husband and my first love, but after a while I found it kept people away. I did not want anyone else to get close to me. I did not want to lose anyone else."

"You will not lose me," he said, his voice husky. "I would never hurt you, Mora, not knowingly." He stared into her eyes for a moment and swallowed. "I should go," he said but could not seem to move away from her.

"Don't." It was a whisper, a plea, and it made his knees go weak and the sizzle return to his skin. "Don't go, please." She kissed him and desire surged through him stronger than before.

All his good intentions to leave her to her own bed tonight fled him. "I do not know how I will ever leave you, love," he answered, pulling her hard against him.

Truer words he had never spoken.

chapter 15

Hours later they lay tangled in the blankets, the fire burned low, and Morainn slept, curled against his side, her breathing calm and even. He breathed deeply, trying desperately to calm the rapid beating of his heart. Possessiveness roared within him. A need to protect her, to keep her safe and happy, joined it. Never had he experienced feelings so powerful and the tenderness, the longing to keep her with him always, was just as strong.

Ailig had wanted little in his life. He had been content to drift along the edges of his family, observing and fixing what he could. He had not expected to be chief. He had not asked for the king's regard and confidence in him. But this he wanted—Morainn.

Desperately he wanted to make her his own, to claim her, to get her with bairns, to comb his fingers through her hair whenever he wished. He wanted to shout from the ramparts that he had found something, someone, to fill his heart and make him glad to be alive—that he was in love.

He marveled at the realization. Somehow, knowing what it was he was feeling calmed him, soothed him, as she did.

He kissed her forehead and murmured her name as he gathered her into his arms and stroked her smooth, warm back, letting his hands glide from shoulder to buttock then down the thigh she hooked over his legs, letting his fingers tease the springy hair just within reach as his hands roamed up again. She mumbled something in her sleep and edged closer to him as he skimmed his hand over her ribs and tickled the side of her breast. He murmured her name again as he ran a thumb over her peaked nipple and sprinkled kisses over her face.

"You are insatiable . . ." she said, her voice dark with sleep.

"'Tis true only where you are concerned. Do you want me to stop?"

In answer she reached for him, a smile flirting over her lips, though she had not opened her eyes yet.

"I find I am insatiable, too." Now she did open her eyes. In the flickering rush light he could not see their color, but he could see desire, white hot, and something deeper, something that mirrored what he was sure shone in his own eyes. He counted himself a very lucky man.

Time stood still as they indulged themselves, exploring, touching, laughing softly together before she took him inside again. This time they were not in a hurry. They savored. They slowed the pace, drawing out the magic as long as they could, reveling in every delicious sensation until at last they could stand it no longer.

"Ailig," she whispered.

He wanted no further urging as he gave in to his passion, his desire, his love, and drove them both into that white hot place once more.

S*ometime very late in the night Ailig had reluctantly left* her. Soon he would not need to, but for now they would give no one reason for gossip. He spent a fitful hour in his own bed. No longer was he content to fulfill the king's command; now he had something, someone, he wanted for himself. And soon, if she felt as he thought she did, they would pledge themselves one to the other. But not yet. First the future must be secured. Only then could he reach for the happiness he had glimpsed last night.

When he deemed it close enough to dawn, he rose again and dressed, then fled his empty chamber in search of Tamas, Skaeth and Baltair. He grimaced at including the champion, but he would need everyone's help if he hoped to accomplish all that must be done.

He found Skaeth in the dark, deserted bailey. The man moved like a lethal dancer as he cut and stabbed at an invisible adversary. Ailig waited until the mercenary slid his sword into its scabbard and resheathed his dirk.

"You are up early," Ailig said from a distance, not wanting to startle the man.

"Not so early," Skaeth replied. His eyes narrowed as Ailig drew nearer. "Something has happened?"

Ailig was surprised at the question. Did happiness show that easily?

"Many things have happened and more to come. If I am to be made chief on Saint Bride's night, I must be prepared. Will you come with me? I want to find Tamas . . . and Baltair. I must find a way to gain his support, or at least to keep him from working against me. We must begin to make plans."

Skaeth's face smoothed to his usual detached expression. "Right . . ."

Ailig couldn't help but smile. "Will you come?" he asked again.

Skaeth motioned for Ailig to lead and he fell into step with him as they headed across the bailey.

"Am I that obvious?" Ailig asked, as they climbed the stair to the Great Hall.

"To me, aye. To others? I suppose you shall find out soon."

Ailig tried to school his features back into his usual intensity, but a smile kept creeping out. He had little to smile about, truly, with Duff's escape and attack upon Morainn's cottage, his unknown parentage, and becoming chief without Neill's blessing looming in the future. He had little to smile about, and yet he could not keep it from his face for more than a moment or two at a time.

He was pitiful. Besotted. And 'twas the best thing that had ever happened to him. All he wanted was to return to Morainn's chamber, to her bed, and spend the entire day there with her. Though even that would likely not suffice.

Tamas was snoring on a pallet near the fire in the Hall, as were many of the clan who would normally return to their cottages up and down the glen were it not for the danger posed by Duff. Ailig nudged him with his foot. Tamas mumbled something and Ailig nudged him again.

"Tamas, wake up!" he hissed, not wishing to wake everyone else just yet.

Tamas cracked open one eye. "Cannot a man sleep in peace?"

"Nay, not in this castle," Ailig said, a grin spreading on his face again. He had slept very little last night, yet he was wide awake and full of energy to take on the day.

"'Tis still full dark without," Tamas said, pulling his plaid up over his head.

Skaeth moved to the other side of Tamas and they each grabbed a handful of plaid. Skaeth raised three fingers, lowering them one at a time. When the last one lowered they yanked, pulling the plaid off Tamas so suddenly he sat bolt upright.

"I'm up, you damned whoresons."

Ailig and Skaeth looked at each other. Laughter danced in the mercenary's eyes, though his mouth was as unmoved as it always was. Ailig couldn't help snickering. He held out a hand to Tamas and pulled his friend to his feet.

"You're in a fine mood this morn," Tamas said, yanking his plaid from Skaeth's grip. "Who gave you a tumble?" As soon as he said it, Tamas's eyes went round.

Apparently, Ailig *was* quite transparent.

"I'll kill you if you hurt her," Tamas said, and Ailig was quite sure he meant it.

"I do not intend to hurt her, Tamas. Far from it. 'Tis part of why I need your lazy arse up and your devious mind working."

He led the two men from the Hall. They slipped into the larder, grabbing enough food to break their fast, before heading up to the ramparts in search of Baltair. They found him sound asleep on a stone bench in the cap house atop the chief's tower. 'Twas bitter cold, but that didn't seem to bother the man.

He awoke more easily than Tamas had, but with stronger words for the trio. Once he was up, they all went down the twisting stair to Ailig's chamber. It took every shred of self-control Ailig possessed not to knock on Morainn's door. He wanted to see if she had a silly smile on her face this morn, too. But he didn't knock. He led the others into his chamber. While he stoked the fire he noticed Tamas had gone to the bed and was studying it and the floor around it, no doubt looking for signs of Morainn.

Tonight there would be signs of her in this room. Tonight.

He threw another peat on the fire as he tried to get the smile off his face. He wished to give Baltair no additional reasons to work against him. When he thought he had his expression back under control, he faced his unlikely trio of advisors.

"I will not recognize you as chief of this clan," Baltair said suddenly. "Neill does not wish it. 'Tis not right that the council will make you go against his wishes. The clan has not even had a say."

"The clan is not against it," Tamas said. "Most of them."

Ailig looked to Skaeth to see if he wished to also damn him with faint praise. Skaeth raised one blond eyebrow, but left him on his own.

"It is my intention to get the clan's blessing, Champion. If you wish to remain in that position after Saint Bride's Day, I suggest you pledge me your loyalty or at the very least, your cooperation."

He glanced at the other two.

"You have mine," Tamas said. "I have already told you that."

Ailig nodded once, then considered Skaeth.

Skaeth stared back at him for a moment, and Ailig began to wonder if the man did support him as chief. At last he said, "I am not of this clan, but you do have my support. I have seen no other here"—and now he looked directly at Baltair—"who would make a better chief."

Touché. Now he had added his faint praise.

Ailig closed his eyes for a moment. 'Twas the best he could hope for at the moment. Perhaps, in time, he would prove to everyone that he would be a good chief for the clan. He would start now.

"Very well. Baltair, if you cannot pledge at least your cooperation, I must ask you to leave."

The champion didn't budge, but neither did he say anything.

"'Tis my preference that you remain champion, but I cannot in good conscience allow that if you will not pledge your support to the clan's chief—whether that is me, Neill, or anyone else. Will you give me your pledge?"

"*If* you become chief, you will have my pledge of . . . cooperation. But you are not chief. Neill has my oath of fealty now. I cannot give it elsewhere . . . even if I wanted to."

And it was clear he did not, but Ailig had to admire his loyalty to his oath, and for now, 'twould have to be good enough.

"I will hold you to that, Baltair. No matter what passes between us personally, the clan needs strong leadership, and strong warriors. 'Tis what will see us through these next weeks and months."

With that settled, he had them draw near the fire and they began to plan. For now, they must concentrate on finding and securing Duff MacDonell so the clan would be safe in their cottages once more. When that happened, these MacDonells, still biding under the hospitality of the MacLeods, would require a delicate touch, or a strong one. They must be prepared for either eventuality. And lastly, they must be prepared for those same MacDonells to do something desperate.

'Twas all complicated, but they would be ready. 'Twas agreed that the warriors scouting for Duff would be reassigned to the defense of the castle and Skaeth, as the least likely to be known by Duff, would begin forays out into the glen to search for signs of Duff and to see if he had others with him. Tamas would do the same, only inside the castle, quietly scrutinizing not only the MacDonells within the castle, but everywhere they went. He'd have to see if any of their own folk had grown friendly with them, just in case. It would not go well for Ailig if his own people were working against him with the MacDonells.

Baltair was given the defense of the castle, though equal attention was to be given to the gates as to the walls Tamas had earlier been so concerned about. As had been determined yesterday, the palisade gate was to be kept closed at all times now, not just at night. Ailig would concentrate on winning over the clansfolk, as well as preparing himself to become chief.

When the others finally left, Ailig stopped pacing his chamber. Morainn was probably off to the kitchen already, but that did not stop him from jerking open his door and quietly knocking on hers. There was no answer, even after repeated knocking. He sighed. He'd have to content himself with catching a glimpse of her elsewhere. He could not wait until they could be alone again.

Tonight.

He broke into another grin as he turned his thoughts
back to the things he needed to do today. But the grin went
sour when he realized that the first person he must speak
to was Angus Mhór.

M *orainn carefully smoothed the covers over her bed.*
Last night was like a dream, except there were certain parts of her body that attested to the reality. Euphoria
made her giddy even as part of her worried that everything
was moving too quickly with Ailig, just as it had with
Hamish.

But Ailig was nothing like Hamish, and her feelings for
Ailig were so much more vivid, so much brighter, so much
more joyful, than she had ever felt with Hamish, that she
refused to listen to her own worries.

The night had been filled with whispered conversation,
laughter and passion. She could not imagine giving that
up. 'Twas exactly as Una had said. She could not focus on
what might be. She donned her cloak and left the chamber
without a backward glance. She would not regret anything.

A quick trip to the kitchens assured her that all was well
in hand there. Before long, she would not be needed anymore. Once they had all gotten past the laziness caused by
the sudden freedom from the Shrew's control, the kitchen
and its staff were running smoothly, with only the occasional temper flare that required her mediation.

The next thing she needed to do was begin the prepara-
tions for the Saint Bride's celebration. They would have to
forgo the hunt. She'd not send anyone out while Duff was
still lurking about. They would make do with salted meats,

and there were other things that must be organized and prepared.

Una had said she would help. Morainn knew Una
would be able to tell that something had happened, just by
looking at her friend's face. The woman had a sense about
such things. Sure, she hadn't known yesterday, but
Morainn had been in shock from the fire. Today she
couldn't keep a smile from her face. She shook her head.
Una would know the moment she opened her door.

And if she did figure it out? Morainn was dying to tell
someone, to share the wonder of what had happened and
Una was really the only one she could tell. But should she?
She wandered across the bailey unable to decide.

She knocked on the bothy door and waited for Una to
open it. She did not want to chance interrupting another
tryst between her and Tamas. A smile of understanding
spread over her face. Suddenly, all of Una's lectures about
not being alone, and her obvious joy at Tamas's attentions,
made sense to Morainn. She understood, at last, why Una
had been at her for months to get out more.

Una opened the door. She wiped sweat from her forehead with the back of her wrist.

"Why did you not come in? I had my . . . what has happened?" She grabbed Morainn's hand and dragged her into
the moist darkness of the bothy, shutting the door firmly
behind her.

"Nothing," Morainn managed to say without grinning.
Una did not look as if she believed her.

"Your mouth says nothing but your eyes say everything."

"All is well," she said, losing the fight with the grin.
"The Saint Bride's Day festivities must be planned. I've

come to get your help. You did promise," she said, trying for a light tone.

Una faced her, fists on her hips and an I'm-not-believing-you look on her face. "I'll help," she said, "but you'll be telling me what's going on before I do. You look like Lili with a honeycake."

"No honeycake," she said. She looked down at her hands as memories of the long night washed through her. Her shifting emotions were making her dizzy. She took a deep breath and looked Una in the eye. "The festivities should begin with the procession, right?"

"Of course, but I'll not be sidetracked. Sit you down there," she said, pointing at a stool near one of the braziers. She pulled another close and the two women sat, their knees almost touching. Una reached out and took Morainn's hands in hers. Surprise lit her face. "They are not cold."

"I did not say they were."

Una sucked in a breath and covered her mouth with her hand. "'Tis Ailig. What has passed between you? I was right, wasn't I? It has taken a braw man to warm you." She giggled at her double entendre. "He's warmed you well, has he not?" Una's smile was so wide Morainn thought 'twould split her face in two. Her friend leaned forward and hugged her, nearly toppling the both of them from their stools. "Tell me! Tell me everything!"

Morainn put her hands on her hot cheeks. She didn't know whether to laugh or cry. "'Tis complicated, Una."

"It does not have to be. How do you *feel* about him?"

Morainn blinked and tried to slow her swirling emotions, tried to grab hold of just one, but 'twas impossible. Each thread of emotion tangled about another, or several.

Nothing was simple. Nothing was clear. 'Twas like a weaving gone mad.

"Morainn." Una's voice was quiet. Her hands rested on Morainn's knees. "Does he make you happy?" she asked, her voice hushed as if they sat in a chapel.

Morainn grabbed that thread. "Aye, he makes me very happy." Another thread was tangled with that one and it made her blush.

"'Tis more than happy, I'm thinking."

"More than happy."

"Do you love him?"

Morainn searched the tangle and found that thread. "I do." She smiled as she remembered how she felt just lying in bed with him, tangled in the sheets, her cheek resting on his chest, listening to the thump of his heart beating. She looked down at her lap, at the work-worn hands of her friend resting there like an anchor in the storm of her emotions. "I love him."

"Have you told him?"

She shook her head. "There is no rush. I do not want to make the same mistake I made with Hamish, and Ailig has many things he must see to right now. I do not want to distract him."

"Hmph. I think you are a distraction whether you tell him or not. 'Tis that you do not trust your feelings. That is what is holding your tongue."

Una was probably right, but that did not change anything. With time she would trust her feelings, and once Ailig was chief they would have lots of time.

"When he is chief and Duff MacDonell is dealt with, then I will tell him. Now I would plan the celebration. I want it to be perfect for you and for Ailig."

Una considered her for a long moment, then sighed and gave in. "What do you need me to do?"

Ailig *made his way to the tiny chamber above the kitchen* the chief had afforded Angus Mhór. Many of the elders preferred the kitchen tower, for 'twas warmer than any other part of the castle, save for the kitchen itself. The elder opened his door on the first knock. He did not appear to be surprised to find Ailig at his door. He motioned the younger man in and closed the door firmly behind him. The room was as austere as Ailig's.

"I've been expecting you," Angus Mhór said. He stood erect, his hands clasped before him and an expression of patient waiting upon his face.

"Then you know why I've come?"

"You have questions."

"I do." Now that the moment had come to ask them, though, Ailig discovered that he was not so anxious to learn the truth as he had thought. He wiped damp palms against his thighs. He cleared his throat, chewed on his bottom lip for a moment, then looked Angus Mhór in his bright blue eyes.

"You are my father." He'd meant to ask a question, but the certainty in his gut had him stating it as a fact.

Angus Mhór didn't flinch, didn't move. He held Ailig's gaze for a long moment before shaking his head slowly. "I am not."

"But . . ." Ailig couldn't seem to get a breath. He'd been certain. The man was lying. "You are. You must be. My fath—Neill hates you. He kept you off the council for years out of spite. And you have always championed my cause, whatever it might be, from as early as I can remember right up until now. Why would you do that if you were not my father?"

"Is it so hard to believe that I saw something in you that your brothers do not possess? Is it so hard to believe that I could look into the future and see that the first four sons of Neill MacLeod were not what this clan needed for leaders?"

"Aye, it is when no one else ever saw such in me." He clenched and unclenched his fists, trying to understand. Nothing was as he expected it to be.

"No one? Neill and his ilk are not the only ones with opinions in this clan, lad." The edge to Angus Mhór's voice felt like a slap. "Morainn, Tamas, even the mercenary, do they not see more in you than most? Did not King Robert himself?"

Ailig tried to relax his jaw, unclench his teeth, as he considered each of the people Angus Mhór named. In each case he remembered each of them telling him, in so many words, that they trusted him, supported him. He nodded, more to himself than to Angus Mhór, then folded his arms across his chest and studied the auld man in front of him.

Auld was not really right. He carried more years than Ailig, to be sure, but not nearly so many as the other members of the council. Indeed, he was probably younger than the chief. And despite his protestations otherwise, Ailig still suspected Angus Mhór of being his true father. He just couldn't figure out why the man would deny it.

"If you are not my father, then who is?" He watched the man carefully, ready to see any sign that he lied, or that he spoke the truth.

"I cannot say."

"You cannot or will not?" Ailig's voice was low. "Do you know who my father is?"

"'Tis not my story to tell."

He dug his nails into his palms and tried to keep his voice calm. "But it is my story to hear."

"I do not deny that, Ailig."

The placating lilt in the elder's voice had the knots in Ailig's shoulders twisting.

"'Tis only that I gave my word," Angus Mhór continued, "many years ago, that I would not speak of your true father to anyone."

"Then who *can* tell me?"

"'Tis up to Neill to tell you. 'Tis his story, too, more than mine."

"But he will not."

"Give him time." Angus Mhór laid his hand on Ailig's stiff shoulder. "Give him time. Once you are chief he will have nothing to lose, or to gain, by keeping the truth from you. But until he is certain he will not get his way in this, he will keep the secret."

"Cannot my true father speak of it?"

Angus Mhór looked away and sighed. "Nay, he cannot."

Ailig's anger was so strong now he wanted to hit something, someone. "If 'tis true and you are not my father, then why does Neill hate you so?"

The older man smiled. "He is afraid of me, I think." He steered Ailig to the door and opened it for him. "You have much to do before you are declared chief. Should you not be about your business?" He gently pushed him out the door and closed it again behind him.

Ailig stood in the corridor for a long moment, breathing

deeply, trying to relax enough to think clearly again. He still was not convinced that Angus Mhór was not his father, but 'twas clear he'd not get any answers out of the man. For now, he had responsibilities, and who his father was, or was not, did not change what he must do. For now, he must concentrate on those tasks, but Neill would be receiving a visit from him before the day was out and Ailig would have his answers.

chapter 16

🌿

Giorsal hadn't let Ailig see Neill that day, nor the next, nor the next. If it weren't for reports from Morainn, he would suspect the chief was dead. His days were filled with the business of running the castle and the clan, sparring with Skaeth and Tamas, hearing petty grievances, and making sure the MacDonells behaved themselves. When no further sightings of Duff had been reported, Ailig had been compelled to release Gofraig from his forced seclusion and the man made every effort to voice his displeasure with Ailig to anyone who would listen, and many who wouldn't. Soon he would have the power to oust the Mac-Donells. But not soon enough.

His nights, though. His nights belonged to Morainn. Each evening, after the meal was done and the kitchen quiet, after the nightly arguments and scuffles in the Great Hall, after the castle had quieted into sleep, Ailig would slip into Morainn's chamber. They were the happiest hours of his life, laughing, talking, loving. Sometimes they would just sit quietly and stare at the fire . . . but not for long. He found he could not get enough of running his hands over her soft skin, twining his fingers in her thick curls, sinking into her heat. And she seemed just as hungry, just as curious, just as needy as he.

He lived for those dark hours spent in her chamber. All else was lived for the clan, for the king, for the good of Scotland. But those few quiet hours each night, those were for the two of them alone.

He left her, each morning, well before dawn and the stirring of the castle, and each morning it was just a little harder to leave than it had been the day before. But today, at last, was Saint Bride's Day. Tonight he would be made chief and he would finally be able to ask her to be his wife.

All day he had waited for the evening's festivities to begin and now 'twas almost time. The feast was over and the procession of Saint Bride's Day revelers spread out behind him, trailing after him at a more leisurely pace than he tried to set as they circled the snow-blanketed fields, scattering sacred herbs to welcome the coming spring and ensure fertile fields and fecund livestock.

He felt odd, wearing his sword on this night and sending out warriors to guard the procession, but he had little choice. He glanced behind him, slowing his pace to allow the crowd to catch up. 'Twas bad enough that Duff could be lurking about in the dark, though Skaeth had seen no evidence of his presence at all, but he was anxious to get back to the hall. Morainn waited there and he needed to see her with a desperation that almost frightened him.

He entered the castle's gate, leading the procession on the last leg of their journey, around the bailey, up the stair to the wall walk and down again to the Great Hall. Happy voices trailed behind him. Quiet singing accompanied their steps. A pleasant hum of excitement shimmered off the crowd. Ailig led them, but he was not a part of them. Even though he was to be their chief this very night, still he did not feel a part of the clan. Only with Morainn did he truly feel like he belonged.

He started the climb to the wall walk, taking the steps two at a time even though he knew the crowd would not keep up. He was done with this foolishness. He needed to be made chief as soon as possible, for so many reasons, and not the least of them was Morainn. Smoke from his torch stung his eyes and he realized he held the torch too low. Raising it over his head again, he waved it left and right to scare away any evil spirits that lingered nearby. Though the only evil spirits seemed to be the MacDonells both within and without the castle. He waved the torch again as vigorously as he could without putting it out, then headed down the stair that would finally take him to the Great Hall and Morainn.

When he entered the hall, she was waiting, a smile on her face. The remains of the feast had been cleared away, though a few tables still stood near the walls, laden with sweets and savories. Morainn held a ewer that most likely held ale or wine, ready to fill the first empty cup she could find.

She pointed him to where a new fire had been laid, awaiting the flame from his torch. He stood by the hearth watching Morainn greet the clanfolk as they filed into the hall and gathered about him, gradually cutting off his view of her.

Twelve lasses formed a semicircle in front of the hearth,

each dressed in white. One placed a poppet's cradle, fit for a small doll, near the hearth. Another placed a poppet made of oat straw in the cradle and a third set a twig of rowan next to it. Several others stepped forward and placed dried flowers and herbs in and around the cradle. Finally Ailig lowered his torch to the freshly laid wood in the fireplace. The new fire blazed to life.

"May Saint Bride bless this castle and this clan," the women of the clan chanted three times. The crowd erupted in whoops and whistles as Ailig placed his torch in a nearby bracket. Soon there would be music, dancing and then he would be named chief and would take the vow. One life was ending. Another would soon begin—as soon as Morainn consented to be his wife.

He looked for her and found her moving about the crowd, filling cups, laughing, hugging a child, whispering to a lass. As he watched, Una's daughter, Lili, ran right into Morainn, who managed not to spill a single drop from her ewer. Morainn stooped down to talk to her, then stood, ruffled the girl's hair and watched as she ran toward the bailey door.

The look on Morainn's face was one of fondness and he wondered if she ever regretted not having a bairn of her own. She had said she couldn't have any, but the image of her holding his child swept through his mind, and he thought perhaps there was hope for that, too.

Musicians struck up a lively tune and people streamed toward the center of the hall. After a minute they organized themselves out of the chaos and the dancing began. Couples swung in circles as they moved their way through a complicated pattern and back to where they had begun. Ailig searched over the heads of the dancers for Morainn and found her standing opposite him, observing the festivities with a smile on her face. The urge to pull her out onto the floor and join in the fun gripped him and he started to circle around the dancers.

He threaded through the onlookers, though no one greeted him the way Morainn had been greeted as she moved through these same people. He was almost there when a discordant shout rang out.

"You'll not dance with my sister!"

The sudden shout jerked Morainn out of her reverie. The dancers stopped. The music stopped. One of the MacDonells had left the clump of his kinsman across the hall and had a MacLeod lass, Freya, the healer's apprentice, by the hand as if he had been about to lead her out for the next dance. Her brother, Rory, stood squarely in the first lad's path. Freya looked angry at her brother and she had not removed her hand from the MacDonell's. Morainn had seen the two together several times in the last few days but had thought little of it. Perhaps she should have.

"I did not ask you to dance, laddie," said the MacDonell. Jock was his name, Morainn thought. "So I do not see where it should concern you."

"Nay, for a MacDonell would never be concerned with aught save what he wants," Rory said, a menacing scowl on his face. "'Tis my duty to see to my sister's safety."

Gofraig stepped forward from the gaggle of MacDonells who crowded about Rory and the couple. "And 'tis my duty to see that my kinsmen are met with hospitality while we bide in this hall. You are quick to blame my kinsmen of ill behavior when 'tis obvious 'tis your own wanton women that keep causing trouble."

"My sister is not wanton!" Rory surged forward.

"Rory, stop!" Freya yelled, grabbing his arm before he could swing at Gofraig and pulling him around to face her.

"'Tis the poor influence of the MacDonells that has clouded your judgment, my sister." He shifted his glare over his shoulder at Gofraig and his kinsmen. "'Tis time they left these walls and made for their own."

"Your words do little to calm hostile tempers, Rory," Ailig said, pushing into the angry knot of men. Morainn released the breath she hadn't realized she'd been holding.

"The MacDonells are our guests," Ailig said, his voice firm and loud enough to carry over the hushed crowd. "'Tis our duty, by custom, to give them every courtesy."

"My sister is not a courtesy!"

Ailig glared at Rory. "I did not say she was, but 'tis a courtesy to allow our . . . guests . . . to dance on Saint Bride's Day. Since there will be no dances of war this night and they do not have any of their own kinswomen with them, 'tis only right that we allow them to dance with some of our own."

The crowd grumbled and no one moved.

"I'll not allow my sister to dance with *him*."

"Fine, is there any lass or lady here who would honor the duty of hospitality and dance with our . . . guest?"

Pride flashed through Morainn. Ailig would make an excellent chief. He understood the needs of the position, the duties, the difficulties, and he would handle them with fairness and justice, but he would still require help, and in this, she could be the one to help him.

She walked to his side, pushing her way past those who would not give way.

"I will," she said loudly when she stood next to Ailig. He looked down at her, startled, and a strange look that was half gratitude and half something else, something wilder, darker, passed over his eyes. "I will," she said to him.

"Thank you, Mora." He turned his attention back to the scowling couple. "Will you dance with Morainn, Jock? Perhaps when Rory sees that you will not harm a lady you dance with . . . you will not trod upon her toes, too much, will you? . . . perhaps then he'll reconsider his opinion about allowing Freya to dance with you."

Rory muttered under his breath and took his sister's hand out of the other man's.

"Come, Freya," he said, pulling her to the far side of the hall, well away from the MacDonells.

The MacDonell lad watched her walk away from him, his face an unreadable mask. Morainn was sad for him, that something as silly as a dislike of his clan might keep two lovers apart. She moved to Jock's side.

"I know I am not so pretty as Freya, but I would like to dance."

He inclined his head to her, then lightly took her hand and led her out onto the floor.

A ilig caught the eye of the musicians and they began a quick tune that required dancers to move so much there was little opportunity for touching or conversation. Ailig could not take his eyes off Mora as she stumbled her way through the rapid foot movements as if she had not danced in years. Yet she was smiling when she whirled past him, caught up in the arms of Jock MacDonell. He had the almost overwhelming urge to charge out into the dancers and knock the man away. But he didn't. He couldn't.

Mora had helped him diffuse a difficult situation and he'd not undo that just because his own jealousy ran rampant. Personally, he did not wish to see *any* of the MacLeod lasses dancing with the MacDonell men, but as future chief he had no choice but to uphold the rules of hospitality. 'Twas his duty, like it or not, and Morainn had stepped in and smoothed the way, as she always seemed to do.

"You ken, if you keep staring at her like a man starved, every single person in this room is going to know what's been going on between you." Tamas said, standing at his elbow and watching the dancers.

Ailig cast a sideways glance at Tamas. "I do not know what you mean." The man was her brother-in-law and Ailig really didn't want to discuss what had passed between himself and Morainn.

"Do you think I am blind as well as daft? You watch her every move."

Embarrassment had Ailig shifting his attention back to the dance floor. Once more he found Morainn and watched her glide through the dance, her steps more sure now, her smile wide.

Tamas sipped on his ale and watched the dancing for a few minutes. "It would be selfish of you to break her heart for but a passing tryst."

"'Tis no tryst," Ailig said with more heat than he'd intended.

"Then what are your intentions? When are you going to ask her to marry you?"

Ailig glanced at Tamas, then back to find Morainn once more. "Soon," he said. "Very, very soon."

"Were you going to ask my permission?" Tamas asked. "After all I am her closest kin."

"Would you say aye?"

Tamas clapped him on the shoulder and looked out at Morainn, too. "I would. She has been happier since you returned than I have seen her in a very long time. Do not hurt her, Ailig. Do not break her heart. My brother did that to her once and I'll not let it happen again."

"I have no intention of hurting her. Can you do something for me?"

"Probably."

"I am tired of waiting. Will you tell Nigel Hunchback to start the ceremony now. There is something I cannot do until I am chief and I do not wish to wait any longer."

Tamas grinned. "That I will gladly do," he said and took off into the crowd.

Ailig took a deep breath and leaned his back against the wall, waiting as Morainn, the comeliest of all the lasses there, made her way back to him. Her face was flushed like it was after they made love, and her beautiful brown hair, normally forced back into a braid, was loose and curling about her shoulders and her lovely face. She smiled up at him and he felt like a very lucky man.

"You are beautiful when you dance, love," he said as she took his cup and drank from it.

Morainn looked out at the crowd still milling about the middle of the hall, awaiting another tune. "Hamish and I used to dance each year on this night to celebrate our wedding. I did not think it right to dance these last two years. I have missed it."

He lifted her chin with his fingertips, pulling her attention back to him, back to now, away from the past.

"Do you still miss him?"

The heat that skittered over him at the merest touch of her skin made him feel overheated, light-headed. Besotted, he thought as she gazed up into his eyes.

"It has only been two years," she said. "Yet I fear I cannot even remember what he looked like, nor the sound of his voice." Her own voice dropped to a whisper. "Am I wicked that all I can think of is you?"

He wanted to crush her to him, beg her to marry him now, here, but he did not dare jinx anything by asking before he became chief. Only then would he have a future to offer her.

"You are wicked, love, but not for that," he said, grinning at her. The flush on her cheeks deepened. He took her hand and squeezed it. "Will you dance with me?"

"I should see to the ale."

"Leave it. Una has it well in hand. Come, dance with me," he said, pulling her out amongst the dancers just as the musicians struck up a familiar circle dance.

To Morainn the dance was like one of her weavings, the dancers twisting around each other like thread spinning on a spindle before she had to reluctantly release Ailig's hand. He moved away from her, weaving between the other lasses as when she sent the weft thread through the warp, binding it all into a complex pattern that was all the more beautiful for the work it took to create it. Ailig was the weft that bound them all together, securing the substance of the community.

The dancers spun and wove around each other three more times before she once more found herself in Ailig's arms. He lifted her up and swung her around as the music came to a stop. The dancers whooped and applauded as Ailig slowly lowered Morainn to the floor. She could not take her eyes off his.

"The ceremony will be soon," he said, cupping her cheek with his hand. She leaned into it, relishing the feel of his skin against hers. "I must speak to you as soon as 'tis done, Mora. I've something important to ask you."

He pressed his lips to hers right there, in the midst of the hall with everyone about, and she didn't care where they were. She wanted his kiss more than she'd ever wanted anything.

"Ailig?" A familiar little voice piped up from beside them, breaking the spell that wove between them. Lili stood there, tugging on Ailig's sleeve. "Ailig, there's a man outside." She smiled up at both of them. "He said to fetch you."

Morainn looked at Ailig. "Who?"

Ailig shrugged. "Give me a moment to see what he wants. Will you find Angus Mhór? Tell him to prepare to administer the oath as soon as I get back. I can wait no longer."

"I will tell him," she said, squeezing his hand. He kissed her again, then ruffled Lili's hair as he set off for the bailey.

"There're honeycakes in the corner," Morainn said, squatting down in front of Lili. "I'll bet you could eat one or two of those."

The elfin girl gave her a gap-toothed grin. "I love honeycakes. The ugly man outside said I could have some, too."

"Then scoot before the lads eat them all." She watched as the lass raced across the Great Hall, only bumping into three people in her mad dash for the sweets. She wondered who the lass thought was ugly. A stranger, perhaps?

Concern slithered up her spine. A stranger . . . ugly? Saints! She searched the crowd for Skaeth, for Tamas, even Baltair would do. She could not see any of them as she raced for the door. Jock stepped into her path, just before she reached it, a huge smile on his face.

"Will you not dance with me again, Mistress Morainn?"

"Nay, Jock, not now. Pardon me," she said, trying to step around the large man.

"I'm afraid I cannot do that," he said, standing firmly in front of the door.

She gaped at him. "You cannot? Let me pass!" she said, loud enough to gather the attention of those around her.

Now he scowled. "Do not do that lass. I do not wish to hurt you."

Morainn could feel her mouth hanging open. She knew she stood dumb, staring at the man. His words had stopped her heart. He would not stop her, threaten her unless . . .

"Get out of my way!" She tried to sidestep him, but he blocked her. She balled her fists and aimed at his nose. He stopped her, calmly gripping her wrists, and spinning her so she stood with her back to him, his arms crossed across her, pinning her to him.

"Tamas! Skaeth! Balt—"

He slapped a hand over her mouth stopping the alarm. But even over the music and the loud sounds of conversation her shout had been heard. Those close by turned and looked. Confusion, then concern washed over them. She took advantage of the moment and bit the hand that covered her mouth as hard as she could.

Jock yelped, but didn't release her. He gave a strange whistle that slashed through the air, cutting through all the noise and music, and she heard the unmistakable sound of daggers being drawn. A cry of surprise rose from different parts of the hall.

"Be still and no one will get hurt!" Gofraig's voice rang out over the gathering.

Morainn struggled against Jock's strong grasp. She had to get to Ailig before Duff—Dogface MacDonell—killed him.

chapter 17

Ailig left the hall, his mind full of Morainn and of the coming ceremonies that would make him chief. He left the bottom of the stair and looked about the dark, deserted bailey. Torches guttered here and there along the walls, casting a weak, flickering light.

"Hello?" he called.

A shadow separated itself from the darkness of the gate tunnel. "I did not think you would come alone."

The shadow came closer and Ailig's stomach lurched as he drew his sword. Duff MacDonell stood before him, travel-worn, but with an eery leer slashed across his face.

"How did you get inside?" Ailig's mind was racing. Baltair was responsible for the gate tonight. The man might betray Ailig, but he wouldn't harm the clan. His loyalties to Neill ran too deep.

Duff moved close enough for Ailig to see the wild hatred in his eyes. "'Tis amazing what guards will do when their clan's champion's life is at stake."

"Where is he? Is he alive?"

"He is where he will do me the most good, trussed up and disposed of in your own oubliette."

Ailig tried to edge back towards the stair that led up to the Great Hall. Everyone was there, except those who'd been assigned to guard the gate . . . and the wall!

He jerked his attention to the heights and found guards in each of the positions they should have been in, but the flickering light showed MacDonells, all facing inward, watching *inside* the castle, rather than outward as his guards would have done. He'd get no help from there.

"Have you killed them all?" Ailig asked.

"A few, but most were content to keep their lives."

"Where are they?"

"That is something you do not need to know. I am in control now and you, you are just a detail to be dealt with."

"What do you want, Duff? You cannot escape the king's men for long. What do you think to gain from this?" All the while he kept his sword at the ready as he moved slowly toward the stair. Duff watched him, but made no move to stop him.

"Justice, that's what I want, and a bride."

"Catriona is wed to another, you know that. My sister would never have wed you anyway. She vowed to kill you in your wedding bed if she was forced into the marriage. You are safer with her wed to another."

"I doubt it not, but still, this clan owes me, and I will have payment. I understand there is another one, a lass who will ensure your cooperation."

Ailig lunged at Duff only to feel the sting of a thrown

knife slice into his calf. He stumbled. Duff shouted something to the MacDonells on the wall as Ailig reached to
pull a *sgian dhu* out of his leg. Then Duff was upon him,
knocking him to the ground and his sword from his hand
before Ailig could regain his balance. The larger, heavier
man hauled Ailig up by his plaid. Ignoring the burning in
his leg, he twisted free of Duff's grip and spun away, drawing his dagger and preparing to fight.

Duff's grin shown in the torchlight. Ailig could feel the
warm stream of blood that flowed down his leg and into
his boot, but Duff did not attack again. Instead he gave an
ear-piercing whistle and the door at the top of the stairs
opened. The silhouette of two figures stood framed by the
brighter light of the hall and Ailig was struck that no sound
of music or laughter or even conversation slipped through
the open door.

"You have the lass?" Duff called.

"Here with me," a voice called that Ailig could swear
belonged to the man Jock, who Morainn had danced with
earlier. Anger surged through him. 'Twas stupid of him to
believe MacDonells would abide by the customs of hospitality. 'Twas stupid of him not to have shoved the lot of
them down the nearest privy chute when first he had returned. He'd not make that mistake twice.

"Bring her," Duff said, and Ailig watched as Jock was
almost pulled down the steps by Morainn. His heart
stopped, then started again, triple time.

"Are you all right?" Morainn's voice was steady, but
sharp. "Ailig? Are you well?"

She was worried for him.

"Aye. Are you? Is all well inside?" 'Twould do no good
to pretend she was not special to him. Jock and all the

other MacDonells had surely seen the kiss they had shared
on the dance floor.

"Silence! Jock, do not let the wench speak again." Duff
stepped closer to Ailig. "You will know how your clan
fares when I wish it, not before. Do as I say and we will
not harm any others. Do not do as I say, and she will be the
first to feel the bite of my . . . blade."

Ailig was in agony. If he did as Duff said, Morainn
would be spared, but the clan would be at the man's mercy,
and he did not think much mercy bided in the heart of Duff
MacDonell. If he fought Duff, Morainn would die, and his
clan would suffer the wrath of all the other MacDonells
within the walls. There had to be a way out of this quag-
mire, but he needed time to figure out a solution.

Skaeth's voice echoed in his head, repeating his odd
ideas of stratagem. Skaeth's way was devious, canny, not
straightforward brute force as was the Highland way. Duff
would not expect such a feint from a fellow Highlander.

Ailig tossed his blade toward Duff's feet. "Do not hurt
the lass. I will do as you say."

"Ailig, nay!" Morainn struggled in Jock's grip but the
man held her firm.

Duff waved a hand as if beckoning someone forward
and two more large shadows detached themselves from the
gate tunnel shadow.

Baltair was taken, but Tamas was still up in the hall as
far as Ailig knew. And Skaeth? He'd not seen the man return from his daily scouting. He said a quick, soundless
prayer that Skaeth had not lost his way . . . or his sword,
then concentrated on the immediate problem. He was on
his own for now, but soon he'd set his plan in motion.

"Mora, do as he says. Do not fight him. I have no doubt that his threats are true."

"Ailig!"

Anguish was in her voice and he wished he could give her some comfort that all was not yet lost. He remembered the way she had laid her hand over his heart after they had made love the first time. Quickly he laid his own hand where hers had been, tapping his chest to make sure she saw before the two MacDonell brutes grabbed him and dragged him toward the chief's tower.

M orainn couldn't believe that Ailig would give up without a fight. And his signal, his hand over his heart told her that he had not. She took a deep breath. What was he up to? Giving in, but not . . . Understanding burst upon her. Of course. Giving in, but not. A feint, a ruse, and she must play her part.

"Ailig!" She struggled, letting tears run down her face. She scowled at Jock. "How could you allow this?" She beat her fists against his chest and played the part of grieving lover all too easily. 'Twas entirely likely they would none of them survive this night . . . especially Ailig.

"Take her to Gofraig's chamber and make sure everything is secured there," Duff said. "I think I shall have a talk with the chief."

Morainn resisted Jock's pull, but only enough to convince him she was unwilling to go with him, not enough to get hurt. She had too much to do this night to allow herself to be hurt.

Jock pushed her into the relative warmth of the kitchen

tower. Good. If there was one part of the castle she knew well, it was this tower.

She straightened her shoulders, lifted her chin and sent a burning glare to Jock. She jerked her arm free of his grip and walked slowly toward the stair that led to the chambers above. As slowly as she could muster, she made her way up the stairs, her mind taking in every passageway, every shadowed nook, but nothing presented itself as an escape. Jock nudged her from behind but she refused to hurry to her prison.

"Was Freya just a tool for you then?" she asked as they passed the first landing. "Did you set out to use her, or did Gofraig tell you to do that after you had caught her fancy?"

"Does it matter?"

"It will to Freya."

"She'll never speak to me again, anyway. It matters naught."

"Hmm."

They walked a few steps in silence. When they passed the second landing, Jock reached out and stopped her.

"What do you mean by *hmm*?"

"Oh, nothing. If you do not have feelings for the lass, then you are right it matters naught what your original motives were." She shook off his hand and continued her slow climb.

"But if I did . . . do?" he asked, coming up even with her now.

Morainn shrugged. "If you do have feelings for her, then why you betrayed Freya's kin and clan might be very important . . . to her. As for me, a betrayal is a betrayal and I care not what your motives were." She continued up to the third landing. "Gofraig was on this floor, I believe."

She looked back and Jock was standing a few steps below the landing looking as lost as she felt. "I'm damned," he said, shaking his head and narrowing his eyes. "I cannot be loyal to my chief and Freya. 'Twill never work."

"And your chief is *so* deserving of your loyalty. No amount of penance will ever absolve you and yours of the sins you have committed this night against this clan."

"Hush, woman," he said, shoving her towards Gofraig's chamber. He pushed open the door and propelled her inside, slamming it loudly behind her. "I'll be on this side, so don't be thinking of leaving," he said, his voice muffled by the thick door.

Morainn looked about the chamber, hoping to find another way out, even though she was sure there wasn't one. There wasn't even a privy in this chamber, though she'd have to be even more desperate than she was now to drop down a privy chute. She shuddered at the thought and continued making her way around the room.

Despair pricked her. Fear poked her. Helplessness nearly strangled her. She sat on the edge of the narrow bed and fought the urge to roll up into a ball and cry. She hated feeling this way.

She never should have left her cottage. She never should have given in to Ailig's request for help. She never should have opened herself up to this kind of pain again.

And yet . . .

If she had not, she never would have felt the joy she and Ailig had shared. She never would have known the happiness and the love. She did love him, deeply, completely and she had two choices. She could sit here feeling sorry for all that she was about to lose, or she could do something about it.

She rose and took a deep breath. The only thing standing between her and doing something was Jock, and she had already found a chink in his armor. Now she just had to figure out how to use it.

She chewed on her lip and started pacing the small chamber. The man clearly had feelings for Freya, yet his loyalty to his clan made him act against hers. His conscience was obviously bothering him. If she could play on that . . .

She paced. First she would need to get him on *this* side of the door. She couldn't talk to him easily through it. Second she'd have to either distract him, or set him at his ease enough to let down his guard. That was harder, but that was where Freya and his conflicted loyalties came in. After that . . .

She looked about again. The only thing in the room she could possibly use as a weapon was the chamber pot. Picking it up she heard the jingle of the castle's keys at her waist. She smiled as she set the chamber pot on the hearth and removed the ring of keys from her belt.

When she was ready she dug down into those emotions she hated and let them roll over her until she could feel the tears coming. "Please, please," she wailed, beating on the door with one fist as she tried the key. That one didn't work so she tried another. "Please, Jock, I need to see Ailig one last time!" It felt good to shout and beat upon the door. It felt almost empowering. The second key turned and she quickly turned it back and held it tight in one fist. "I must tell him that I love him before . . ."

Sobbing as loudly as she could, she beat sporadically on

the door. Jock's voice was so muffled, even if she hadn't been wailing she wasn't sure she could have understood him.

"Please, Jock, just open the door and listen to me." She sobbed another few moments as she tried to think of another tactic. Just as she was about to give up, the door swung inward, opening just enough for Jock to stick his head inside.

"I cannot let you see him," he said. "Duff said to keep you here and that's what I must do, so get ahold of yourself, Morainn."

Anger at his callous words threatened to still her tears, but she did not let it.

"I do not know what has come over me," she said around sobs. "I love him so. I do not know what I will do if Duff kills him."

She moved away from the door to the far side of the chamber, squatting in front of the fireplace as if to tend the fire. She grabbed the chamber pot by the handle and rose. She kept her back to the door, hiding the keys in her hand in a fold of her arisaid and holding the pot so he could not see it. All the while she kept her crying up and listened to see if he would come in the room.

"I imagine Freya is as upset as I am," she said, dangling the bait.

"Nay, she is a strong lass," he said and she heard the crunch of his footsteps in the rushes. Good.

"She is independent," he continued. "She will be fine."

"That is what everyone says about me, too, but 'tis different when you are in love."

"She's not in love with me." His voice was right behind her now. "Is she?"

Morainn slowly faced him, keeping what she held out of his sight. "I do not think Freya would risk the displeasure of her brother for anything less than love."

She whipped the chamber pot out from behind her, aiming it in an arc for his head. At the last second he realized what she was doing and managed to get his arm up to shield his face, but the pot still shattered on his head, sending him staggering to the side. She dashed for the door, only to feel a tug on her skirt strong enough to rip the fabric. She spun, trying to free herself from Jock's grip. He stumbled. She pulled a stool in his way and he crashed over it onto the floor and lay still. She flew for the door, slamming it behind her. She jammed the key in the lock, threw the bolt, yanked it out again and ran.

D*uff led the way into the chief's chambers. Ailig was* dragged along by the two large MacDonells he had not seen before, come from Dun Donell with Duff no doubt. He was surprised, when the two tossed him to the floor in the outer chamber, to find Neill sitting calmly at his desk as if nothing was amiss. Gofraig stood, one hand on his sword hilt, in front of the fire.

Slowly, Ailig rose, taking in his surroundings and noting where everyone was positioned. He was neatly surrounded. He flung a smile, sharp enough to cut, at Duff.

"You fear me this much? You need all these men to assure that I do not kill you?"

"You cannot kill me. Broc tried and failed. The king did not even get a chance to try. You can do nothing. I am the one in power now."

The ugly man strutted around Ailig, his nose wrinkled as if he circled a dung heap.

"Did you really think to let this boy become chief in Broc's place?" Duff directed the question to Neill, still seated behind his desk.

"I never wanted him to be chief and your timely arrival has prevented that from happening. At least now the council will see the error of their judgment. He could not even keep the castle safe from interlopers."

"You are most welcome," Duff said with a mocking bow.

"Tell me how Broc died," Neill said. "You were there, were you not?"

"You do not teach any of your sons well. If Broc had known what loyalty was, he would not have panicked. We would have escaped your bitch of a daughter and her bard and had the king. But he was too stupid to be patient. Broc turned on me, then fell upon his own blade."

"And you were so brave you whimpered like a babe, begging for your life when you were brought before the king," Ailig added.

Duff grabbed him by his tunic and lifted him until his toes were all that touched the ground. Ailig tried to stay calm.

"At least I am alive to see justice done. 'Tis more than you can say for your brother!" He pushed him away and Ailig stumbled backwards until he stood near Gofraig.

"'Tis true, then," Gofraig said, his voice ominously quiet. "You really were intent on taking the king?"

"We were."

"But why? Why would you do such a dangerous thing?" Gofraig had stepped forward until he stood in front of Duff, leaving Ailig outside the ring. He took one small step towards the corner Gofraig had stood by while the others in the room were busy watching what was unfolding.

"Dangerous? Life is dangerous. We figured the risk and decided 'twas worth it to gain the respect of the Highlanders. 'Twas to prove that the MacDonells are not to be taken lightly."

"Respect? For drawing the ire of the king upon your clans? You will draw only ridicule and 'tis well deserved!" Gofraig shouted. "Did you not see how this would affect your clan? The king seeks you and will punish all of us, all MacDonells, for aiding you! We are lost!" He paced the confines of the room. "'Twas but a game to you, was it not? A game to prove you were good enough to be chief—but you are not. You would take advice from Broc, a man known for causing trouble, and then you would keep all but the betrothal to the Shrew a secret? You would follow a man like that instead of consulting your kinsmen? At least Broc is dead so he can pose no more risk to the MacLeods, but we, we are stuck with you."

"You are not stuck, Gofraig," Duff snarled. "I release you from your champion's vow. You are no longer anything to me."

Gofraig stared at Duff for a long moment, then slowly looked about the room. "I am sorry we have brought this upon your clan," he said to Neill. "And I am sorry I cannot stay to help you, but someone must warn my clan of the disaster that is about to befall them—and why," he added, glaring now at Duff again.

"Go," Duff said. "Any who are still loyal to me will stay. The others I do not need anyway. Go!"

Gofraig looked to the other two MacDonells, but they would not meet his eyes. He glared back at Duff. "You shall rot in hell," he growled as he left the chamber.

Ailig took advantage of the argument to secure the fire tongs, which he held down along the side of his leg, in the hopes that Duff would not notice. He glanced at Neill and realized he was watching him. He raised an eyebrow, but the auld man simply returned to watching the glowering Duff.

"'Twas not supposed to end this way," Neill said quietly, leaning forward. "Broc assured me . . ."

"You knew what Broc planned?" Ailig asked, watching the chief carefully.

"Nay, I did not know he was after the king, only that he had made a pact with Duff as a way to prove himself worthy of becoming chief. 'Twas me who set him the task."

"So you allowed this to happen? You handed the responsibility for the welfare of the entire clan over to him in order to see if he was capable?"

Duff stood between them, leaning a hip against the table, his arms crossed over his chest, looking first at one, then at the other, with a feral grin on his face. All at once Neill hooked his hands under the edge of the table and surged to his feet, upending the table and flipping it on top of the off-balance Duff.

At the same moment Ailig swung the fire tongs at the nearest guard, taking him by surprise with a swift bash to his head that had him crumpling to the floor. The other guard had drawn his sword and approached Ailig with care.

Out of the corner of his eye he saw Duff stagger out from under the table and send Neill flying against the wall.

Duff drew his sword and faced Ailig, who held his tongs as if they were his sword. Not a very effective offensive weapon, but at least it would take the blows of a sword.

He waved the tongs in front of him as the two men closed the distance, backing him away from the fireplace toward a corner. Between them, on the floor, he noticed Neill's ink bottle, unbroken, lying on its side. The stopper was still in it, though a black puddle was slowly forming below the neck. Skaeth's voice echoed in his mind and he dove between the two MacDonells, rolling and snagging the bottle as he did, then smoothly regaining his feet on the other side of them. He flicked off the stopper, then let the guard come close, parrying his attack as best he could with the tongs. He let the man come even closer, close enough to nick his arm. The guard's face burst into a grin that proclaimed Ailig's defeat as he moved in for a killing thrust. Ailig waited until the last possible moment, then, as if 'twas only one of Skaeth's dancelike exercises, he twisted out of the blade's way and threw the ink bottle as hard as he could at the guard's head.

The unexpected miss sent the man off balance. The unexpected missile stunned him enough to make him drop his sword and claw at his eyes where ink had splashed him. Ailig lifted his tongs to finish the job.

Duff's ominous voice came from behind him. "I would not do that were I you."

Ailig swung anyway, catching the blinded guard at the back of the head. This man dropped as hard as his kinsman had and Ailig did not know if he was alive or dead. Nor did he particularly care, as long as he was out of the fight.

He grabbed the man's sword, threw the tongs to the far side of the room, and quickly faced Duff only to find he held Neill up by the back of his tunic. Duff's dagger was held to the limp chief's ribs.

Ailig's breath burned in his chest but he did not react, at least not as Duff was expecting.

"You would kill a defenseless, unconscious auld man?"

"I would kill your father if you do not drop that sword and kneel in the center of the room."

"Good luck," Ailig said. "If you find my father, let me know."

Duff was perfectly still for a moment, as if he didn't understand what Ailig had said. Ailig held his breath and tried to determine if Neill even still lived. Something about the way his arm hung, as if caught in his plaid, didn't look quite right. A slight twitch of the plaid told Ailig the auld man was still alive, and he realized there was still a trick or two that Neill could show them. A new respect for the chief glimmered to life. Ailig didn't smile, but he wanted to. 'Twasn't often Neill surprised him and yet he had been full of surprises of late.

"I think I shall keep my weapon," Ailig said.

Duff pressed the tip of his blade against Neill. There was no response from the chief and Ailig had a momentary doubt about whether he was truly conscious or not.

"Drop the sword and step to the center of the chamber," Duff said, his voice strident.

"Do you think I care one whit for that man's life? He is not my father. I care not what happens to him, but you, *you* I care about."

Duff snarled and in that moment Neill struck faster than Ailig ever remembered seeing him move. Before he could take a step, Neill's *sgian dhu* was protruding from the hollow at the base of Duff's neck. Neill fell away from the man who was grasping at his throat, a horrible sucking noise coming but no voice, no screams.

Ailig ran to Neill and helped him sit up. Blood seeped from a gash in his side.

"You're hurt," Ailig said.

"'Tis nothing. Tie those two up," he said, pointing at the guards, "then you must secure the castle."

Ailig righted the chair and helped Neill into it, then disappeared into the bedchamber, returning with a blanket and a sheet. As he tore strips from the sheet, Neill rested, sucking in his breath only when Ailig pressed a piece of linen to the wound and tied it in place with a strip of cloth. He used the other strips to tie the hands and feet of the two guards. The sucking noises had stopped and Duff lay still clutching his throat, with a surprised expression on his face, though his eyes stared at nothing. A small knife lay on the ground next to the body. Ailig threw the remains of the sheet over Duff and returned the quickly cleaned knife to Neill.

"Do you know what has happened to Baltair?" Neill asked as Ailig settled the blanket around the man's shoulders.

"Duff said he was in the oubliette."

"Get him free. Tell him I said 'tis over. Tell him I say he must help you."

"He'll not believe me."

"He will. Just say those exact words: 'tis over. He'll understand. Go. Get Baltair, and anyone else you can trust, and get those damned MacDonells out of my castle!"

Ailig gathered up Duff's dagger and slid it where his belonged. He grabbed a sword from the ground and laid it in Neill's lap.

"As soon as I am able I shall send Giorsal to you. In the meantime stay here, rest and watch over these fools."

He checked once more to make sure Duff was dead, then slipped out of the room. The clan's future lay in his hands now more than ever.

chapter 18

Morainn scurried down the stair and into the darkness of the corridor at the bottom. The torches in the corridor had long since burned themselves out and for once she was grateful they had been neglected. Carefully she made her way towards the Great Hall. Tamas was there, or at least he had been when Jock had taken her away. She needed to find a way to get him out of there. She needed a strong sword arm if she was to free Ailig.

Gripping the keys so they would not jingle and give her away, she crept into the shadows behind the carved wooden screen that separated the near end of the hall from the rest of it, inching her way toward the opening. She needed to see where everyone was before she could devise a plan.

Mostly, it was eerily quiet, but two voices were quite clear, as if the men were just on the opposite side of the screen from her. Of course they were. The ale cask had been set there for the celebration, a celebration gone terribly wrong.

"Damn, 'tis empty," one voice said. "We missed all the ale guarding one man."

"Aye, but he was the important one. I heard from Malcolm that without him, the rest fell like rotten timbers. He'll wake in the morning with enough pains to remind him that the MacDonells are a force to be reckoned with."

"If he wakens at all."

Morainn's heart stopped. She covered her mouth with her hand lest a sob escape her.

"'*Twas* a long fall into that pit."

Pit? The oubliette? They had thrown Ailig in the oubliette!

As quietly as possible she crept forward to the opening in the screen and peeked into the hall. The MacLeod men and older boys were lined up against the fireplace wall, their hands and feet clearly bound. Tamas was there, in the midst of them, too far away for her to get his attention without risking drawing the MacDonells' attention, too. She could not see either Baltair or the mercenary. Perhaps they had escaped and were already plotting a way to rescue Ailig and the clan.

Or maybe they were dead. She pushed that worry aside. For now she chose to believe they were alive and busy plotting a way out of this trouble.

The women were huddled at the far end of the hall, sleeping weans and bairns held in their laps. Giorsal and Freya sat together to one side of the women, both glowering at the milling MacDonells.

There was little she could do here, but at least she had learned where Ailig was. Now she'd just have to find a way to free him, then together they would figure out what to do to free the rest of the clan. As quietly as possible she backed out of the Great Hall. Once she was safely in the shadows of the outer corridor again, she breathed and planned the best way to get to the gate tower without being seen.

The kitchen was dark and deserted as she opened the door that led down to the larder, then pulled it shut behind her. She had to feel her way down the stair and across to the door that led out to the bailey. Unlocking that door, she pulled it open just enough to peer out. The bailey itself seemed empty, though there were men illuminated by torches, gathered in groups of twos and threes along the top of the wall, some looking inward, some outward. She gauged the depth of the shadows along the edge of the bailey and the brightness of the torches lighting the wall walk and decided, if she moved slowly, she was unlikely to be seen. Of course there were probably more men guarding the gate and the oubliette itself.

Fear tingled at the base of her spine, sending irritating tendrils up her back, making her skin crawl and her hair stand on end. But that fear also focused her mind. She searched her memory for something, anything, that might be in the larder that could be used as a weapon. Nothing, except perhaps for a smoked haunch of venison that would be too heavy for her to do much more than lift from its hook. She looked again at the heights, counting the men there. Nine. At least there were nine she could see in the torch light. The shadows might hold more.

Torches. There should be torches—burned out, true— in the bailey. Those she could swing with some force. Before she could have second thoughts, she opened the door just wide enough to escape the larder and stepped into the inky blackness of the deserted bailey. A muffled noise in the direction of the gate had her freezing, not two steps from the larder door, reconsidering her plan. When there was no more noise, she found the first torch and twisted it from its bracket. The keys, still gripped in her left hand hampered her a bit, but she decided they were too valuable to leave behind, and too noisy if she slid them back onto her belt or even stowed them in the small sack that hung from her belt. With the torch in hand she made her way to the gate.

She was surprised when she got there that no one seemed to be on guard. A lone torch flickered outside the guard's room and the gate was closed and barred, but no one . . .

There was someone. He just happened to be crumpled up on the ground next to the doorway that led to the oubliette. She watched him for another moment to make sure he was not simply lying in wait for her. But she did not wait long. Darting across the gate tunnel she pushed the door open that led to the chamber over the oubliette. As she closed the door again, she gasped as a hand grabbed her over her mouth and pulled her against a hard chest. The distinctive feel of a dagger at her ribs had her holding very still. Before she could think what to do next, the dagger was removed and a very familiar voice whispered in her ear.

"Mora?"

She dropped her torch, spun and threw her arms around Ailig's neck and kissed him. The fear she'd been holding at bay made the kiss both desperate and joyful all at the same time.

"How did you get out? I thought they had hurt you. I thought the oubliette was inescapable. I thought I had lost you."

A ilig held her tightly to him, amazed and grateful that she was here, in his arms.

"What are you doing here?" he asked instead of answering her rapid-fire questions.

She kissed him again. "I came to free you from the oubliette. We have to do something to rid ourselves of these verminous MacDonells and I could not do it alone."

He wanted to laugh. He wanted to lift her up and swing her about until he could hear her sparkling laughter. But they could not indulge in the kind of reunion he had envisioned when he imagined freeing her from her own prison. He did smile then, even though she couldn't see it in the dark. He should have known better than to think she would sit quietly by and wait to be rescued. Here was his Mora, coming to his rescue, only he didn't need rescuing, either. He sought her lips once more then whispered to her.

"Baltair is the one in the oubliette, love. Let us free him, then we must get away from here and figure out how to eradicate the vermin from these walls."

With two of them to search the small chamber, they quickly located the trap door, secured only with a toggle, and opened it.

"Baltair," Morainn whispered. "Are you there?"

"Aye," came the terse reply.

"Is anyone else with you?" Ailig asked.

"Nay," came the equally short answer.

"The chief said to tell you *'tis over*," Ailig said, waiting a moment for a reply. All he got was a grunt. "Baltair, will you help us?"

"The chief said 'tis over, so I have no choice. I swore to him I would give my oath of loyalty to you when he said to. You have my oath. Now throw down the damn ladder!"

"Move to a wall," Ailig said as he groped in the dark for the rope ladder, then looped the ends over the hooks in the floor and let it unroll into the pit. Moments later Baltair was at the top.

"Did you have to kiss her so much before you let me out?"

"I did," Ailig said. "Baltair, the gate guards are . . . not a problem for the moment. Open the sortie gate. Skaeth never returned from his scouting today. If he is alive, I've no doubt he's nearby. 'Twould be good to have his arm and his mind for strategy in this fight."

"What are you going to do?"

"Mora and I will try to find out what is going on and where everyone is being held."

"I know!" Morainn said, then quickly filled them in on her own scouting expedition.

"Baltair, after you open the gate, go to the chief's chamber. Neill is there, safe, but he is hurt and will not be able to defend himself if this fails. Mora and I will try to find a way to free the men in the Great Hall."

"I have an idea," Morainn said, squeezing his hand. "If you see Skaeth," she said to Baltair, "tell him to make his way to the kitchen larder if he can."

Baltair grunted and Ailig led them out of the antechamber. In the faint light of the guardroom torch, Ailig could see that Baltair's face was swollen, half of it covered in dried blood.

He quickly checked Morainn and was relieved to see no signs of violence upon her, only worry and determination. The three of them stared at each other for a moment, then Baltair made for the gate and Ailig pulled Morainn along behind him as they disappeared into the shadows.

When the larder door was closed behind them, Morainn told him to wait there and moments later he heard the sharp sound of iron against flint and shortly a candle flamed to life, sending out a gentle glow that pushed against the darkness.

"What is your plan, love?" he asked, wanting to ask so many more questions, but they would have to wait.

"They have finished the ale and will be wanting more. If we take the sleeping draught Giorsal has been giving your father—Neill—and add it to the ale . . . It may take a while, but eventually they will become sleepy. If we can get word to the women—"

"The women?"

"Aye, the men are tied up, but the women . . ." She smiled. "The women are not considered a threat. But they are." Her smile turned almost feral and Ailig knew he never wanted to be the focus of that particular smile. "If we can get word to the women to watch for when the Mac-Donells succumb, they can release the men and the Mac-Donells will be the ones surprised this time."

"But how do we get word to the women?"

"Let us see who comes for the ale. You find ewers. There are several casks against the wall. Two are tapped in case they were needed for the celebration." She grinned. "Turns out they are. I must get to Giorsal's workroom."

"Nay, Mora, 'tis too dangerous."

She smiled again and kissed him quickly. "Aye, but it

must be done and I have the keys, and I know where she keeps the draught. There should be several ewers on the shelves over there," she said pointing at the far wall.

Reluctantly, Ailig realized he could not dispute her logic and he let her go. 'Twas her clan, too, and each of them would do what they could to see the MacDonells bested. Each minute she was gone, though, felt too long and every tiny sound, even those he made himself moving about the larder, had his heart pounding. The faint jingling of her keys told of her return just before she appeared at the top of the stair, a tall earthenware pot in her hands.

In quick order they had filled several ewers a quarter of the way with the sleeping draught—enough to do the job without changing the taste of the ale, not much anyway. Then they shielded the candle and settled down to wait in the shadows. Ailig indulged himself and pulled her close, wrapping his arm around her so they sat hip to hip. After a little while she rested her head on his shoulder, her silky hair tickling his cheek.

"As soon as we are sure the Great Hall is secure, we must take care of those on the walls outside," Ailig said quietly.

"Do you have a plan?"

"I thought you would," he teased.

"The kitchen is my purview. The wall is yours," she said, snuggling closer. "But I will help in any way I can."

"I ken that, love. I do have a plan, but I am hoping Skaeth will turn up before I have to put it into action. 'Twould help if Tamas and the other warriors were free, too, so we will wait a bit longer to see if this ruse will work."

Just as the last word was out of his mouth they heard the

door at the top of the stair open. Several lasses descended the stair, a lantern held high lighting the way. They waited to see if any of the MacDonells would follow the lasses down into the larder, but as they neared the tapped casks Morainn could wait no longer. She put a hand on Ailig's chest as if to tell him to stay put and she rose quickly.

"Freya?" she whispered.

The girl jumped, nearly dropping the lantern.

"'Tis me, Morainn," she said, moving into the light.

Two other girls crowded around Freya now, their eyes wide in the pale light.

"I need you all to do something," she said, lifting one of the prepared ewers and quickly explaining the plan. "You must warn our people not to drink of the ale, though they must appear to, so they do not draw the suspicion of the MacDonells. Can you do this?"

The girls all nodded and Freya set the lantern atop the cask and began drawing off the ale. That was when she noticed Ailig sitting there. Her hands stilled and Ailig managed a smile as he placed his finger to his lips.

The lass nodded her understanding and finished her task, handing filled ewers to each of the other lasses, then taking her own and returning up the stairs without so much as a backward glance.

"Will she do it?" he asked Morainn, who had settled back by his side.

"Aye. She has been betrayed by the MacDonells as badly as any of us have, and more personally. Freya will see 'tis done."

Moments later the door from the bailey inched open and someone edged into the larder, holding to the darker shadows. Ailig heard a quiet rhythm tapped out on something hard. 'Twas a rhythm only a few people would understand and he happened to be one of them.

"Skaeth, over here," he whispered.

The mercenary made his way across the larder as if he could see in the dark and hunkered down in front of them, his body a blacker shadow than the chamber behind him.

"Are there more MacDonells outside the walls?" Ailig asked.

"Nay. As near as I can tell from their tracks, Duff was traveling with only two others."

"They are dead, or as good as," Ailig said.

"And Duff?"

"Dead."

Morainn's gasp had him squeezing her tighter to him. "Neill killed him."

"Where are the others?"

"Ten are in the Great Hall," Morainn said, leaning a little forward. "Nine on the wall. Jock is in Gofraig's chamber, locked in."

"And Gofraig has left. At least he said he was leaving," Ailig added. "You've become quite the spy, Mora," he said, pride filling him.

Skaeth cleared his throat. "Why are you just sitting here?" he asked.

"We are waiting for Mora's plan to work, then you and I are going after those men on the walls." Quickly, they filled him in.

Ailig could feel Skaeth's skepticism. "Do you think it has worked yet?" he asked Morainn. He felt her shrug.

Just then Freya and her two helpers opened the upper door and Skaeth dove for the shadows next to Morainn. The girls returned to the cask, saying nothing as Morainn

rose to pour the sleeping potion in the once-more empty
ewers. They refilled them but Freya paused before they
left.

"They've each had a cup of ale already. A second cup
should have them snoring very soon."

"Well done, Freya," Ailig whispered.

She nodded at him and her eyes widened as she spied
Skaeth there, too. Morainn touched the girl's elbow and
drew her attention away from the men.

"Are there any MacDonells in the kitchen above?"

"Nay, they let us come alone this time."

Ailig saw Morainn look over at him. Something about
the set of her face told him she was up to something.

"Let's follow them up. We can hide in the corridor. 'Tis
very dark. You'll need to know the men in the Great Hall
are taken care of before you approach those on the wall,
else the entire clan will be at the mercy of the MacDonells'
blades. We cannot risk the weans and bairns that way, and
I cannot abide sitting here and waiting another moment."

"The lass has a point," Skaeth said.

"I know," Ailig allowed. "I know."

The three lasses led the way with Morainn and the two
men following a discreet distance behind, but they
didn't wait in the corridor. Without so much as a word, all
three of them continued into the screened area of the Great
Hall, hugging the shadows as they listened and waited.
Freya kept up a chatter, as she poured the ale, which served
to give them an idea of how the MacDonells were spread
about the large chamber. It sounded as if most of them

were gathered near the bailey door, but several were closer to the screened end.

A crash signaled the first to succumb, followed by confused shouts and another crash. Ailig and Skaeth surged to their feet and rushed into the hall. Morainn clutched a knife she had grabbed from a table in the kitchen as they had passed through, and now she ran to the nearest man and cut his bindings. Other women were struggling to unknot bindings, but her knife sliced through the twine with only a little effort.

When she got to Tamas he grinned at her, holding his hands up for her to free. When his feet were free, too, he surged to his feet and signaled another man to grab the far end of a bench, then they rushed several MacDonells who were busily engaged in a sword fight with Skaeth. They barreled through the melee, knocking MacDonells to the ground. A veritable wall of women were throwing trenchers and cups at the MacDonells while hiding their children behind them. 'Twasn't long before the half-score of MacDonells found themselves overcome and outnumbered by angry MacLeods.

Ailig quickly called Tamas, Skaeth and several others to him. Morainn hurried across the room, unwilling to be left out of the last battle.

"Four of us will go up the chief's tower, the other four, the kitchen tower. If we split, two in each direction, we'll trap them all between us. They'll either face our swords or have to jump to their doom."

"You'll need a distraction," Morainn said. "You'll need someone to draw their attention as you make your way to the chief's tower."

"Nay, Mora," Ailig said. "We do not."

"She is right," Skaeth said.

"Aye," Tamas agreed. "There's no way to the chief's tower except through the bailey. A diversion will help us. We'll keep the element of surprise."

"I shall be fine, Ailig," she said. "I have a right to help. 'Tis my home, too."

"Very well. What do you propose?"

"Don't worry. I have a plan."

"You always do."

She grinned. "Come on. I'll go ahead of you into the bailey, from the larder. You'll have no difficulty getting to the tower." She left them no choice but to follow her.

Moments later she walked to the center of the bailey and began to scream, pulling at her hair like a madwoman, wailing and beating her breast. "They're dead! MacDonell scum have killed them all! Babes and children, women, men, dead, they're all dead!"

She repeated this performance, turning in circles and working her way away from the towers, until she was sure she had the attention of every guard upon the wall and Ailig and his men had made it to the chief's tower unnoticed. But still she kept it up until she heard the shouts of surprise and watched as Ailig and the others quickly overcame the remaining MacDonells. She dusted off her hands, smoothed her hair and made her way back to the Great Hall.

In short order the now-sleeping MacDonells were lined up along a wall and bound, as the MacLeod men had been before. Skaeth and several others brought in the surviving men from the wall. Skaeth spoke to Giorsal, who then ran out of the hall, while others bound the MacDonells and had them join their kinsmen.

"Where is Ailig?" Morainn asked Skaeth, suddenly fearful that something had happened to him.

"He's gone to the chief's. I've just sent Giorsal there. Ailig is fine, lass. 'Tis the chief who's in need of Giorsal's attention. Ailig said to tell you he'd be back here soon. Not to fret," he added with a grin. "He kens you well."

"He does." Reassured, she poured out the remainder of the drugged ale and sent the kitchen staff to work. 'Twould soon be dawn and everyone had earned a good meal this night. She stifled a yawn, knowing full well that 'twould still be a long time before she could seek a bed—Ailig's bed, she thought with a new lightness to her heart. She hastened to the kitchen to see what needed tending there.

Freya passed her in the corridor and she stopped the lass. "Thank you. You were brave to serve the ale, and you helped Ailig and Skaeth by speaking to the MacDonells."

"'Tis glad I am I was able to help."

"Freya, Jock is above stairs, in Gofraig's chamber. Do you wish to speak to him?"

Hurt passed quickly through Freya's eyes and was replaced with a stony-eyed look of disgust. "I have no use for a man who could betray me that way. I'll find a lad with honor, or I'll not have one."

Morainn hugged the girl and let her continue on her way. Tamas trooped by, two more MacDonells being carried by others in his wake.

"Tamas," she called after him. He stopped and let the MacLeods bearing the MacDonells go past him into the Great Hall. "Jock. He is still above stairs."

"Aye. Ailig said to leave him there for now. I think he wants to deal with Jock himself."

"Oh, dear."

Tamas smiled. "Not to worry. I'll make sure Skaeth or Baltair or I am there, too. We wouldn't want Ailig to be accused of murder." He grinned. "I'm glad you are well. Una was beside herself with worry."

"For me *and* you."

"No doubt."

"You should marry her soon," she said. "She has had too much grief and worry in her life. She deserves to be happy."

"The same could be said for you."

Surprise sliced through the clutter in her mind, alerting every nerve to sudden possibilities. She did deserve to be happy; she had learned that this past sennight with Ailig. And he was the one who made her happiest. She opened a door in her heart that she'd been trying desperately to keep closed and savored the feel of Ailig there, allowed herself to envision him by her side as they grew old together.

She smiled at Tamas. "There is much yet to be decided," she said, hugging him.

"Not so much." He kissed her on the cheek and headed for the Great Hall.

Ailig *moved through the Great Hall, acknowledging* the folks he passed with a smile, a word, or a pat on the back. He was grateful that all of these people had come together to rid the castle of the MacDonells. He still had to find someone to get word to the king and they had to find a way to hold so many prisoners until the king's men arrived to take them. But all that could be dealt with—after he found Morainn.

He spied Tamas with one arm wrapped around Una, and

the other around Lili, who sat upon his hip. A lick of jealousy burned along his spine as he made his way to the happy trio.

"Do you know—"

"She's in the kitchen, of course," Una said before he could finish. "Get you in there!" Una gave him a friendly shove towards the doorway.

Ailig tried not to run. When he burst into the kitchen, the cook took one look at him and pointed at the larder door with his long wooden spoon. Ailig waved his thanks and strode to the door.

"Mora?" he called as he descended into the dimly lit chamber.

"I am here," she said. Her voice, strangely quiet, came from the corner where they had hidden only a few hours ago.

They stared at each other for a moment, and then Ailig closed the distance between them and crushed her to him.

"'Tis over," he murmured. "'Tis done."

"I know, but I cannot stop trembling." She looked up at him. "I was so afraid you would die. I could not bear the thought of never seeing you again. Everyone I have ever loved has left me . . . died. I did not want to love you, Ailig."

"Do you, Mora? Are you in love with me?"

"I am," she whispered, reaching up and framing his face with her hands. "I love you." She pulled him into a kiss that had his mind spinning and his body humming with need. She locked her arms around his neck and he picked her up, holding her close, kissing her still.

At last he set her on her feet again, but he could not bring himself to release her. "Do you regret loving me?"

She smiled up at him, her eyes sparkling. "For a moment, just after Jock took me away and I was sure I would never see you again I did. But then I realized that I would not trade the joy we've found with each other, the love . . . you do love me, do you not?"

He kissed her again, then rested his forehead against hers. "I do love you, Mora, with all my heart."

"Then how could I regret loving you?" She pulled away just enough for him to see the sparkle in her eyes turn impish.

"But . . . ?" he asked.

"But I am selfish," she said. "I want you for my husband, Ailig. I do not plan to watch you wed anyone but me. Will you marry me?" she asked, the impishness turning suddenly vulnerable.

"Selfish, huh," he said, running the pad of his thumb over the softness of her cheek. "We are well-matched then, for I too am selfish. I was only waiting to be made chief before I asked you to be my wife, but here you have beat me to it."

"Is that a yes?" she asked.

"'Tis."

The vulnerability that looked so out of place on her beloved face blossomed into the greatest joy he had ever seen, though he knew it was mirrored on his own face and in his heart. He swept her up and twirled her around, her sparkling laughter twinkling around them in the air.

"You'll have to cease whatever private celebrating you two are doing down there," Tamas's voice called from above.

"Nay, we shall not!" Morainn replied, hugging him tightly.

"What do you want, Tamas," Ailig asked, not taking his eyes from his bride.

"You are both summoned to the Great Hall. The chief awaits you!"

"I suppose we shall have to go," Ailig said.

"Aye, but later we shall continue this celebration," she said, kissing him so thoroughly he had to follow her slowly up the stairs, lest everyone know where his thoughts lay.

As they entered the Great Hall, Ailig could see all the tables had been cleared away, though the clan was still gathered there. Neill was seated in the ornate chief's chair on the dais at the far end of the chamber, the council of elders ranged on either side of him, and Skaeth stood just behind him to the chief's right. Neill wore the white cloak of office, a formality Ailig had not seen in many years. At his feet was a large gray block of stone, set upon a brightly colored carpet brought back from the crusades many years ago.

Morainn squeezed his hand. "Ailig." Her eyes were filled with pride and he was very glad she was there, for his knees had gone a little weak at the sight of the stone, the *Clachan à MacLeod.*

They quickly cut through the crowd and came to stand before the stone and the chief. Neill rose to his feet with Skaeth's help and Ailig could see that the effort cost him as sweat popped out on his face. Giorsal stood at the back of the dais, scowling at Neill, but she did not stop him. The crowd hushed.

"Ailig MacLeod, you have proven your ability to lead this clan. You have proven your worth."

A sense of accomplishment and pride accompanied the long-awaited words, but they were nothing compared to the completeness he felt as he glanced over his shoulder at Morainn. He realized that while he appreciated Neill's acceptance of him, he no longer needed it to feel worthy of his place in the clan. Morainn's love made him feel worthy. The loyalty of men like Tamas, and Skaeth, and even the hard-won loyalty of Baltair made him feel worthy. The support of the clan made him feel worthy.

"The council was right," Neill continued. "You have the loyalty of these good men," he waved at the warriors gathered around him, "the trust of this council, and me. And the support of King Robert." He glanced at Skaeth, who gave a slight bow in acknowledgment.

"Skaeth?" Answers swirled around questions in Ailig's mind. "No mercenary, then?"

"Nay, I am not a mercenary, Ailig," the man said, an enigmatic smile on his austere face. "I work for the king." A gasp raced around the hall. "I was sent to watch you, to aid you if necessary. King Robert will be quite pleased with the outcome of all this."

Ailig nodded to himself. He had the king's charge, but not his complete confidence. The king was even wiser than he had thought.

Neill cleared his throat. "Will you take the oath and become chief of this clan?"

Ailig locked eyes with the auld chief, then raised his voice so the entire gathering could hear him. "I will—on two conditions."

The crowd muttered but Neill just watched him, his face nearly expressionless, except for a faint narrowing of his eyes.

"And they are?" he asked.

"One . . ." Now Ailig faced the clan, for 'twas they who

must agree or not. "Neill shall remain as a member of the council as long as he is willing."

A cheer went up in the hall and he glanced over his shoulder to the council. Heads were bobbing in agreement, and he let out a breath he hadn't realized he'd been holding.

"Two . . . Morainn MacRailt shall be my wife." He reached for her hand again and pulled her to his side. "I cannot hope to lead this clan without her level head and courage."

Morainn blushed as he kissed her there in front of everyone. He heard whoops from Tamas, Una and others and he dared a look at Baltair, who was not smiling but nodded his agreement. Morainn laid her hand over his heart then stepped back into the circle of people around him. He faced the chief again.

"Step up upon the *Clachan à MacLeod*," Neill said as he loosened the tie of the white cloak.

Angus Mhór took it from the auld chief and signaled Ailig, now standing on the stone, to face the crowd once more. As he draped the white cloak over Ailig's shoulders, he whispered, "My brother would have been very proud of you this day and all days, as your mother was."

Startled, Ailig locked eyes with the elder. "His eyes were the same pale gray . . ." Angus Mhór said. He clapped Ailig on the shoulder and returned to his place by Neill.

Neill came forward then, slowly, holding the chief's sword aloft, like a cross. He stood in front of Ailig and intoned the ancient oath of the chiefs of MacLeod, the Gaelic words flowing like a river through the crowd. Ailig repeated the oath, then kissed the amber imbedded in the hilt of the sword. Neill held the sword out on his palms and Ailig took it, sliding it home in his sheath.

As simply and as quickly as that the responsibilities for the clan passed from one chief to the next. Ailig stepped down from the stone and cheers ripped through the crowd, with scattered hoots and loud applause. He found Morainn in the crowd, smiling, though tears ran down her face.

He swept her into his arms. "What's wrong, love? Why are you crying?"

"I never dared dream of such a day as this," she said, wiping the tears away.

He grinned at her and spun her around in the air. "And yet, here it is. What shall we dream of next?"

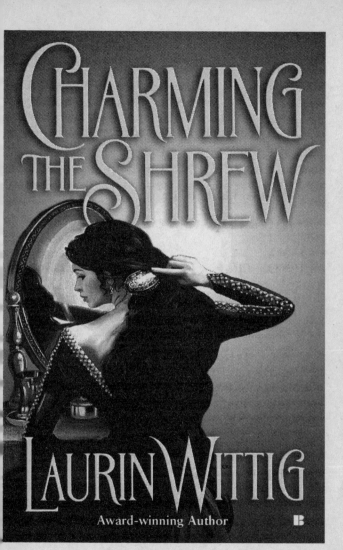

CHARMING THE SHREW

LAURIN WITTIG

Award-winning Author

A Berkley Sensation Paperback
0-425-19527-9
www.penguin.com

Jane's Warlord

by Angela Knight

The sexy debut novel from
the author of
Master of the Night

The next target of a time travelling killer,
crime reporter Jane Colby finds herself in the
hands of a warlord from the future sent to
protect her—and in his hands is just where
she wants to be.

"CHILLS, THRILLS...[A] SEXY TALE."

—EMMA HOLLY

0-425-19684-4

**Available wherever books are sold or at
www.penguin.com**

B865